# EVIL WAYS

To

Kirsty

Best Wishes

Gordan Waugh.

# EVIL WAYS

## GORDON WAUGH

Stoater Books

Published in 2019 by Stoater Books

ISBN Paperback: 978-1-9993227-2-4
Ebook: 978-1-9993227-3-1

A CIP catalogue copy of this book can be found in the
British Library.

Published with the help of Indie Authors World
www.indieauthorsworld.com

IndieAuthors
World

For Jean,
whose constant support makes everything possible.

# ACKNOWLEDGEMENTS

My deep and grateful thanks, to all those connected with Indie Authors World for all their help in making this my second publication possible. Especially to Sinclair and Kim Macleod, who always seem to go that extra mile to ensure we get there in the end. Again a special mention to Suze Clarke- Morris for her patience and once more making things work. Also to Jim Kennedy and his vast experience in regard to Taekwondo.

To the many family, friends and former colleagues for their very kind and positive remarks on my debut novel Dark Days. They spurred me on to complete this my second book which I sincerely hope they will all enjoy in equal measure.

# CHAPTER ONE

Joseph McGarvie had won and retained his seat on Glasgow City Council in three previous elections. He was a rising star in the Labour Party, both locally and nationally. Only twenty-three years old when first elected, he could definitely look forward to a bright future. He was a married man with three young children and lived in the Calton area of the city. This was where he came from; he loved the east end and serving the people he represented.

Life was good for Joseph and it came as no great surprise when, in 2005, the Party selected him to stand for a seat at Westminster. The election was set for Thursday 5th May and campaigning began to gather pace. Things were going well. Labour felt McGarvie would win easily but still ensured he had plenty of people out on the streets canvassing and knocking on doors. The more people they got the message across to, the better results that would be achieved.

McGarvie wasn't tall, dark or handsome but he had a charismatic personality. When he told the voters his thoughts on any given subject, they tended to believe that he meant what he said.

One of his activists was a twenty-five year old local woman, Moira Henderson, who was a shop assistant. She was passionate about her politics and had worked hard for the Labour Party and Councillor McGarvie during the council campaigns in 1999 and 2003. Moira was just an ordinary woman, neither plain nor beautiful, but she did possess a bubbly personality which endeared her to her fellow activists. She was besotted with Joseph McGarvie and he was attracted to her.

On the evening of Tuesday 3rd May 2005, just two days before the election, Moira had arranged to meet other party members at the shop premises in London Road that were being used as a campaign headquarters for the area. She never arrived. It was very unusual for her to let anyone down. The next day one of her friends went to the shop in Argyll Street where Moira worked to see if she was alright. She had not appeared for work either, which had never happened before. Her home address was also checked but there was no trace of her. She was reported as a missing person to the police.

In the course of the police enquiries it came to light that Joseph McGarvie had been the last person to see Moira the night she had apparently disappeared. He was subsequently interviewed at London Road Police Office. During his interview Joseph admitted that he and Moira had been having an affair. This changed everything and he became the number one suspect in the disappearance of the young woman.

On the day of the election Joseph McGarvie easily won his seat for the Parliament at Westminster but he was destined never to take it up. Once the news of his indiscretion got out his marriage came to an end and so did his political career. He had no option but to resign.

When Moira didn't turn up, it was obvious that the police suspected that she had been murdered. In the absence of a body however, there was insufficient evidence to charge

McGarvie, who was released after questioning and quickly disappeared from public view.

In the early summer of 2007, two years after her disappearance, Moira Henderson did turn up again. Early one morning a milkman came across a body wrapped from head to foot in cling film at the side of the Peoples Palace on Glasgow Green. The body was frozen stiff although it was starting to defrost. The police attended the discovery and the remains were taken to the city mortuary.

After allowing the corpse to completely thaw out the authorities were then able to carry out a post mortem examination. This revealed that the body was indeed that of Moira Henderson, who had been strangled. The media had a field day. The killer was dubbed 'The Ice Man'.

In between being harassed by members of the press, Joseph McGarvie was again interviewed by the police. It was purely procedure as there was still no evidence to tie him to the crime. At this time McGarvie was back in his old profession as an estate agent working for an old school-friend, Kevin Reilly, whose company was based in Shettleston.

This was the first murder case in which newly promoted Detective Sergeant Audrey Lynch was involved since her move to London Road. It was to be the first of many. Just one week after the body of Moira Henderson had been found another woman was reported missing.

Avril Paterson, thirty from Shettleston, worked in the same estate agent's office as Joseph McGarvie. She had not been seen for a couple of days and her family were worried about her. Once again Mr McGarvie was interviewed. On this occasion it seemed that he had a watertight alibi. On the afternoon Avril had last been seen he had been taking clients to view a couple of properties in Dennistoun. He admitted having seen Avril at lunchtime that day in the office but not after that. The only other man with the firm, the owner Kevin Reilly, was also interviewed but nothing new was learned.

It seemed more than suspicious that another woman had gone missing and McGarvie was once again closely involved with the woman but there was no evidence against him. As time passed, as with the first case, it was suspected that Avril had also been murdered. Nobody was arrested for the crime, although the police felt, as did the public, that there was little doubt Joseph McGarvie was somehow involved.

McGarvie himself, not wishing to cause a fuss or any problems for the firm owned by his old friend, left his job and once more disappeared. Soon afterwards Reilly sold the business and he too moved on to pastures new.

# CHAPTER TWO

Linda Coyne had dressed in a certain way for a reason. It was not just because it was such a bright sunny afternoon. Company rules dictated that female members of staff must wear a grey pencil skirt and white blouse. Linda had adhered to the dress code, although her blouse was purposely quite revealing, and her skirt was slightly shorter than normal. Sometimes when meeting a male client, it paid to flirt a little. All's fair in love, war and the property business.

She was at a flat in Calton, Glasgow, for a 2pm appointment with a Mr McLean. Linda was showing the apartment on behalf of her employers, the West of Scotland Property Agency, with a view to the gentleman renting the property out on a long lease.

At 1.55pm Linda unlocked the front door and entered the living room. She liked to have a couple of minutes to have a quick look about the place, just to make sure everything was in order before the client arrived. A few moments making sure everything was in place was always worth the extra effort.

As she walked back into the lounge,the cupboard door under the stairs suddenly burst open. There stood a man wearing a dark blue boiler suit, workmen's boots, gloves and a woollen hat. His face was covered by a stocking mask. Frighteningly he carried a large knife and threatened Linda, warning her not to make a sound, or she would be killed. She was petrified and believed him. The man then proceeded to grope Linda and tear off her blouse. She braced herself, fearing that he would rape her at knife point. But that didn't happen. The attack was over almost before it had begun. The culprit forced Linda into the cupboard under the stairs, which he locked before escaping.

Realising her attacker had gone Linda used her mobile to call her office and the police. By the time they all arrived she had forced the cupboard door open. Although not injured in anyway, Linda was really annoyed with herself getting caught out in the way that she had. She and her colleagues had been warned time after time about attending viewings alone. It was for their own safety and everybody knew that, but when they were short staffed and there was a chance of commission, everyone Linda knew would have done exactly the same, given the circumstances,.

Later when giving her statement to the police, Linda would recall that the man seemed overly excited, as though this was something he had never done before, or perhaps he was somehow sexually immature. The only other thing she could say about the man was he was about six feet tall and had a Glasgow accent. Strangely he had cut a piece from her blouse and taken it with him.

One thing the police did discover - there was no sign of forced entry. Whoever was responsible either had a key for the front door or had picked the lock. It was certainly a mystery, which DS Audrey Lynch was happy to take on and add to her growing list of enquiries.

Nothing linked this attack to those of the so called 'Ice Man' but the public were getting slightly twitchy and on edge. This attack came only weeks after the body of Moira Henderson had been found and Avril Paterson had gone missing. Somebody was killing or attacking women in the east end of Glasgow. It was enough to make everyone nervous.

# CHAPTER THREE

It was now the height of summer and for once, Glasgow was enjoying some warm weather. It wasn't exactly sweltering but was a change from the dour temperatures the locals were used to.

Whatever happened to those long hot summers? The ones when kids set off all the fire hydrants in the streets to use as showers to keep cool. People had moaned when the fire service couldn't extinguish fires, due to low water pressure. Thankfully that risk had passed for another year as the schools had just started back after the summer holidays.

As usual on a Friday the offices of QLM Investigations Ltd, on Alexandra Parade in Glasgow, were a hive of industry. It wasn't always possible, but Gerry Lynch and Sandy Morton had always asked their staff to try to be as up to date as possible with their paperwork before the weekend. Just a thing they had about starting afresh on Monday morning.

When it came to paperwork, Sandy Morton was the top man. No surprise there, given that he was an ex-detective chief inspector who, over a thirty year police career, had got through mountains of the stuff. He seemed to be able to breeze through his workload, while his partner Gerry Lynch always struggled. Perhaps Sandy was more used to computers. Gerry was useless when it came to technology and no amount of tuition from the secretaries Jenny and Sarah, or indeed his wife Audrey, had helped. They all said the same thing - he had the attention span of a gnat. Gerry did own a laptop which was back in his flat buried somewhere under all Audrey's clothing from her flat. He couldn't recall the last time he had used or even seen it.

It was only approaching mid morning but Gerry was distracted and had already had more than enough. He left his desk, crossed the hall and spoke to Sandy in his office.

"Sandy" Gerry announced, "I'm going to get some ice cream from Angelo's cafe, do you want some?"

It was a stupid question and Gerry knew that before he had asked. It was well known locally that Angelo made the best ice cream in the west of Scotland. Well that was his claim anyway.

Mind you, didn't every Italian cafe owner make the same claim about their ice cream? As far as Gerry was concerned there was no argument. Angelo's ice cream was good. It was very good indeed.

In the end Gerry had to take his car, as he could not carry all the orders he had been asked for.

There were now several new members of staff and they all wanted some. It was amazing how the company had grown in such a short space of time.

Having made his purchases from Angelo's cafe, Gerry returned to the office and handed out the goodies. Suddenly, it was very quiet whilst a group of contented people all tucked into their ice cream treat. It wasn't a day for being stuck in the office but, unfortunately, it was Friday and the paperwork wasn't going to do itself .

Gerry had finished his tub of vanilla heaven and was not looking forward to renewing his battle with the reports piled on his desk. Thankfully, he was saved by the bell. Sarah buzzed through to his office to tell him that he had received a message. A lady from Easterhouse wanted him to contact her mobile number, which was supplied. Gerry had no idea who she was, but the message said Effie needs your help, which made a massive difference. Effie McGuire and her husband Bert had been his parents' friends and next door neighbours in Easterhouse for many years. Although not actually related, Gerry had always called them Auntie and Uncle. If Effie needed his help he would be there. She was the nearest thing to family he had, and there was no way Gerry was going to let her down.

The phone call had come as a huge relief to Gerry as he hated Fridays with all the paperwork. He much preferred to be out and about. As he made the short drive to Easterhouse, he thought about how his life had changed so dramatically since his release from hospital in 2005, following his break-down two years earlier.

Gerry had been a police officer, part of a group that took down a leading member of a Glasgow crime family. In the ensuing carnage his parents and two colleagues had died, one of them his best friend, Paul Corrigan.

Now he was a private investigator, in partnership with his old gaffer, ex DCI Sandy Morton. In the short time they had been together the firm had grown arms and legs. From small beginnings they had more than enough work to be getting on with. Recently he and Sandy had been talking about expanding the business even further by opening a second office in Glasgow. As usual Sandy had taken on the task.

# CHAPTER FOUR

The Brady brothers, Noel and his younger brother by two years, Keith, lived in a flat in Milnbank Street, just off Alexandra Parade in Glasgow. They originally came from Roystonhill which was just across the M8 motorway.

Their father, had been a career criminal and had initiated the two boys into the family business at an early age. Like his own father before him, he was a housebreaker and often took one or both of the boys with him on jobs. They could climb through smaller windows and let him in to rob from houses. As Noel and Keith grew into teenagers they became well known to the local police and spent quite some time in young offender's institutes.

Nothing was then heard of them for quite a time, they went right off the radar. Some people thought they had perhaps learned their lesson and gone straight.

What had actually happened was the lads had rented an industrial unit just along Alexandra Parade, less than half a mile from their flat. They employed a mechanic, Derek McVey, who dealt mostly with MOT tests and a few minor repairs. This side of their business was strictly legal and above board.

The brothers kept two or three vehicles separately in another unit at the back of the premises which had its own entrance. This was because Keith had met a young woman named Charlene Crainey, who liked to be known as Charlie, and she had taken them in a new direction and changed their lives.

Why risk capture by the police breaking into property or stealing cars? According to Charlie, being a bogus workman or sneak thief was the way forward. Prey on the old and infirm, steal their cash and belongings and be long gone before they knew what day it was. If by some misfortune the old dears twigged that they were getting turned over, they were hardly in a position to stop anyone making off.

The brothers had obtained a car and two vans which they made to look like those belonging to utilities companies and the Glasgow City Housing Department. They wore identical type polo shirts when out and had smartened up their appearance to give the illusion of genuine employees. They really did look the part.

Their new way of life had proved to be very profitable and Charlie had been right; they had never even come close to being caught. They struck all over Glasgow and beyond, never returning to the same area for several months. They had stolen thousands of pounds in cash and jewellery and left a trail of misery, as well as more than a few elderly people bewildered. The three had been very active especially in the last few months. At various times, they had hit areas they knew well, Riddrie, Springburn and Clydebank, which was Charlie's home town.

They knew the elderly were an easy target. Despite all the warnings that were out there, older people seemed not to care much for all this new technology, having no time for internet banking. They tended to be creatures of habit who struggled down to the nearest post office or bank to collect their pensions and kept their cash at home. Prior to

2005 it had been so much easier taking their pension book to the post office. Since then, despite having been forced by the government changes to have their pensions paid into either a bank or post office account, it seemed that very few pensioners trusted these establishments and once back home they hid cash, sometimes huge amounts, in the same obvious places believing they were safe.

Favourite places included in an old handbag, in the wardrobe, under the mattress or the back of a kitchen drawer under other documents.

The brothers and Charlie simply took up observation points and then followed likely victims home. Once happy with their targets they swung into action. Many people were so gullible. The pickings for the trio were rich and the risks minimal. If they were in any doubt that they'd been rumbled, they simply beat a hasty retreat in the knowledge that their elderly victim was hardly able to give chase. They would then just give that area a miss for a few months in case of any increased police activity.

It wasn't hard to persuade a lot of the elderly that they were genuine officials or workmen - they just needed bottle and some patter. Noel and Keith Brady had plenty of both and so did Charlie Crainey. She, like the brothers, had been involved in crime all her life. Her mother, Bessie, took her along when she and her gang went shoplifting. It was a highly organised group. They would use Charlie to distract staff whilst the other members of the team stole large quantities of goods. Bessie and four or five other women travelled the country from Clydebank in cars, on an almost daily basis, to carry out crime. This was a very lucrative business.

The three crooks had decided that particular week they would check out the area along Edinburgh Road from

Cranhill up to Easterhouse. It was just after the end of the summer holidays and all the schoolchildren were back in school. That meant less witnesses out on the street and they hoped to take a nice quiet break in the sun once they had finished this area. They already had enough cash to pay for a holiday, but a little more spending money wouldn't go amiss.

Effie McGuire was an eighty-four year old widow, who lived alone in a semi-detached house at the end of Lochend Road in Easterhouse. Despite her age she still managed to do most things for herself, including going to the bank in Bogbain Road on one Monday each month, for her pension money.

Twice a week a local woman, Lynne Gormley, came in and cleaned for Effie and did any washing. The two women had an arrangement and Effie paid Lynne cash in hand. She didn't want to bother the council asking for help and Lynne was glad of the extra cash. Charlie Crainey had followed Effie from the bank, marking her as a possible target. It wasn't hard to pick up her name as Effie spoke to all the people she met, and also had a nameplate on the front door of her home.

Once the Bradys and Charlie felt they had enough targets to make it worth their while, they began visiting the different houses in the area. It had been decided that Charlie would go to Effie's house pretending to be from the local housing office, whilst Keith would slip into the house and see what he could plunder.

It was late one Thursday afternoon when they hit Effie's house. Charlie knocked on the door and when Effie answered, she produced a fake identity badge and Effie let her in. They went into the living room and Charlie engaged Effie in conversation,

"Just a few questions, Mrs McGuire." she began, "It's to see which of our residents are exempt from a new tax the government are about to bring in."

"Nae bother, hen" Effie replied. She liked the new girl from the housing as she seemed so friendly and it was nice to have somebody different to talk to. After about fifteen minutes Charlie left with Effie's thanks ringing in her ears.

'Stupid old sod,' she thought, as she walked around the corner to meet Keith, who was parked in a van.

"Great lift," he said as she sat in the vehicle, "the old doll was loaded."

They both laughed as they drove away having robbed their last victim for that day.

The following morning Effie went into her wardrobe in the bedroom, to get money to pay Lynne. She kept it in an old handbag at the back of her wardrobe, behind her shoes. Since her Bert had died three years earlier she had kept her money there rather than in the bank. Effie lifted the handbag from the wardrobe onto the bed.

When she opened it she got the shock of her life. It was empty. 'How could that be?' she thought to herself. Nobody, not even Lynne, knew where she kept her money. Effie didn't know what to do. She knew there had been over £2,000 in the handbag as she had counted it recently after sending money down to her daughter in England, to give to her three grandchildren for the holidays.

Ten minutes later Lynne found Effie still sitting on her bed, in a flood of tears. It took her some time to find out what was wrong but when she had she immediately phoned the police. They were not long in attending as the office was literally only two minutes from Effie's house. The young constable took a statement and description of the supposed housing office lady. A quick phone call to the local housing office confirmed his worst fears, nobody was carrying out any type of survey with the residents. Also the description of the woman did not fit anyone working in their office. Effie had lost over £2000 at the hands of bogus callers.

Later that morning two CID officers called to see Effie and they also interviewed Lynne Gormley, who was initially a suspect but was quickly eliminated. It was little comfort to Effie when the officers told her that she had not been alone. Three other local pensioners had been duped in the same way earlier that same day. In all the culprits had got away with over £4000 in cash and a quantity of jewellery.

Once the police had left Effie asked Lynne if she would contact Gerry Lynch. "He was a policeman," Effie said, "until his poor mum and dad were killed in the fire next door. He'll know what to do."

Lynne found Gerry's contact number in Effie's address book, phoned and left a message. It was less than half an hour after she had called that Gerry Lynch was at the door.

As soon as Effie saw Gerry walk into the room, she struggled to her feet to give him a hug. He hugged her in return. She began crying again and took some time to repeat the story. When Effie's husband Bert had died Gerry had been unaware of his passing, as he himself had been hospitalised. He had liked Uncle Bert. He always had a beautiful garden and as Gerry's father was an invalid, he took care of the Lynch family garden as well. Gerry had many happy memories of helping Uncle Bert back when he was a boy.

Gerry was able to reassure Effie about the money. He, thanks to his late friend Matty McGowan, would replace her cash but she had to keep it in her bank account from now on.

Matty had died the previous year but not before he had stolen well over one million pounds from the men who had killed his brother. He had left the cash and a letter to Gerry in the hope he would do the right thing. And that was not to hand it in but spread it out to people who needed a hand. Gerry had been doing his best. Sometimes he felt like a modern day Robin Hood. The money had been the proceeds of crime but now it was being used for good.

He told Lynne Gormley that he would be back with the full amount in cash on Monday morning and he asked if she would ensure Effie paid it into the bank. Lynne assured him that she would go on Monday morning and make certain that Effie paid the money into her account.

"No more saving money at home, Auntie Effie," Gerry said.

"Whatever you say, son," Effie replied.

Being called son brought a tear to Gerry's eye. He left hurriedly, heading for the local police office which was only a few hundred yards away. He stopped for a few moments just around the corner to compose himself. He was upset Effie had been robbed; in fact he was bloody angry. What had upset him most though, and taken him somewhat by surprise, was how he had become so tearful and sentimental. Possibly the close proximity to his old house had not helped, or maybe he was now just a big softie.

Gerry called into Easterhouse Police Office just to let them know that he would be looking into the robbery from his Aunt Effie's house. He knew they would warn him off, which they did. But it was always better to be up front with the law - he never knew when he might want them on his side.

# CHAPTER FIVE

In the last year everything in Gerry Lynch's life had changed. Towards the end of 2006, after waiting far too long, he had finally arranged to ask Audrey Jennings to marry him over a romantic dinner at their favourite Italian restaurant. Before he could pop the question, he was shot by a would-be assassin. Two bullets in the chest had put pay to his romantic evening. He had also sustained a fractured skull but had survived. After a few weeks in hospital he had been released and told to take it easy.

He had then arranged to buy an old run-down property in Baillieston. His intention was to demolish it and clear the garden before building a dream home for himself and Audrey, but a woman had beaten him to it. Fortunately, that woman had been Audrey. Not only that, but not wanting to lose him again, she had arranged for them to get married the following Saturday.

Family friend Richard Jonson, an American millionaire businessman had arrived late at the reception with a present: two weeks in a beachside villa in Bermuda, which the Jonsons owned, for their honeymoon. They had jetted off and had a fabulous time. Gerry was feeling much better when they landed back in Glasgow. Not long afterwards they attended Richard's wedding in Hawaii when he married Audrey's friend, Aimi McLeod on Christmas day.

Once back in Scotland, early in 2007 they learned that Audrey was to be promoted. The new detective sergeant would be moving to start work at London Road Police Office. Unfortunately, Gerry's doctor had less good news. Gerry may well have felt better but his doctor insisted that he take at least two months off work and continue attending physiotherapy. With Sandy still sporting his arm in a sling due to also having been shot, things at work were difficult.

Not for the first time Jenny Galloway took up the strain, ably assisted by Pamela Gibson. The firm had won a contract with Steinberg & Williams who now had five clothing stores in Scotland, in Glasgow, Falkirk, Stirling, Inverness and Aberdeen, and the company were also in negotiations for a sixth store in Edinburgh. All the existing stores needed security staff and the contract was due to commence at the beginning of April.

Pamela and Jenny already knew the model by which Gerry and Sandy worked. They liked to employ people from a police background. After a hurried meeting with Gerry and Sandy it was agreed that the two ladies would do the necessary. After a series of telephone conversations, several meetings were arranged around the country. Two weeks later Pamela and Jenny returned for a second meeting with Gerry and Sandy. They had files on a number of people whom they had selected as prospective office managers. All that was required was the rubber stamp from Gerry and Sandy. Nobody wanted to get this wrong as this was a massive boost for the company.

In the end it was an easy task as Jenny and Pamela had done a brilliant job. All that remained was to let the candidates know they had been successful. During their discussions Gerry and Sandy realised that suddenly the size of the workforce had exploded. Back when Gerry took over the reins there had only been Jenny and himself. Now there were approximately sixty employees scattered across the land. Further matters needed to be put into place to ensure the smooth running of the company. In the meantime, QLM Ltd set up offices near the sites of all Steinberg and Williams current stores.

Former DCI in Grampian Police Neil McKinnon was the new office manager at the Gallowgate in Aberdeen which was near the Bon Accord Centre. George Mason, a former detective superintendent in the Central Scotland Police was in place at the newly acquired office in Barnton Street, Stirling just along the road from the Thistle Centre. John Clelland, an ex-uniform inspector, was in charge at East Bridge Street in Falkirk near to the Central Retail Park and finally, Ex DI John McLeod had the helm at the Academy Street office near to the East Gate Shopping Centre in Inverness. They were all busy recruiting their own staff and vehicles locally.

Alison Pearson was engaged as the company wages clerk and each office had to deal directly with her with regard to all matters pertaining to pay and expenses. They would soon discover that she was quite a formidable lady. She was based at the Alexandra Parade office as was David Gray, a recently retired inspector, who had worked in the Scottish Criminal Records Office within the headquarters of Strathclyde police in Pitt Street, Glasgow. His job, amongst other things, was to deal with matters concerning criminal intelligence. It was his task to collate any knowledge of criminal activity passed from the various offices and ensure that it was made available to all the other offices for their information.

It was still Gerry and Sandy's intention to use the money left by Matty McGowan for the good of all. They were the only two who knew about it and it remained within the safe in Gerry's office.

They already used the local bank for the company account and Tom Kane & Sam Bryson solicitors dealt with all their legal requirements. They were looking for an accountant and decided to go with the one who Jean Morton had used for her business for years, Jackson Cairns and Company of Tollcross.

Once Gerry did get back to work full time things changed dramatically. If he had thought he was under pressure previously, he soon discovered it could get worse. With Audrey moving into the flat, life was chaotic to say the least. The flat was just too small and with all her clothing filling the spare bedroom and beyond, the new house was required urgently.

Audrey had found herself inundated with work as soon as she moved into her new job. Gerry was under the cosh as well. He and Sandy wanted to make sure that the contract with Steinberg & Williams went well. For the first few weeks it seemed they were in constant contact with their offices around the country. Thankfully their new colleagues didn't take offence as they were all really in the same boat; none of them had ever been in this situation before. Things would settle down.

One good decision bore some fruit almost immediately. A notorious gang of shoplifters and till snatchers were sighted one day at the Bon Accord Centre in Aberdeen. Thankfully, Neil McKinnon and his staff had managed to frighten them off empty handed. The gang were known to live in the central Scotland area so it was felt that they would try at least one other raid in the north before making their way south again.

David Gray circulated the information to all QLM offices. Just three days later a car used by the gang was spotted in Inverness. John McLeod and his staff were ready. The local police had also been alerted. This resulted in four members of the gang being arrested, caught in the act, attempting to make off with thousands of pounds worth of goods.

Steinberg & Williams were delighted with the result as was everyone at QLM, not to mention all the other retailers when the news filtered through to them.

Gerry and Audrey badly needed new accommodation. They had to overcome a battle with the planning people over the proposals for their new home in Baillieston first. Their architect had submitted numerous drawings for their new home, but each time they had been denied. Eventually after several visits to the planning office they finally got the go ahead to begin. Their dream home was about to become a reality.

Gerry knew he had the skills to carry out most of the work on his own, which had been his original intention, but he wasn't fit enough to contemplate the work himself. In addition to that, things were so busy at QLM he couldn't spare the time. He decided to employ the builder who had renovated the offices and his flat but was worried about cost. Gerry and Audrey set up a meeting with the builder and came to an amicable agreement. The work had started back in February when the existing old house was demolished. Whilst awaiting planning permission they cleared the gardens and removed all the rubble and rubbish. The plot was now a blank canvas. As the summer arrived the first job was to lay the foundations and then it was full steam ahead.

On top of all the other work that QLM had, they also supplied the security for The Buckingham Terrace Trust at their property just off Great Western Road. This was a charity which Gerry had helped to set up for women and their families who had been the victims of both sexual and domestic abuse.

The founder, Vivien Henshaw, was the widow of Maurice Henshaw QC and had wanted to do something to redress the despicable behaviour of her deceased husband, whose family had owned the property. The idea was to create a safe environment for victims, in a place that had previously been anything but when her husband had been alive. She had asked Gerry to undertake the renovation of the building to prepare it for purpose. It had required far more of his time and attention than he could possibly have envisaged. It also meant his builder would be even busier than before.

The business had grown so fast and more work kept pouring in by the day. Gerry and Sandy realised that they would require a few cars for the staff to use so turned to their former colleague Ken Brown for help. He too had left the police force and now ran a garage. Ken was only too pleased to help and worked out a lease deal which gave them three new cars and three vans for themselves and the staff to use.

Through all of this and despite still recovering from being shot Sandy Morton had been a tower of strength. His association with the company had not only meant a huge increase in work but also former police officers were queuing up should any vacancy or new job be advertised.

Although also very busy, Audrey was really enjoying the extra responsibility her new job brought. She loved working with her new detective inspector, Brian Wallace. It turned out that he had been a colleague and friend of Sandy Morton's for years. The nice thing for Audrey was that Brian was very much a chip off the old block; it was just like working with Sandy.

Although it was only a few months since they had extended their business premises in Alexandra Parade, Gerry and Sandy both agreed that a second office would be of benefit. To this end they put out feelers which soon bore fruit. A solicitor who was an old friend of Sandy's contacted him. He was about to retire and wondered if his offices would suit. Given that they were on Gordon Street, right in the centre of the city and next to Central Station, it was an easy decision.

Once the solicitor retired at the end of March, Gerry and Sandy took over the offices which were perfect for the needs of the company. After freshening up the decor, half of the staff moved from Alexandra Parade down into the city. Pamela Gibson, an ex-detective inspector, was to be the office manager. She had already shown her worth to the company by assisting Jenny Galloway to recruit the new staff for the satellite offices. Louise Cadden was the secretary. The rest of the staff were all former detectives who had mainly worked in Glasgow during their police careers: Barbara Rice, John Johnstone and Alex Burnett.

# CHAPTER SIX

John Sinclair took the carrier bags of shopping from his car and struggled towards the building where he lived with his mother. He managed to press the button to call for the lift and took it up to the third floor. He had his front door key ready and as the lift stopped at his floor, he blocked the door with his bags. He opened his front door, then collected the shopping and brought it into the flat.

He popped his head round the door to his mother's bedroom and found that she was asleep. Quietly he put away the shopping in the fridge and kitchen cupboards before boiling the kettle for a cup of tea. It always worked. Immediately the kettle boiled he heard his mother's voice.

"Is that you, John?" she croaked.

"Yes Mum, I'm just making you a lovely cup of tea."

He took it through to her on a tray with a packet of custard cream biscuits. They were her favourites.

"You're a good boy to your mum," his mother said. "I don't know what I'd do without you."

Marie Sinclair was bedridden. Fifty odd years of smoking had reduced her lung capacity drastically and she relied on bottled oxygen to get her through the day. She only took the mask off to smoke the cigarettes she had sworn blind to the doctor that she'd long since stopped. In truth she was not long for this world.

Her son John was forty years old and as far as Marie knew had never had a girlfriend. He was a bit of a loner. His good-for-nothing father had disappeared years before. Thankfully, John and his grandfather got on really well.

Big John 'Jock' McLeod was a Highlander who, like many others, had been enticed down to Glasgow from up north with the chance of working as a officer in the city police force. At the time Glasgow had recruited big strong highlanders whose sole purpose was to clean up the streets of the city. They were frightened of no one and struck terror into the hearts of many a wee hard man, back in the day.

Jock McLeod had been a legend when the local police worked out of Tobago Street. He was renowned for never having drawn his wooden baton in anger in all his thirty years of service. He had no need for batons. If there had been a bare knuckles championship in the city, that would have been a different matter. Jock would have been one of the main contenders. He certainly knew how to handle himself.

There had been lots of drunken husbands who had come home and beat their wives, before feeling Jock's wrath. He had handed out many beatings to those he deemed deserved it. Never one complaint against him in all his years of service. Back then that's the way it was, just a way of life.

When he had finally taken his retirement, he went to live with his daughter Marie and grandson John, who was named after him. The young lad adored and idolised him and Jock regaled him with many stories of the 'Glesga polis'.

Young John couldn't wait until he grew up and was old enough to join up and emulate his grandfather. Unfortunately, it was not to be as he was found to be colour blind. Something else for Marie to blame on her errant husband. In the end John became a taxi driver instead.

He did pick up one thing from his grandfather and that was a love of all things to do with locks and keys. For many years Jock had been fascinated with different keys, and over time he had collected an enormous amount. He could open just about any lock known to man.

Young John loved anything to do with Jock and soon learned all his ageing grandfather had to teach him. He had a set of keys for cars known as jigglers and numerous different skeleton keys for various types of lock.

Old Jock lived well into his 80s and regularly received visits from the local beat constables from the new police office in London Road which was just across the road from their flat in Fielden Street. They usually called for a cup of tea, particularly in the winter or when it was pouring with rain. Whatever the reason, Jock loved to see them.

You could see right over the wall into the car park of the police office. Jock and young John had been shown around the new building when it had first opened. They would sit at Jock's bedroom window pointing out which office was which. The offices facing their flat were occupied mainly by the CID.

John didn't particularly like his job. He preferred working the night shift, so that he could watch daytime television, before grabbing an hour or two of sleep. Over the years he became obsessed with watching mainly programmes featuring young women. He would fantasise that he knew them or that they were his girlfriend.

One morning he came home from work to find his mother in tears. His beloved grandfather had passed away quietly during the night. John couldn't remember how he got through that time. He was never the same person again. Not only had he lost his grandfather, his hero and mentor but also his one and only friend. He was distraught.

John was an introvert and he moved into old Jock's bedroom, sitting for hours watching the police station from his room. Soon it became an obsession. He bought himself a very expensive pair of binoculars with night vision, which he mounted on a tripod. When he looked through them, he felt as if he was right there in the room with the detectives across the road.

He soon realised that he could read what was written on the white board on the wall of the detective inspector's office. In his own little world, he became a detective and pretended to be involved in enquiries. Because of his grandfather, John had been given the nickname locally of 'Little John' and everyone called him by that name.

After her father died, John noticed that his mum had started smoking more and more. She was also prone to drinking the odd bottle of cheap firewater from the local off sales. Her health soon deteriorated and after a prolonged stay in hospital she came home and took to her bed. Marie now relied on John for her every need.

# CHAPTER SEVEN

The family of Robbie Collins had been known to the police in Glasgow for many years. His grandfather, Freddie 'The Fox' Collins, was just twenty years of age when he married his wife Chrissie back in 1930. She was only sixteen and pregnant. They didn't have much and at first lived in a room and kitchen in Tannock Street in the Possilpark area of Glasgow.

Freddie was a petty thief who worked part time as a runner for the local illegal bookmaker in Possilpark. He also had another claim to fame - he was the main man in a bunch of thugs known as the Possilpark Young Team or PYT.

At that time Glasgow was beset by gangs of razor toting thugs, who defended their own territory with manic pride and frequently carried out vicious attacks on members of rival gangs.

Freddie was venerated by his fellow gang members. He was the local hard man - razors, fists, it didn't matter, Freddie could handle himself. He was a hard man and he treated his wife like dirt.

Chrissie gave birth to a son she named Archibald after her father. Much to her annoyance, Freddie immediately began calling the lad Archie, just to be awkward and to make the point to his wife that what he said was law. As Archie grew up, Chrissie looked on in dismay as her husband turned him into a young hoodlum who was frightened of no one.

Freddie would give young Archie regular beatings and then beat him again if he cried.

"It's to toughen him up" he would tell his tearful wife.

In time he turned his son into a cold-hearted monster. It was not surprising then that he followed Freddie into a life of crime. Archie was just like his dad; he could fight with his fists or use the razors his father had given him as a birthday present one year.

After giving birth to Archie, Chrissie had more than one miscarriage. The doctor eventually told her she would never have any more children. She was glad in a way. It was a terrible thing, but she didn't want more kids if they turned out like Archie.

In 1945, just as the war was coming to an end, Freddie Collins was killed in a fight outside a pub in Springburn, Glasgow. He was only thirty-five years old.

He had been a heavy drinker all his life, and on that particular evening he was very drunk. As was often the case, he picked a fight with a young lad in the pub and they took it outside. Before Freddie could think what was happening, the young man had stabbed him in the heart. He fell to the pavement dead. The police attended but didn't show much interest and, as usual, nobody saw or heard anything.

Archie was only fifteen years old at the time and, despite the war and rationing, was big and powerful beyond his years. The PYT wanted revenge for the loss of their leader; someone must pay. It was not difficult to learn the identity of the person who had killed Freddie. He was an eighteen year old lad from Springburn called James McCann. He worked in the railway yard in Springburn, known as 'The Callie'.

Most nights he could be found drinking in the Vulcan Bar. He had been boasting about killing Freddie Collins to anyone who would listen.

One Friday night Archie went to the Vulcan Bar with a couple of friends. Although three years younger, Archie handed out a vicious beating to McCann, then used his father's razor to cut him so badly he was lucky to survive with his life. He did survive but spent the rest of his life in a wheelchair and never spoke of Freddie Collins again.

Partly because of that incident and many others, Archie's reputation soon grew. He wallowed in the nickname of 'Animal'.

When Archie was eighteen years old, he married a local girl called Annie Jamieson. They quickly had a son called Robert, who Archie insisted on calling Robbie. In an effort to replicate his own upbringing, he used to beat his young son, making him cry, saying it was just to toughen him up. Annie was having none of it and would intervene. On many occasions it was her who took the beating which was handed out.

In 1954 she fell pregnant again and gave birth to a girl she called Sandra. Archie was elsewhere at the time and it wasn't until a few days later he learned he had become a father again. Sandra's birth was a great annoyance to him. Not only because she was a girl, but up until then the family had managed in a wee room and kitchen in Fruin Street. Now they had to move to a bigger tenement flat in Ardoch Street. That meant a few more pence a week rent and less for Archie to spend on drink.

As he grew up Robbie Collins came to hate his father with a passion and although he followed in his footsteps becoming involved in crime that was where the similarity ended. Robbie was always smartly dressed in a suit with a crisp white shirt. His tie always matched the handkerchief he kept in his breast pocket and it became his trademark. Over the years he spent thousands to ensure that he always bought the best of everything.

When he was drunk Archie would insult his son calling him a 'poof' or a 'gay boy'. Robbie did not respond, never rising to the bait. Archie eventually stopped saying anything. Robbie was a man now and, in truth, Archie was afraid of him.

Robbie was always good to his mother as he knew what she had suffered at the hands of his father. He also spoiled his little sister. Sandra was a bonnie wee thing with piercing blue eyes. As she grew Robbie was always giving her sweeties or a new dolly. He used to give Sandra half a crown to clean his shoes and she always made sure they were spotless.

By the time he was just twenty years old, Robbie was the top man locally. His father had not yet reached forty but was an alcoholic and a spent force.

The big difference between Robbie and his father was that Robbie had class. It was well known locally that he paid the rents of some families and old folk who were struggling. Robbie was more of a benefactor to the locals. That's not to say he didn't have a steely grip on business - he just preferred to persuade people to do things rather than bully them.

Outwardly he was the quintessential Glasgow businesses man. He very rarely drank alcohol and kept his friends close. He was, however, by this time heavily involved in crime, mainly theft, housebreaking and stealing cars. He soon branched out into the sale and supply of drugs, which he didn't really care for, but it was good business.

Another member of the gang was eighteen year old, Malky Gourlay who just lived nearby in Killearn Street. He was trusted by Robbie and soon became his second in command. This meant he regularly went to the Collins home. Malky took a shine to Robbie's wee sister who was now almost sixteen. He asked permission to take Sandra out, just to the local cinema or a local cafe for a coffee. Archie was having none of it.

"Over my dead body," he told the family, "over my dead body."

One Saturday night Archie went out as usual for a beer. He was found on a railway embankment the next day with two bullet holes in him. Nobody was ever charged with his death and Malky began taking Sandra out, with the permission of her mother and big brother.

The romance blossomed and Malky asked if he could marry Sandra. Annie was beside herself as Sandra was only sixteen, and she didn't want the same life for her girl as she'd had with a gangster. She was pleased when Robbie saved the day. He told Malky he wasn't against the marriage, but they would have to wait as Sandra was too young.

What Robbie said was law. Malky waited until Sandra was nearly twenty. By this time, he almost lived with the Collins family, he was at their flat so often and Annie had warmed to him. Yes, he was a criminal, just like Robbie, but he was a nice lad, who she knew loved Sandra.

The couple were married in the Registry Office on Martha Street in Glasgow on 7th January 1974, Sandra's twentieth birthday. Robbie paid for the reception in a local pub.

The happy couple had a week honeymooning down in the Lake District, before they were cruelly separated by the law. The following week Robbie and Malky were up in court on charges of assault and car theft. They were both found guilty and sentenced to eighteen months imprisonment.

Sandra was beside herself - she'd been married for less than four weeks and her husband and brother were in jail leaving her with her mum.

To cheer her up a couple of pals took Sandra dancing in Glasgow. Feeling sorry for herself she got drunk and ended up having sex with some boy she met at the dance. All she knew about him was his Christian name. The inevitable happened, she fell pregnant. She missed her period in February, so was looking for it in March. When it didn't happen, she felt sick and Sandra realised she was in big trouble. The only option was to tell her mum.

Annie was upset and very disappointed with her daughter but, in a way, she understood. What frightened both of them the most was Robbie or Malky finding out. Thankfully they were both in jail. Annie and Sandra spoke about how best to deal with the situation and, in the end, however hard or painful it would be, they decided that Sandra should have the baby and then put it up for adoption.

They concocted a story for the neighbours; Sandra was going to look after a fictitious aunt in Girvan who was ill. In actual fact, six weeks before the baby was due, Sandra moved into a home for mothers and babies, Atholl House in Partickhill Road, Glasgow. Up to that point Sandra had hardly looked pregnant.

The house was full of girls and women all in the same position as Sandra. It was a long six weeks but eventually her time came and at 2.20pm on Tuesday 19 November 1974 Sandra gave birth to a beautiful baby boy. He looked like his father except he had Sandra's piercing blue eyes. It was a cruel situation to be in. The baby had been put up for adoption but in the following six weeks Sandra breastfed and tended to the needs of her son, who she named Craig after his father. It was all she had to give him.

Then one day she was told to dress her baby, as the new parents had arrived to collect him. Sandra would remember that day for the rest of her life. She could hardly see through the floods of tears. Her eyes were red and puffed up with crying, she had a pain in her chest so severe she thought she might have a heart attack. She had dressed her son in a little woollen suit with a matching hat, which had a small teddy bear motif on the front.

When the people came to take the baby she broke the rules and peeked out of the bedroom window. Sandra saw a big car parked in front of the house and a very smartly dressed man and woman with her baby son. They looked like a nice couple and she prayed they would care for the boy.

Once the couple had left Sandra was told to pack her bags straight away and go home, with no compassion. She caught a bus back to Possilpark where her mother was waiting for her. As Sandra opened the front door Annie was there and they fell into each other's arms and wept. It took Sandra a few weeks to get back to any semblance of normality.

When Malky got out of prison in July 1975, Sandra realised how much she had missed him - without her son she needed to be loved. She soon realised she was pregnant again. In April 1976, Sandra found herself in the Royal Maternity Hospital, commonly known as the Rottenrow. The circumstances of this birth were so different from the first - the doctors and nurses couldn't have been nicer. Malky always kidded on after she gave birth to their daughter Christine, that Sandra had timed it just perfectly right before dinner was served. As she lay in bed that night with her daughter in a crib next to her, there was a tear in Sandra's eye. She was thinking of her son and offering up a prayer, as she had often done in the preceding year, that God was keeping him safe and that he was well. Sandra swore nobody would take her wee girl away from her. She was true to her word; Christine was always by her side. Indeed, Sandra was perhaps a little too over protective sometimes.

Malky and Sandra Gourlay lived in a tenement building on Balgair Street in the Possilpark area of Glasgow. It was an area of the city that had seen better days and things were only going to get worse as the disease of drugs polluted Scotland. Things were not so easy but growing up Christine soon realised that she and her parents had a head start over everyone else in the scheme. Christine's dad worked for his brother-in-law, her uncle Robbie Collins. Both were known as local 'hard men' so there was no way anyone was going to give them any bother, unless they were prepared to accept the consequences.

Uncle Robbie was not married and loved nothing better than spoiling his niece. He always made certain that she had the latest new toys, and when she moved into her teen years, the latest fashions. Sandra could hardly complain as he had spoiled her in exactly the same way when she was young. There was just one thing that Sandra insisted of her brother and her husband: Christine was never to become involved in anything criminal.

Christine was a happy child and did well at school. She went on to business college and got herself a diploma in business studies. She wanted to get involved in the property market and she soon got a job with an estate agent in Bishopbriggs. It meant two buses to work and two back home again. Christine didn't mind.

Over the next couple of years Christine worked hard learning the various aspects of the business. Eventually she realised that she was doing the bulk of the work. It was the estate agents who were the ones benefiting, not her. It was time to try and breakout and go it alone. The only problem was finance. She had some money of her own, but not enough, Christine visited every bank she could think of. All gave her the same answers: she was too young, had insufficient funds of her own and was too big a risk.

Her uncle Robbie had offered to give her the money more than once, each time she refused. Sandra had tried to shelter Christine from the business that Malky and Robbie were involved in, but she wasn't stupid. Christine knew people would talk if she took money from her family, and she was determined to prove that she could run a legitimate business.

Just around this time Glasgow City Council decided it was time to have a spot of urban regeneration and began demolishing some of the older tenements in Possilpark, replacing them with new flats. Malky and Sandra moved out and bought their own house in Bilsland Drive. Robbie had been living in a small house in Springburn for years by then with his friend and secretary, Noel Freeman. They had met years before in prison and on their release, Robbie had bought the house in Springburn rather than return to live with his mother. Although they were very discrete it was known that Robbie and Noel were a couple. Whereas Robbie was more reserved, Noel was very flamboyant and always a snappy dresser.

The changes in Possilpark also meant Granny Annie would have to move. Christine was either going to have to remain living with her parents or buy her own place. As usual Uncle Robbie solved the problem. He told Christine that he was looking for a new larger house nearer to Glasgow city centre, as he wanted to be nearer his business interests and had plans to expand his empire. He also wanted to buy a couple of small hotels.

Robbie proposed that he pay Christine commission for obtaining these premises, and in the meantime, he would loan her the money to get started and she could pay him back once she was on her feet. Christine still wasn't sure until he hit her with the sucker punch.

"You would be helping put a roof over Granny Annie's head."

Such emotional blackmail. But she could not refuse after it had been so subtly put.

Christine found herself some premises in Springburn Road near to the Willow Shopping Centre and called it 'CC Properties'. It stood for Christine and Collins Properties but if anyone asked it would be City and Countryside. The minute she managed to repay her uncle she would change the name again. She also bought a small flat nearby and got to work.

Robbie had told Christine that money was no object. She took him at his word and set about the task of finding suitable premises. Within the month she had found the perfect house in Kirklees Road in Kelvindale, near to the Botanic Gardens and not too far from Possilpark.

Robbie was delighted with the house which was set in its own grounds and surrounded by a walled garden. It was a detached five bedroomed property and had large outhouses to the rear. The sale went through quickly and Robbie soon had builders renovating the place.

When they had finished, the outhouses had been turned into a two bedroomed, self-contained annexe for his mother

Annie and the main house had been totally refurbished. Christine realised her uncle had been right, money was no object. Annie moved into the 'wee hoose' as she called it. Robbie and Noel moved into their new home as soon as it was finished.

By that time Christine was negotiating for two small hotels. The first was a ten bedroomed property in Belgrave Terrace, just off Great Western Road and a fourteen bedroomed property in Hillhead Street around the corner. Both were in walking distance from Robbie's new home.

Having viewed both premises, Robbie agreed to purchase both. He called the first the Balgair Hotel, after the street his sister and her husband had lived in. The second was named the Ardoch Hotel, after the street in which his mother had lived. Both premises were extensively renovated before they opened.

Unknown to Christine, Robbie turned them into brothels, and in the Ardoch Hotel, he turned the large basement into a small licensed casino. The hotels were to be used to launder money from his growing drugs dealing empire. Although frequented by a largely criminal element, the casino was Robbie's only legitimate business.

The commission Robbie paid to Christine enabled her to repay his original loan, and also to pay a sizeable amount off the mortgage for her flat.

From the beginning Christine worked every hour she could, soon diversifying into purchasing property on her own behalf as well as buying and selling for clients. With her business expanding she moved to new office premises in West Nile Street in the city centre. She also renamed her company the West of Scotland Property Agency, turning it into a limited company. This was for tax reasons, on the advice of her accountant. Christine now owned twenty houses and was collecting rent from over one hundred flats, mostly student lets in and around the area of Glasgow University.

No matter how hard she was working, or how busy she was, every Wednesday night without fail she took Annie and Sandra to the bingo at Possilpark. There they met lots of friends from the old neighbourhood and spent time having a good old fashioned natter between games.

# CHAPTER EIGHT

There was one thing which Robbie Collins had learned early on. As long as he looked after the locals, then the locals would look after him. Unlike his father and grandfather before him, Robbie showed a degree of benevolence to the people of Possilpark. Just because he no longer lived amongst them didn't mean he had abandoned them, far from it. If anyone had any money problems or needed help Robbie gave his assistance. This assured that there was no way that anything he did which was illegal ever reached the attention of the police.

Over the years the Possilpark Young Team gang had ruled their own area of Glasgow by fear. They were prone to sort out any trouble, no matter whether petty or serious, with violence and the weapon of choice which in their case was the razor.

Robbie Collins changed all that once he took over. His way of running things in a different way soon earned the locals' respect. That was not to say he was an easy touch, far from it. If violence was called for Robbie and his associates could be more vicious than their predecessors had been. Petty matters often just resulted in a harsh word, but anything serious ended with someone getting a severe beating or being slashed. But if what had been done warranted it, then Robbie and his gang had no problem at all in killing those responsible.

There was no doubt that the locals looked upon Robbie as an almost benevolent father figure to those in Possilpark. None the less, he was feared as he was not one to be crossed.

Back in the day the gang's headquarters was a warehouse situated in Stronend Street, between Panmure Street to the west and Balmore Road to the east. It was quite a large site and at one time numerous stolen vehicles passed through the yard, as well as large quantities of drugs and cash. When the regeneration of the area took place, new industrial units were built nearby as well as a large housing estate springing up across the road to replace the old tenements. Once Robbie decided to move house to Kirklees Road then the headquarters moved with him. Rather than have everything in one place, he moved the flow of drugs and cash to the casino below the Ardoch Hotel. Various other parts of the business were sited elsewhere in separate locations.

One of the oldest members of the gang still alive was John 'Spud' Murphy. He had been an integral part of the firm for more years than Robbie could remember. Now in his eighties, at one time he had been an enforcer for the gang and had earned a fearsome reputation as a hard man. As the dynamics of the criminal world changed, Spud was slow to change with it. He had difficulty with the drugs scene and the new technology that criminals were now using. In other words, he was old school.

Rumour had it that he had once done a ten years prison sentence rather than give up one of the gang bosses. When he came out of prison, he was a broken old man. By this time Robbie was the main man and he ensured that Spud was taken care of. It was a matter of honour.

The thing was John Murphy was a proud man and would not take any handouts. It was obvious though to Robbie that he was of little use to the business. It had been Malky Gourley who had come up with the answer.

Robbie sent for Spud and told him that he had a very important job for him. He wanted Spud to move into the old headquarters. There was an office with a kitchen and sleeping facilities on the premises. Robbie told Spud that for all the new methods that they used, one thing they could never buy was loyalty. Robbie explained that he didn't want to put all his eggs in one basket. He was going to be leaving a substantial amount of cash and drugs in the office safe. It was a form of security for the gang. He gave Spud the combination of the safe, knowing full well that he would never open it. In this way Robbie was giving him a roof over his head, paying him to do the job of watchman and allowing the old man some dignity in believing he was still working as part of the gang.

This had all worked perfectly for nearly three years. Robbie ensured that Spud received regular visitors, different gang members called to make sure he was alright and to pay him his wages. Spud made himself at home in his little flat within the warehouse at Stronend Street.

There is an unwritten law amongst the criminal fraternity to never to do business in another firm's territory or you will suffer the consequences. It was unfortunately the case that some younger gang members in various parts of the city were in a hurry to get where they thought they should be. Over the years this had caused numerous acts of retaliation, even murder. These youngsters didn't want to be patient, learn their craft and climb up the ladder. They wanted it all, now.

Way back Spud had served time in the Army and still kept his little living area as clean as the barracks he had been billeted in with his fellow recruits all those years before. Some days he even had ladies from across the road bringing him meals. He was a character in the area, well known to everyone. At weekends he could be found in the corner of the public bar in his local pub. He liked a dram to say the least - sometimes the landlord had to make sure he got home in one piece. After all he didn't want to answer to Robbie Collins if anything untoward happened to the old man.

When in the pub, especially when he was drunk, Spud was prone to brag about the fact Robbie Collins relied upon him to look after the firm's stash which he kept in his safe in case of emergency. As with all tall stories, it grew arms and legs and eventually fell upon the wrong ears.

One Friday night Spud had as usual been in the local bar longer than he should, the landlord had a couple of the local lads help him back to the warehouse. They lay Spud on the bed. He was snoring soundly when they left.

The following day there was no sign of Spud at his local. Nobody thought anything of it, sometimes when he'd gone over the score he gave the pub a miss for a few days.

On Sunday lunchtime, one of the women from across the road, Betty Fitzpatrick, went across to the warehouse to give Spud some lunch. She knocked on the office door but got no reply. However, she had detected a strong smell of burning. She tried the door and found it wasn't locked. She cautiously opened the door. What confronted her caused her to let out a blood curdling scream and would haunt her for the rest of her life. Betty somehow managed to run back home and telephone the police.

A few minutes later uniform officers arrived followed by CID. The whole warehouse and yard was cordoned off as a crime scene.

What Betty Fitzpatrick had come across was quite horrific. Someone had tied old Spud to a metal chair and subjected him to a vicious attack, before pouring petrol over him and setting him alight. The feeling amongst all the police officers who attended was the same. They hoped he had died from a heart attack rather than suffer the flames. Fortunately, that is exactly what had happened.

Soon after dark on the Saturday evening, Spud was readying himself to go to his local for a hair of the dog. He knew that he drank too much but at his age, what the hell, why not. Just as he was about to leave a car pulled into the yard. As Spud looked out of the window of his wee room he saw four young lads he didn't recognise. They weren't members of Robbie's crew. They were, in fact, four members of a gang from the Barmulloch area. As with many other teams they couldn't be bothered waiting to rise up to the top of the ladder. They wanted it all now.

The leader of the group of four was a nasty piece of work called Kevin Kennedy. He was rising up towards the top of his gang but was impatient to get there. He loved handing out beatings and, being a big lad, he was more than able to dispense violence. Over and above that he was an evil, sadistic bastard. His three companions were all petrified to go against Kevin's wishes. They didn't possess a backbone between them. They could not do anything unless Kevin told them what do.

Word had reached this team about what old Spud supposedly kept in the safe. Kennedy thought that they would only have to slap the old boy a couple of times and he'd give up the combination. But he didn't know John Murphy. The three goons tied Spud to a chair in the flat and knocked him about for quite some time. He refused to say a word. Kennedy ordered the three to intensify the assault and after several hours Spud finally gave up the combination, but not before he had taken an horrific beating. It was a miracle it hadn't killed him.

Kennedy strode over to the safe, which stood against the back wall, with a smug sense of self achievement. He input the combination and pulled the large, heavy metal door open to reveal its contents. Nothing. The safe was completely empty.

All that could be heard in the room was Spud's laughter. Kennedy was enraged, almost running across the room, punching Spud hard in the face. The tough old boy just shook his head and continued laughing, spitting out his broken dentures onto the floor.

This just made Kevin Kennedy even angrier. He looked about the room for something to use as a weapon and saw a petrol can over by the door. It was full. Not hesitating Kennedy poured the contents over the old man and without saying another word, set him alight. Kennedy's three companions stood open mouthed and watched in horror, as the old man let out blood curdling screams before eventually his heart gave out and he died.

Kevin Kennedy just stood and watched as old Spud died. He had a smile on his face and told his associates, "Nobody takes the piss out of me."

There was nothing worth stealing from the flat so the four made off empty handed after murdering an old man. They had no idea who they were messing with or that their problems had only just begun.

The next morning Robbie Collins was sitting having breakfast when he learned what had happened to John Murphy. He was furious and ordered that his gang find those responsible immediately. It didn't matter what it took, Robbie wanted those responsible before the law got anywhere near them. He had to put down a marker. It was a matter of honour. Someone had broken the unwritten code and must pay. Besides that, whoever had killed Spud in that manner also needed putting down.

The word soon got out and urgent enquiries were made. The last thing that any other crime family in Glasgow wanted was a war with Robbie Collins. That night, although it was only a Monday, the casino below the Ardoch Hotel was full to capacity. There were gang leaders from all over Glasgow there. None of them were there to gamble, their only purpose was to assure Robbie that they were not responsible. If somebody knew who was, they weren't saying.

It took longer than usual, six weeks to be exact, to track down those responsible. As is normally the case, it only took one wrong word in the wrong place. One of the others who had accompanied Kevin Kennedy on the night he had murdered John Murphy was to unwittingly cause the ensuing carnage. Since that night he had gone off the rails and was hitting the bottle. One night in a pub he let slip about the murder. The following morning Robbie Collins had the names of the four who had been present when old Spud had died.

It was dark outside, the rain battered down upon the metal roof of the old warehouse. Robbie Collins entered the dimly lit building accompanied by Malky Gormley. Several members of his crime family were already present: Ricky Mathews, Joe Cassidy, Billy and Charlie Henderson.

They had been taking care of the four naked young men who were hanging secured and suspended by chains from the steel roofing beam. All four were in agony, having suffered a severe beating for what, to them, seemed like hours.

On Robbie's command the four young thugs were lowered to the concrete floor. They were then helped over to the old office which Spud had used as his living quarters, and where he had died. The four stood trying to keep warm but failed miserably, shivering with fear. They all recognised the smartly dressed man who stood before them.

Robbie Collins spoke, "So you are the four hard men who came here a few weeks back and beat the shit out of a defenceless old man."

None of the four spoke - they were too afraid.

Robbie continued, "Beat an old man to get the combination to the safe. Then when you opened the safe and it was empty you poured petrol over the old man and set him on fire."

One of the four went to speak but was slapped down by Ricky Mathews.

"The funny thing is the safe wasn't empty," Robbie said. "Old Spud would never have taken the job in the first place if that had been the case. He gave you the combination 5934, didn't he?"

Robbie directed these remarks to Kevin Kennedy who just nodded.

Robbie walked across the room to the safe which had once again been locked. He punched in the combination and opened the door. Everyone could see that again there was nothing inside. He then punched in the numbers again, only this time backwards, 4395. A panel at the back of the safe sprung open. Inside was over £50,000 in cash and two kilos of cocaine.

"You know old Spud was his own worst enemy. At one time he had been a top man in the PYT but he was well past his best. His only pleasure in life was a wee dram and, okay, he talked too much. But he didn't deserve to die like that. To be fair, three of you didn't really have anything to do with his killing, but then you didn't help him or stop it either. Therefore, me being a benevolent soul, I'll make sure my men go easy on you."

At that Robbie's men left Kevin Kennedy in the room and took the other three back out to the main warehouse. Three shots rang out and Kennedy knew he was now alone.

"As for you, son," Robbie turned to Kennedy, "you are going to die a very slow agonising death, just so you can feel exactly what old Spud felt".

With that Robbie and Malky left the building. The others had their orders.

When the police eventually found the four bodies, three had been shot once at the back of the head. A classic gang-land type execution. The fourth body, or what was left of it, had suffered terrible torture. So mutilated were the remains that the identity was only confirmed by examination of the teeth and checking dental records. Kevin Kennedy had indeed died in agony.

Just a few weeks later, as part of the further regeneration in the area, the old warehouse was completely demolished to make way for new housing. By that time the criminal fraternity had been brought up to speed as to what had happened in the old warehouse that night. It was never spoken about again. Robbie Collins had made his point and laid down his marker.

John Murphy was laid to rest with a magnificent send off, befitting a member of the Possilpark Young Team. As well as gang members, a large number of local residents attended the service and thereafter toasted Spud in his favourite pub, all paid for courtesy of Robbie Collins.

# CHAPTER NINE

Despite the best efforts of Audrey and her new colleagues, the police were no nearer apprehending a suspect for the attack on Linda Coyne. They were not helped by the fact that the culprit had left no forensic evidence, such as DNA, at the scene.

Over the next couple of months there were another three similar incidents, all involving female estate agents, all of whom worked for the West of Scotland Property Agency. Whether or not there was anything significant in this was yet to be established. Each time there was no sign of forced entry to the premises, but each attack was more serious than the last and, worryingly the level of violence had escalated.

It became apparent to Audrey and her boss Brian Wallace that there were two different perpetrators on the loose. One was attacking women working as estate agents and the other strangling women, before freezing the bodies for some reason which had, as yet, not become apparent.

The next incident took place in Dennistoun in November. It happened one Saturday morning.

Alice Brennen, again from the West of Scotland Property Agency, had an 11am appointment with a client, a Mr Sharpe, to view a flat in Harcourt Drive just off Alexandra Parade and less than half a mile from the office. Alice drove to the appointment and took young Carol McVey with her. Carol was a schoolgirl, who only worked on Saturdays to earn a few pounds spending money.

They arrived ten minutes early and Carol sat in the car while Alice went into the building, to see the client. Carol spent her time texting some of her friends on her new mobile phone. It had cost her a lot but that was why she had her Saturday job, to buy the extras her dad couldn't afford. She had only just got it and still had not worked out all the new functions, but she had mastered sending text messages.

When Alice had not returned thirty minutes later Carol went to investigate. She found Alice in the bedroom. Her clothing had been torn off and she had been stabbed in the side. She told Carol that a man had tried to rape her. Thankfully the stab wound was not too serious and would heal but it would take Alice much longer to get over her ordeal.

It was obvious to the police that the culprit was the same person who had committed the previous attacks. The description was exactly the same as for the other incidents. A tall man with a Glasgow accent wearing a dark blue boiler suit, workmen's boots, a woollen hat and a stocking mask. Once more there was no signs of any forced entry to the property. The police had not found any forensic evidence at any of the incidents. Just as in the previous attacks the culprit had taken a trophy. On this occasion he'd sliced off a piece of material from Alice's skirt.

Even though Alice had not gone alone, young Carol had not seen anyone either entering or coming out of the same building. She just remembered seeing a man come out of the building next door. He was carrying a holdall and walking towards an empty taxi cab, which was parked on the corner facing towards Alexandra Parade. He was dressed in a beige coloured sweatshirt and a pair of brown coloured trousers.

Enquiries revealed that no taxi driver lived in the building next door. Whoever it was carrying out these attacks was getting more and more violent. Alice had come the closest to being raped. The police knew if they did not catch the culprit soon, they would, without doubt, end up dealing with, at the very least, a rape or, even worse, have a murder on their hands. Just fourteen days later the unthinkable happened.

Carol McVey knew she should have been home hours ago. Her dad was going to be really angry with her. She was almost sixteen years old but despite this fact, she felt that her father still treated her like a child. As she hurried across Alexandra Park down towards Alexandra Parade, she wished she hadn't bothered going to her pal Sheena's house in Don Street in Riddrie. It had been okay, there were a couple of boys there and one seemed to have taken a shine to Sheena. Carol didn't fancy the other one much and he obviously had felt the same about her or he might have offered to walk her home across the park to Dennistoun.

The cheap vodka she had drunk was wearing off and she needed to go to the toilet. The lighting in the park was not the best and, if she was honest, she was a little scared. As she passed the boating lake Carol was just thinking that she would be too tired to go to her Saturday job that morning. That would be another reason for her dad to be angry. Since the attack on Alice Brennan she wasn't sure she wanted to work there anyway. Perhaps she should just be honest and tell her father that.

Carol thought that she heard a rustling noise and suddenly a dark figure emerged from the bushes. It was the last thing she would see...

At 6am Gerry Lynch was a familiar figure, partaking of his usual daily morning run in the Park. There was a frost on the ground and a bite in the air. It seemed that winter had finally arrived.

Gerry saw a man out walking a wee dog. Over the last year or so, he had got to know all the early morning regulars in the Park and that included Andy Gemmell from Eastercraigs and his Jack Russell bitch, Jinny.

As he approached Gerry, saw that the dog was straining on its lead trying to get into the nearby bushes. Andy was talking to his dog, "What have you got there, lass?"

Seconds later he was bent over vomiting and frantically gesturing towards the bushes. Gerry stopped and took a look into the foliage. The dog was sniffing around the dead body of a young girl. He used his mobile phone to contact the police and awaited their arrival.

Having given a statement to the first officers on the scene Gerry returned to his home for a shower and some breakfast before going to his office. The police knew where to find him if he was needed. After all that had happened in the previous twelve months or so, he had become something of a celebrity in the area, and he was married to a police detective.

Down in his office within London Road police office, Detective Inspector Brian Wallace and Gerry's wife, Detective Sergeant Audrey Lynch, were going over the initial report on the death of the young girl in Alexandra Park. Local enquiries had quickly identified her as Carol McVey, just fifteen years of age who lived with her father Derek, a single parent, in nearby Sannox Gardens.

The two officers had paired up as soon as Audrey had arrived at London Road. The DI was an old friend and colleague of Sandy Morton's and he'd heard great things about her. They already had the job of investigating all the recent sexual assaults and attempted rapes. On top of that they were also delegated the enquiry regarding the two women who had been strangled and then frozen solid. Now, as they had feared, a murder in their first enquiry had occurred. Other than the victims of these crimes, young Carol McVey had been their only independent witness.

Around lunchtime they would attend the post mortem examination at the city mortuary down in the Saltmarket, Glasgow.

Door to door enquiries had already begun in the streets adjacent to the park. The next step was to get some support unit officers in, to make a thorough search of the park and pond to see if they could come up with anything which might aid the investigation, such as the weapon used. There was also no trace of the victim's handbag at the scene.

Later that same morning, before the post mortem, Wallace and Lynch attended at the home of a distraught Derek McVey to offer their condolences and interview him regarding his daughter's death. He tried to explain to the officers how he had found the last five years really hard. Trying to raise a young girl on his own had not been easy. His wife had died of breast cancer, after a long battle with the illness. As Carol had only been eleven years old at that time, she had taken the loss very hard. Derek explained that he was a motor mechanic at a garage just along Alexandra Parade. He had taken the job to be nearer to home and his daughter if needed.

"I knew she was going to visit a pal last night, but she didn't tell me who. I told her to be home for 11 o'clock at the latest. She didn't answer her mobile phone and I was up half the night waiting for her." He again broke down and began sobbing uncontrollably. Who could blame him? He had now lost not only his wife but also his only child.

Wallace and Lynch knew that they had also lost their only independent witness in the attempted rape and wounding of Alice Brennen. Was this just coincidence or was Carol's murder planned? If so, why and what did she know that had got her killed? The two officers once again expressed their deep regret to Derek McVey and took their leave. The next job was to attend the post mortem of his daughter at the city mortuary.

The pathologist, John Smillie, had taken over the job when Audrey's friend Aimi McLeod had left. He told the two detectives that Carol had died as a result of a single stab wound to the heart. It appeared that she had been violated after death and that the culprit had been less than gentle.

"Almost frenzied," were Dr Smillie's words.

Tissue samples had been taken and the results were awaited. As to time of death, the doctor felt it had occurred between 1am and 2am. The officers thanked Dr Smillie and as they were leaving the mortuary DI Wallace's mobile rang. He answered then turned to Audrey.

"The troops have detained a suspect back at the office," he said.

"Did they say who?" Audrey enquired.

"No, they just want us back as soon as possible to conduct the interview."

\* \* \*

Gerry Lynch had borrowed an old van from Ian Bell's garage to remove a load of rubbish from the back of his building. It was something he had promised Jenny Galloway that he would attend to. Jenny and her daughter Sophie had moved into Matty McGowan's old flat. Gerry had bought it for her as a thank you for all her hard work and support to him when he had first started out on his own. As per Matty's will, the money from the sale had gone to Sadie Gleason, a prostitute and old friend of his mother. She had burst into tears at his generosity towards her. But he had only repaid her many kindnesses to him over the years. Now, hopefully she could retire in comfort.

Jenny had been delighted. It had, however, been somewhat of a rush job to leave her mother Brenda with her latest boyfriend. His name was Terry Banks and Brenda had met him on an online dating page. There was something about her mother's latest flame that Jenny couldn't put her finger on but the move into Matty's old flat couldn't have come at a more opportune moment. She had cleaned the place from top to bottom and done a bit of decorating. It was only once she moved in that she had some work done and it was the rubbish from this which was now in the back garden for Gerry to move.

No way was he using one of the shiny new company vans. Gerry put on an old pair of overalls, filled Ian's old van and headed for the council tip. After that he had an appointment with the builders in Baillieston. He had asked Ian if he could keep the van for a while, for a surveillance job. After what had happened to his Aunt Effie, Gerry had decided on a plan. Later he would cruise around the Easterhouse, Riddrie and Baillieston areas looking for bogus workmen. He reckoned that it was about time for them to return to the area. They were known to be creatures of habit.

Gerry parked his van, leaving it along the road from the site of his new home. As he walked along the street he saw a woman in the garden of a house across the road. She was speaking on her mobile phone. Gerry was just about to go and introduce himself when a marked police vehicle came speeding around the corner and skidded to a halt right next to him. The two officers jumped out of their vehicle, placed him in detention and handcuffed him.

Gerry was stunned - it was like something out of a Keystone Cops movie. The next thing he knew he was at the charge bar within London Road Police Office. The duty officer was explaining to him that he was being detained, as a suspect responsible for a number of sexual assaults and a murder that had occurred in the area. He was asked if he wanted a lawyer.

"No," Gerry replied. "Please can I speak to Detective Inspector Wallace?" He was placed in a locked detention room.

Twenty minutes later the door of the detention room opened and there was Brian Wallace and Audrey. Gerry walked to the door. "Come on Gerry," Brian Wallace said, "let's get you booked out and we can have a chat."

Gerry fully understood; it was a genuine mistake. No one could blame the woman for phoning the police given what had happened recently. She had never met Gerry before and even he had to admit that perhaps he looked a bit shifty in his workman's outfit. There was no harm done but Gerry gave up on work for the rest of the day and didn't bother with the surveillance. He made a mental note to go and introduce himself to the lady who had phoned the police and would soon be his new neighbour but decided it would perhaps be better to wait until Audrey could come with him.

# CHAPTER TEN

It was Friday evening and it had been raining for days without end. In the London Road police office every available radiator seemed to be covered with a raincoat or some part of police uniform drying on it. The air was damp.

In the CID office Detective Constables Willie Wilson and Charlie Ross were wading through a backlog of paperwork which had accumulated over a busy period just prior to Christmas. At this time of year, it was always crazy. DS Audrey Lynch was reviewing some case papers before they were sent to the Procurator Fiscal's office.

It was always busy, although the enquiry into the murder of Carol McVey and the sexual assaults on four other women had stalled. Forensics had come up with nothing of any use. One potentially important piece of the jigsaw was missing. They still had to trace the dead girl's handbag and her mobile phone. The phone had not been found at the scene and there was a possibility that the culprit had taken it. As yet the team had failed to determine where Carol had been in the hours prior to her death. There was always the hope that she may have lost or misplaced the phone which was just waiting for somebody to find it.

Detective Inspector Brian Wallace had taken pity on his troops and was boiling a kettle to make some tea. Just then the telephone rang, breaking the monotony.

"Hello, CID, DI Wallace speaking".

The voice at the other end of the line spoke and then hung up.

"Right gang," Wallace said. "Grab your coats, Hamilton's Jewellers in the Gallowgate has just been done."

They all made for the cars in the back yard. It was just after 6pm. They had been thinking of going to get something to eat. They could forget that idea.

Hamilton & Sons Jewellers was situated on Gallowgate near to Biggar Street, not five minutes from the police office. When DI Wallace and his officers arrived, they were met by two uniform officers, Constables Alan Smith and Joe Collins, who were soaked to the skin. They had been first on the scene as they were on foot patrol in the area and had responded to the activation of the shop's automatic alarm system. At that time of day, they had at first assumed it would just be the shopkeeper locking up for the evening. They quickly realised things were much more serious and proceeded to do everything by the book.

Their first care was for the sales assistant Kate Jaclson, who had been hysterical on their arrival. Every display cabinet in the shop had been smashed open and almost every single item of jewellery stolen. When they entered the rear office, they realised that the manager, Craig Hamilton was dead and had apparently been stabbed. There was a very large amount of blood pooling around the body. They also saw that the door of the wall safe was lying open and the contents had been removed. After that they ensured no one else was allowed access to the shop until the CID arrived.

Once she had calmed down a bit, the initial statement given by the twenty year old sales assistant indicated that it was just about closing time when three men burst into the shop. Two carried baseball bats. One stood at the door whilst the other two demanded that the manager open his safe.

He refused at first until one man produced what looked like a very large knife or sword. He had threatened Mr Hamilton and when he spoke, she recalled Mr Hamilton saying to this man, "Is that you Bosh?" or something similar.

The man with the knife forced Craig into his office while the other two smashed open the display cabinets and stole everything inside. All the assistant then heard was the sound of a scuffle coming from the office and the robber ran out carrying what looked like the contents of the safe. All three men then ran out of the shop taking the stolen jewellery with them. She'd had the presence to activate the alarm when they were gone.

The raiders were described by the girl as all being tall, all wearing blue boiler suits and balaclavas which covered their faces. Not surprisingly she had been scared for her own life and couldn't even remember the CID arriving.

DI Wallace knew that, at a later date, she would need to be interviewed again. To be fair, the uniformed officers who had taken her statement they had managed to get quite a bit of information from her despite the fact she had been in a state of severe shock. Hopefully a good night's sleep would help her remember something to help them further.

After giving the premises a quick once over to take in what had happened, Wallace set his team to work. They knew exactly what was required of them. Ross and Wilson began door to door at houses and other shops nearby. DS Lynch was taking general notes regarding the state of the premises - the robbers had not left much. It appeared that a large quantity of jewellery had been stolen from the display units. They would need a full list of the stolen property if at all possible.

The two uniform constables were stood down. They returned to the station to submit full statements and attempt to somehow dry out, the thanks of the detective inspector ringing in their ears for a job well done. Arrangements were made for the Police Casualty Surgeon to attend as well as the Scenes of Crime Officers (SOCO).

Just then DC Ross entered the premises and spoke to the detective inspector.

"Boss, I've got a Mr Joseph Hamilton in my car outside. He says he is the owner of the shop and that his son Craig was the manager. I believe he is the deceased, sir?"

Wallace went outside and sat in the back of the police car with a very elegantly dressed older man. Ross made the introductions.

"Sir, this is Mr Joseph Hamilton, the owner of the shop. Mr Hamilton, this is Detective Inspector Wallace from London Road Police Office." The two men shook hands.

The next few moments were the worst part of being a police officer. Wallace had to tell the man that his son was dead. Nobody can train you for such a moment. It was only natural that the older man broke down in tears.

"I am sorry to meet you in such terrible circumstances, sir," Wallace began. "You and your family have my deepest sympathy. Please rest assured we will leave no stone unturned until we get to the bottom of this matter."

"Thank you, Detective Inspector," Joseph Hamilton replied once he had composed himself. "It is such a shock. What kind of person could have done this?"

"I don't know," Wallace answered. "In the meantime I will have you taken home and I shall contact you tomorrow regarding obtaining statements".

Wallace instructed Ross to drive the gentleman home and then return to the police office.

"Audrey," Wallace said, "there is nothing more I can do here tonight. When the casualty surgeon has finished can you arrange for the body to be removed. Once SOCO finish up, arrange to leave someone on the premises and make sure the place is secure overnight. You could maybe ask if uniform could take the young salesgirl home. You know where to find me if you need me"

Thus, began the weekend from hell. What had happened to the season of goodwill? So far 2007 had been a hell of a year for crime in the Division and a baptism of fire for Audrey. Everyone hoped the new year would give them all a fresh start. In the meantime there was work to be done.

Once everyone had done what was required, Audrey left the jewellery shop. Uniformed police had taken the sales girl home and another of their colleagues had been delegated to remain on the premises to protect the scene overnight. Given the weather outside, it wasn't a bad job, at least he'd be warm and dry. The body of Craig Hamilton had been taken to the city mortuary. Another post mortem for Wallace and Lynch to attend tomorrow.

It was a very wet and tired detective sergeant who returned to the Dennistoun flat in the early hours of the morning. Gerry was waiting up for his wife with a large glass of white wine. It was then she realised she had eaten nothing. It was too late now. Audrey drank slowly before lowering herself into a piping hot bath. Sometime later she wrapped herself in a towelling dressing gown and walked barefooted into the bedroom. Gerry had long since gone to bed and was already asleep. She quietly slipped off the dressing gown and slid under the duvet next to his warm body. Almost immediately she too fell into a deep sleep.

# CHAPTER ELEVEN

When Gerry returned from his daily run the next morning, Audrey was already up, showered, dressed and eating a slice of toast with a large mug of coffee. She had a feeling it was going to be a long day. After giving Gerry a quick kiss, she dashed out of the front door.

First thing that morning after the daily briefing, she and DI Wallace were going to interview Craig Hamilton's parents. Joseph Hamilton and his wife Magda lived in a spacious Victorian house on Haggs Road in Glasgow, not far from the Haggs Castle Golf Club.

Wallace and Lynch arrived at the Hamilton residence at 11am. They parked on the gravel driveway outside and rang the doorbell. The door was immediately opened by a tall regal looking lady who looked about sixty years of age.

The officers identified themselves and the woman let them in, after telling them she was Mrs Hamilton, the mother of the deceased. It was obvious to both Brian and Audrey that Mrs Hamilton had been crying and looked to have had little sleep. She showed them into the sitting room where her husband Joseph was sat at the window, staring blankly out across the garden. He too looked to have had a sleepless night. They had obviously interrupted the Hamiltons as they were taking decorations down from a Christmas tree. Given the circumstances who could blame them.

DI Wallace began.

"We are so sorry to have to intrude upon you both at this time Mr and Mrs Hamilton. Unfortunately, we have many questions, and anything which you can tell us that will aid the investigation would be greatly appreciated."

"Yes, Detective Inspector," Joseph replied. "Please, both of you, have a seat."

He then turned to his wife and asked, "Magda my dear, could we have some tea for the officers?"

His wife left the room immediately to deal with her husband's request, happy to keep her mind busy on other things.

Wallace continued, "I wonder, sir, if you could first of all give myself and DS Lynch some family background and how you came to be a jeweller?"

"Certainly Inspector, I shall start at the beginning."

Joseph then told Wallace and Jennings the history of his family. It took some time and so the tea and cake supplied by Magda Hamilton was most welcome.

"It will be no surprise to you to learn that my family are of Jewish extraction. We only had the tree up for Craig and now he is no longer here."

Mr Hamilton seemed to be lost in his own thoughts for a moment before he was able to continue.

"I'm sorry," he said, "it's just that Craig loved this time of year and although we in the Jewish faith do not celebrate the holiday, our son did and so the tree was the least we could do"

He paused in thought before he said, "Anyway, where was I?

"Oh yes, my grandfather, Abel Hammelmann, and his wife Anna were German. Abel was, like his forefathers before him, involved in the jewellery trade. They were married in

Leipzig in 1914 and as the First World War was looming, they fled to Britain. They came to Scotland where friends advised them to do what King George V had done and change their family name to something less German sounding. So, we were no longer Hammelmann but Hamilton.

"They only had one child, my father, Jacob, who was born in 1924. He followed Abel and became a jeweller. He married a Scots girl, my mother Greta, and I was born in 1947. I never met my grandparents they died before I was born. Between the world wars my father was very successful in his business and travelled over to Holland where he studied the Dutch method of diamond cutting at the diamond house owned by Levi Van Der Berg. The Van Der Berg's were very kind to him.

"At the outbreak of World War II Levi sent his wife Sarah over to Scotland to stay with our family so that she would be safe from the Nazis. In 1943 my family got news that Levi Van der Berg had been killed. He was apparently one of the main leaders of the resistance. After the war Sarah returned to Holland where she married again. A gentleman called Ruben Meijer who also worked in the jewellery trade. They had a daughter, Magda, in 1949.

"My father continued his connection with our Dutch friends and once he thought I was old enough to join the family business, he took me over there so that I too could study their method of cutting diamonds. When I was twenty-one years old I asked for permission to marry Magda. I shall be forever grateful to them for agreeing. We will have been happily married for forty years next year.

"Once we were married my father gave me the capital to start my own business in Glasgow. I have been blessed and now have three shops. One I run in the Argyll Arcade, my son James has the one in Ayr and Craig managed the Gallowgate shop for me.

"Our son James will be thirty-seven next year, he was born in 1971. Magda and I had both hoped to have many children but we were not fortunate. After James, Magda was unable to have any other children. We adopted Craig in 1974, it was just before Christmas. It was always my intention, as with the generations before, for the boys to follow me into the business. James has always been with me since he was a small boy but as Craig was growing up, he wanted nothing to do with the business. All he was interested in was the Army.

"I must say he was always a clever boy and did well at school. He went to university in Edinburgh and I still harboured hopes of him choosing a different career but it was not to be. Immediately he left university he enrolled as an officer cadet with the Black Watch. He, of course, passed with flying colours. To cut a long story short he ended up as a captain and served in many places including, Northern Ireland, Germany and Iraq. He was returned home towards the end of 2005 after suffering head injuries in Iraq.

"As soon as he got back to Glasgow I knew right away when I saw him something was wrong"

He was no longer the happy go lucky man that I knew. He was sulky and became withdrawn. It cost him his marriage. In 2004 he had married Joanne Hanson who was a model. She is now involved in interior design. They lived in a beautiful apartment and seemed to have everything but when he came back things changed. They drifted apart and were divorced earlier this year. Thankfully there were no children involved.

"My eldest son James lives in Dunure near Ayr with his wife Christine. She is a property developer here in Glasgow.

They don't have any children either, so it looks as though Magda and I will not be blessed with grandchildren.

"Craig resigned his commission and came to work for me. He didn't want to be part of the business like James and so he was just the manager of the shop in Gallowgate. James dealt with the stock for the Gallowgate shop as well as his own shop. He was in and out of there all the time.

"I know that we live in a changing world, Inspector, but why would someone do this terrible thing. Who would want to kill my boy? Why didn't they just rob the shop? I tell you now, Inspector, my wife and I will never get over this tragedy. I intend to offer a reward of £100,000 to anyone who can help catch the person who did this terrible thing.

"For the last few years James has been the one who has gone to Amsterdam to purchase any diamonds or pearls we might require for our business. Perhaps, after this terrible thing happening to Craig, it is time for me to step down altogether and let him run the whole business."

The two detectives obtained the details of the home address of James Hamilton and his wife Christine as well as the home address of Joanne Hanson, Craig Hamilton's ex-wife. There was nothing more to be said.

Joseph Hamilton had indeed given them a thorough background to the family and business. They finished their tea, thanked the Hamiltons and left.

It was time to go back to the office for an update on any progress being made. By the time they had got through the pile of outstanding statements in relation to the murder of Craig Hamilton, Saturday had almost gone. It was a weary pair who left to make their way home. Little did they know that it would not be long before they were back in harness. The weekend from hell was just going to carry on.

# CHAPTER TWELVE

It was 2am on a very damp Sunday morning and Tracy Reagan was calling it a night. Tracy was a nineteen year old prostitute from Rutherglen. She lived in a small council flat with her twenty-five year old boyfriend and their two year old daughter. She knew that her boyfriend would be a happy man when she got home as she had earned a fair bit of money. They had planned a special Christmas with their daughter.

Weather wise the night had been a horrible one, however she had still attracted quite a few punters. As with most of the girls, some of what she had earned had gone to feed her drug habit, but she still had money to feed her family. Tracy hailed a taxi down near Glasgow Green and told the driver where she wanted to go. She never made it home.

Her partly clothed body was found on waste ground in Dalmarnock. She had been brutally raped and stabbed through the heart. As with the previous similar murder in Alexandra Park, Tracy's handbag was not found. It was only when her boyfriend went to Rutherglen Police office to report her missing that her identity was confirmed. The following morning Tracey's boyfriend and her father identified her officially for the police at the city mortuary.

Once more DI Wallace and DS Lynch had been given the inquiry. As usual, pathologist Dr John Smillie carried out the post mortem examination.

"It's almost exactly the same MO as the last one in Alexandra Park," he told the bleary eyed officers. "As you will recall, Carol McVey and now this girl, Tracy Reagan, were both stabbed through the heart with a sharp bladed instrument, but this time the perpetrator has gone a step farther and raped his victim before she died. I have taken swabs but have no doubt there will be spermicidal fluid present. Whether we get lucky and get any DNA is another thing."

"So you believe the two murders may have been carried out by the same person?" Wallace enquired.

"Unfortunately, yes I do," Smillie replied.

"That's just great," Wallace moaned. "All we need are two killers going around killing young women. One stabbing and raping his victims, the other strangling women, wrapping them in cling film and freezing them."

So far, as part of the inquiry, DI Wallace had ordered checks to be carried out at all drop-in centres and hostels in city centre, asking about anyone who might be causing women trouble or annoyance or if there was anybody stalking 'girls' on the drag.

All previous offenders were checked out to see if there was any possibility that they could have been involved. The modus operandi was checked on both the Scottish Intelligence Database and the Home Office Large Major Enquiry System (HOLMES) to ascertain if there was any intelligence on crimes of a similar nature. Nothing came to light.

In the afternoon DI Wallace and DS Lynch decided to go visit Kate Jackson who worked in Hamilton's jewellers in the Gallowgate. They wanted to go over her statement with her and just as they had hoped it proved fruitful.

She recalled that the two men with baseball bats and the one carrying the long knife were all Scottish. She was even more precise.

"They all had a Glasgow accents," she said. "Oh, and the one with the knife had a bad limp."

Wallace asked her "You said the man with the knife spoke and you thought Craig said 'Is that you Bosh?' "

"Yes, that's correct," Kirsty replied.

"Can you try to remember exactly what the man with the knife said to Craig?" he asked.

Kirsty thought for a while and then replied, "It didn't make sense to me, he said something like, 'Hurry it up Cap.' "

"Can you remember what kind of knife the man had?" Wallace asked.

"It was a big knife, almost like a sword," she replied.

DI Wallace thanked her for her time and he and Audrey left.

They were suddenly making progress. They busied themselves about the office for the rest of the day and awaited the return of their colleagues who were out dealing with delegated enquiries, from a few different cases. At 5pm they held a meeting to review the days progress.

Brian Wallace addressed the murder inquiry team in the conference room at London Road Police Office.

"Alright folks, if you could just settle down and listen up. The sooner we get this over with the sooner some of you will be getting home. Firstly, I'd like to thank you all for your efforts so far. You are all doing a fabulous job. I know you are missing your families and, no doubt, with a few exceptions, they are missing you. Perhaps tomorrow will bring a breakthrough. But don't be disheartened, we have made definite progress. The deceased Craig Hamilton was formerly a captain in the Black Watch and saw action all over the world. Now, myself and DS Lynch went and spoke again to the sales assistant from the jewellers. She remembered the robbers all had Glasgow accents and the one with the knife had a pronounced limp. Also, she recalls the suspect saying something to the deceased along the lines of 'HURRY IT UP CAP.'

"It sounds to me as though we could be dealing with an ex-soldier who knew Mr Hamilton possibly from Iraq. Enquiries are underway to try and identify the suspect through army records.

"Now DS Lynch and I were also at the post mortem of Craig Hamilton. It seems that he died from a single stab wound to the heart. The weapon according to the pathologist, was a twin bladed knife, similar to the old 'commando' dagger and very sharp.

"I have passed on our thanks to the uniform boys, who found a witness for us on Gallowgate. A barman was going to work when the incident took place and, apparently, saw three men running near the jewellers and getting into what he described as a grey coloured Ford Fusion. He also got a partial registration number SE07B. A PNC check revealed a car of that description had been stolen earlier that day from the car park of Lenzie railway station. The full registration number is SE07BKE. A lookout for the vehicle has been broadcast and Kirkintilloch police are checking the CCTV at all local shops to see if we have any sightings of the car and occupants.

"Now, apart from trying to trace that car, Audrey, can you check out all the members of the Hamilton family, including spouses, to see what the financial investigation unit has come up with? Okay folks, that is where we are so far with the murder/robbery at Hamilton's Jewellers. Let's keep going and try and find out what happened to the stolen jewellery. Hopefully tomorrow we'll learn more from the Army.

"As far as the Carol McVey murder is concerned, we still need to trace the victim's handbag and mobile telephone. Both are still unaccounted for. It is still early days with the murder of Tracy Reagan but her bag and mobile phone are also missing. There are other similarities which may connect both cases, not least that both were stabbed through the heart with a sharp instrument. I have to tell you that the pathologist believes that both women were murdered by the same person. Now I want you to keep that information to yourselves, it must stay in this room. If the press get hold of that they will have a field day. Over and above the killer of Craig Hamilton, it appears we have at least one serial killer operating in our area.

"On top of all that we still have to get to the bottom of the killing of Moira Henderson and there is a possibility that Avril Paterson who has still to be located, may be another victim. Despite all of this, thanks again for all you are doing and bright and early tomorrow, let's get back to it".

There was nothing else to say or do and so everyone headed for home, hopefully for a well-earned rest.

Audrey phoned Gerry to let him know she was on her way home. Really it was his prompt to organise dinner and put a bottle of wine in the fridge. She hoped he wasn't having second thoughts about their marriage as he was fast turning into almost a house husband. She also hoped he didn't resent her being so busy in the job he had once loved so much.

When Audrey arrived home the table was set and a home-made lasagne with garlic bread and salad awaited, together with a large glass of wine. Gerry had put in a great deal of effort for her.

They didn't speak much and as soon as dinner was finished Audrey was fast asleep on the settee.

She awoke around 2am and tiptoed into the bedroom. Gerry was oblivious to her presence, snoring his head off. Audrey knew that something would need to change for the relationship to last. It couldn't continue in this way for much longer. They had not been married very long but now they were seeing less and less of each other.

# CHAPTER THIRTEEN

**A**t the briefing the very next morning, Audrey had updates for the team. She started with the bad news. The Ford Fusion had been recovered, totally burned out on a country road at the back end of Easterhouse. There was nothing of evidential value.

"As you will recall DI Wallace tasked me to send all we had on the Hamilton family and the spouses to the financial investigation unit, which I did. We are still awaiting their reply. I also took it upon myself to contact the registrar at Martha Street in view of the fact we know the deceased Craig Hamilton had been adopted. They are making enquiries regarding that matter. What did come up though, which I thought was very interesting, is the brother James Hamilton or, to be more precise, his wife. She is Christine Gourlay, the daughter of Malcolm, as in 'Malky' Gourlay and the niece of one Robbie Collins."

Suddenly indiscriminate chatter broke out amongst the squad.

"Okay folks let's settle down again," DI Wallace interjected. "Yes Audrey, once again well done, a very interesting piece of information. I can hardly wait for the report from the financial boys. Anyway, in the meantime, let's get back out there and find our killer or killers."

Audrey allocated out all the various tasks for the day to each officer present. The meeting then broke up with everyone chatting excitedly as though there had been a major breakthrough. All that had happened was they had a link to one of Glasgow's best known criminals. It may be that perhaps his niece and her husband were lily white. Consensus of opinion on that piece of information was pretty much one hundred percent 'Aye right!'

Nothing much was happening regarding the robbery at Hamilton's Jewellers and the murder of Craig Hamilton, although the investigation was still in the early stages. DCs Wilson and Ross had been tasked with checking on all known receivers of stolen goods, to try to trace the stolen jewellery. They had so far come up empty. The word was out on the street that there was a £100,000 reward and hopefully someone would come up with information sooner rather than later. The next stop for DI Wallace and DS Lynch was Ayr, to interview James Hamilton. Although it was only a couple of days since his brother's murder, they decided to try his shop in the High Street first. The two detectives said little as they drove down to Ayr. Both were glad to get out of the city, if only for a short time.

James Hamilton was indeed at his shop premises, as was his eighteen year old assistant, Grace McAuley. DI Wallace introduced himself and Audrey and told James Hamilton how sorry he was about the death of his brother. The detective inspector then asked James a few questions.

"Your father tells us that you are the one who travels to Amsterdam to purchase diamonds and pearls for the business Mr Hamilton, is that correct?"

"Yes Inspector," James Hamilton replied. "I go perhaps two or three times a year, depending on how many are required or how busy the firm is."

Wallace went on, "Did you know that your father is thinking of retiring and handing the whole business over to you?"

"No, I did not," Hamilton replied looking somewhat surprised. "I knew that eventually that may be the case, but we have never discussed it."

"Just one last question for now, Mr Hamilton," Wallace went on. "Did you love your brother?"

"Yes Inspector, we were very close," He lied.

Wallace and Lynch thanked Hamilton for his time and after taking his fingerprints as a matter of routine for elimination purposes, they made their way to the shop doorway. As they did so Wallace noticed a brand spanking new, white Jaguar with the registration number JH 1 parked outside.

"Nice car," he remarked.

"Yes," Hamilton replied, "a present from my wife."

As they walked back to their three year old Ford Escort DI Wallace said, "Never mind Audrey, let's go have a look at Hamilton's house while we're here, and then as a treat I'll buy you lunch at the Harbour Inn at Dunure. I mean, what are expenses for?"

They drove south out of Ayr along the coast road, past the Heads of Ayr where the Butlin's holiday camp had once been. Past the hamlet of Fisherton and turned right towards the village of Dunure with its small harbour at the foot of the brae.

As they went down the steep hill, they both noted the Hamilton's house. It was an impressive detached property sitting, as several other similar houses did, looking out to sea. The view was breath taking. No doubt the cost of such a property would be well above their pay grades.

The officers parked their car and had lunch in the hotel, right at the side of the harbour. As they sat enjoying lunch

Wallace had told Audrey that sometimes it was nice to step away from an investigation and get a clearer prospective on things.

On their return to Glasgow, Wallace sat in his office and tried to clear his mind. He realised that what he had said to Audrey earlier was indeed true. They could have spoken to James Hamilton at any time but they had taken the chance to fit in a wee 'time out' from the pressure of all the other investigations. It had worked, Wallace switched his attention to the murder of Carol McVey. He realised that if the culprit had not taken her handbag, which hopefully would contain her mobile phone, at the time of the murder, then the police would require to up their game in an effort to find it. With any luck it may contain vital evidence. Perhaps an appeal on television and in the press might have the desired effect.

Wallace contacted the television companies asking for their help and Audrey put together a press release for all the local newspapers. The appeals would go public the next day.

Brian Wallace knew that the pressure was on. He and his team now had a growing list of outstanding crimes and no suspects or culprits for any of them. Headquarters would soon be looking for answers and results and he knew whose head would be on the block.

Things were just about to get even worse for DI Wallace and his team. The body of Avril Paterson turned up.

She was found at the rear gates of Shettleston police office. Whether there was something symbolic in this or it had been picked at random was anyone's guess. Avril's body was in exactly the same state as Moira Henderson's had been. Frozen stiff and wrapped in cling film. Once more the remains were taken to the city mortuary and allowed to thaw before being examined. The result was also the same as Moira. Avril had been strangled.

The pathologist, Doctor Smillie, once again gave Wallace the bad news. There was, without doubt, a second serial killer operating in the east end of the city. Just what Wallace didn't need to hear.

Not for the first time, suspicion fell on Joseph McGarvie. But the police still had no evidence to go on. Again, they went through the motions with McGarvie and again after interview he was released without charge.

He was now employed as a driver by a care home in the local area. He admitted that he had only got the job as his old friend, Kevin Reilly was the manager. McGarvie went to great lengths to outline the fact that he did not have much to do with any other members of the staff. He only drove the minibus for the elderly inmates.

By now, although he was only forty-three years old, he looked much older. He was no longer the young man in the smart suit with a shock of dark hair trying to persuade people to vote for him. He was almost bald and had a very sallow complexion. He was skin and bone and his shabby clothing hung from his scrawny frame.

Just one week later, in a repeat of history, a third woman went missing. Irene Rooney was a thirty-five year old care worker from Barlanark. She worked at the same care home as McGarvie. Unsurprisingly, he was yet again interviewed and eliminated from the enquiry. Despite appearing to be innocent the public had their view that there was no smoke without fire so, of course, he must be involved. They already had him charged and convicted. They were sure he had killed all three women.

Once more McGarvie resigned from his job and sought refuge in his small flat in the Gallowgate. He became a recluse hardly setting foot out of his flat for fear of being hijacked by some journalist or other. They would not leave him alone. He had his telephone disconnected as he was constantly receiving calls asking for a comment or quote.

# CHAPTER FOURTEEN

After his visit from Detective Inspector Wallace and Detective Sergeant Lynch, James Hamilton was delighted with himself. Things were falling into place much better than he had expected them to. His brother was out of the way and now his father was thinking of retiring early and handing the business over to him. This was excellent news. He locked the front door of the shop and put the closed sign up. He then went into the back office and called for his assistant.

"Miss McAuley, would you step into my office for a moment?"

"Yes sir," Grace McAuley giggled. "I'll be with you in a minute".

She checked her appearance in one of the many mirrors and stepped into his office. Half an hour later she was back in the shop serving a customer.

James Hamilton was quite good looking and had always fancied himself with the ladies. Young Grace was in awe of him. She had worked in his shop since leaving school at sixteen and he had always flirted with her. Recently the relationship had become more intimate and they'd engaged in serious petting. Today James had made love to her for the first time and she was on cloud nine. What she didn't realise was that James was just stringing her along. He had ambitions in other directions. Certainly not with a busty teenager, she was just a distraction.

That night James Hamilton locked up the shop himself, having let Grace leave early for being such a good girl. As he drove home, he was in a really good mood and decided that he would treat his wife Christine to dinner at the inn by the harbour side in Dunure.

Christine arrived home from Glasgow around 6 30pm. The couple walked down the hill to the inn where they were regular visitors. As they were enjoying a brandy after yet another superb meal the owner came over to their table to speak to them.

"I had the police in at lunchtime, James," he said, "asked a lot of questions about you."

"Really?" James replied dryly. "They are investigating my brother's murder and I recommended this place for lunch," he lied.

"What did the police say to you?" Christine asked her husband.

"Oh, you know, just the usual questions," James replied. "To be honest, I don't think they have a clue."

As James lay next to Christine in bed that night he couldn't sleep. His mind was full of thoughts of the past and the present.

From the start James had always resented his adopted brother. Until he'd come along his parents only had eyes for him. When they adopted Craig, all that changed. His father had always made it plain to James that he would be following him into the family business. If he made any complaint about this arrangement, his father simply told him it was tradition. Nobody asked James if that was what he wanted to do.

As soon as he was old enough to leave school, James went to work in his father's jewellers shop in Argyll Arcade in Glasgow. James hated it, but not as much as he hated Craig. It seemed he could do what he wanted. No working in the jewellers for him. He went to university in Edinburgh and then joined the Black Watch as an officer cadet.

James worked for years under his father's tuition as well as spending two years in Holland. When he reached twenty-one years of age, his father announced that he was going to expand the company. Joseph purchased a shop in the High Street in Ayr, with the intention that James would run it. Once again James was never consulted to see if this was what he wanted. At first James was not too keen on the idea but then realised it may be his chance, at last, to shake off the shackles and do things his way. To hell with tradition.

James told his parents that he would take on the shop in Ayr, but only if he lived down there. This was something his parents were not happy about at first, as from their home it was a short journey by car to Ayr. Then James explained that should something happen at the premises, such as the burglar alarm going off, he would need to drive all the way from Glasgow instead of just living nearby. And in the winter, he had pointed out, the journey over Fenwick Moor would be impossible. Eventually his parents were persuaded.

So, in 1992 James bought a small house in Ayr and opened the second jewellers shop owned by Joseph Hamilton and Sons. As part of the purchase agreement with the previous owner the Hamilton's were required to keep on the existing assistant. James had no objection to that as she was a 24 year old young lady who was quite pleasing on the eye. The fact that she had just recently got married did not stop James flirting with her, but he never got anywhere. A year or so later the assistant left as she was expecting twins and never came back.

Over the next few years James had lots of young assistants, but none stayed too long. Apart from flirting with his staff, James found his work boring. His only release was that his father was now allowing him to travel alone to Amsterdam to obtain diamonds and pearls for the business.

James had always enjoyed his trips to Holland when he was a boy. His father had taken him for quite a few years and he loved that Grandma Sarah spoiled him rotten when he was there. But the thing he loved the most was the fact that Craig wasn't there as this was business. This made James feel special again, just as he had done when an only child. He soon got to know his way around the diamond house owned by his grandfather Ruben Meijer.

When he was about eighteen years old Joseph had sent his son to Holland to stay for two years and learn all there was to know from Ruben and his staff. Each one of these diamond merchants could tell by looking at a stone by which expert it had been cut. They all knew each other's work. It was like fingerprints. He also acquainted himself with the more unsavoury red light district in the city. He did like the ladies and was soon one of their best customers.

When he had been down in Ayr for a few years he decided he needed a better house. He had seen one which he fancied out by Ayr Racecourse. The company selling the property was the West of Scotland Property Agency (WSPA). He had arranged to meet an agent to view the house one day in August when, for once, it was actually sunny in Scotland. The viewing was arranged for 3.30 pm and as James parked in the road outside the house in his Triumph Stag sports car, he saw a new, white Mercedes Benz convertible already parked in the driveway.

He remembered thinking to himself, 'This agent must be doing well'.

He walked up the driveway and the front door of the house was opened by a beautiful young woman. She was tall with long auburn hair and was wearing a lightweight grey coloured jacket and skirt with a white blouse. She was very pretty and slightly younger than James. He couldn't help staring at her.

"Hello, Mr Hamilton?" the woman asked. "I'm Christine Gourlay from WSPA."

"I'm very pleased to meet you, Miss Gourlay," James replied.

They got on very well, James bought the house and eventually also got the girl. She wasn't even an agent. Christine Gourlay was only twenty-three years old and she owned the company.

# CHAPTER FIFTEEN

John Sinclair liked looking across to the police station. He was in his own wee fantasy world and pretended that he was helping the police out with some big case. How he envied his grandfather Jock being what he had long hoped to be, a policeman. He really missed him, for when Jock was alive John would never have thought of doing anything wrong.

Now he wasn't around John had become more and more interested in watching daytime television. He loved to see all the beautiful women who dressed in lovely clothes. John especially liked those on the property shows. It was his fantasy to meet them. He thought that perhaps he might try and meet some women who were local. It was around that time he decided to start a scrapbook in which to keep little snippets from the newspapers or any small items he might pick up from the women. He had never had a girlfriend. He was so full of anticipation and excitement, and it was this that had prompted him to take the next step. Meeting one of these women had become an obsession.

John was responsible for the attacks on the estate agents:, Linda Coyne, Alice Brennan and the rest.

Having never been with a woman before he had been left frustrated, not knowing what to do. But when he'd got over excited, he had to abandon his first couple of attacks. He knew what he'd done was wrong but something inside him kept urging him on. He had only killed the young girl in the park to get her mobile phone as he was sure she had taken a photograph of him getting into his taxi in Harcourt Drive. She didn't have her telephone with her but at least he'd had sex with her. The fact that she was already dead when he had didn't even register with John. Mentally he was too far gone.

Then he decided to try again with the young woman in his taxi. He couldn't understand why she had been so nasty to him. She was a prostitute. He had sex with her as well but afterwards he'd stabbed her. To cover his tracks, he took her handbag and phone. He hadn't wanted to kill anyone. In his mind, it was their fault not his. He took all the stories about the attacks on the women from newspapers and put them in his scrapbook, together with the various pieces of clothing and locks of hair he had taken from his victims.

Anyway, now he had finished with all that. He had a new lady in his life. In recent months a new woman had arrived at the police station across the road and John thought she was lovely. He now centred all his attention on her and soon found out she was a detective sergeant called Audrey Lynch.

John could look right into her office from his bedroom window. Some nights he didn't bother going to work. He stayed at home staring at Audrey through his binoculars and fantasised about being with her. He knew everything about her: what car she drove, where she lived, who her husband was, everything. A plan was forming in his head. He needed her to be in his world.

\* \* \*

Just a couple of days after DI Brian Wilson had made his television appeal and the story was highlighted in the national and local newspapers, the murder team had their first big breakthrough. A witness had contacted the office regarding Carol McVey's mobile phone.

Fifteen minutes later Brian Wallace and Audrey Lynch were at a house on Don Street in Riddrie. They were there to speak to a sixteen year old girl called Sheena Halliday who'd called the police with information about Carol McVey's phone.

When Wallace and Audrey got to the house the girl was with her mother in the living room. It wasn't the cleanest house they had ever been in. Sheena seemed reluctant to say much in front of her mother and Audrey asked if they could speak to her alone. She was sixteen after all.

Mrs Halliday didn't seem best pleased at being put out of her own living room, but she wasn't about to start arguing with the polis. Eventually when she had gone both officers sensed Sheena seemed to be more at ease. She was soon telling DI Wallace and DS Lynch what she knew.

"I was Carol McVey's best pal. We were at school together. The night she was killed she had been at a party here. My mother has a boyfriend further down the street and sometimes when they go to the pub she stays with him. It's okay if I have pals around when that happens. That night Carol came to my house and I invited a couple of boys I know. We were listening to music, one of them had brought some cheap vodka. We had a laugh and a dance. One of the boys took a shine to me and we went to my bedroom. I thought the other guy might have fancied Carol but he told me later he didn't. Anyway, a wee while later, it was quite late when me and the boy came back to the living room. His pal was asleep on the settee and Carol had gone home on her own. I found out the next day that she had been killed in Alexandra

Park. There was nothing I could tell you then that would have helped you but the other night, I saw the appeal on television. It got me thinking. I know Carol always has her mobile phone with her and if she didn't have it when she was found, I thought maybe she left it here when she went home. As you can see, my mum is not housewife of the year. Anyway, Carol never left this room, so I had a right good look and found this. It must have fallen from Carol's bag onto the carpet and been kicked behind the curtain."

It was Carol McVey's mobile telephone.

It was switched off, which was why her father hadn't been able to reach her on the night she died. Carol hadn't wanted to get a telling off for being out late. Audrey took down a full statement from Sheena and got the names and addresses of the two boys who had been at the house. They would need to be interviewed to corroborate Sheena's story.

The two officers gratefully took possession of Carol's phone. Hopefully it would give them a clue to the identity of her killer.

On returning to the police office DI Wallace was told that SOCO had been in touch to inform the team that their enquiries in relation to Hamilton's Jewellers were now complete. Nothing of note had been found. No fingerprints, nothing as regards DNA. When Wallace got off the phone he turned to Audrey who had been examining Carol McVey's mobile.

She had been sitting quietly engrossed in what she was doing. Brian Wallace looked over to her almost willing her to give him a result. She suddenly exclaimed, "BINGO!"

There on the screen was a photograph which Carol had taken while waiting in the car for Alice Brennan in Harcourt Drive back in November. It showed a man walking away from her towards a parked black taxi cab. He was as described in Carol's statement, wearing a beige sweatshirt and a pair of brown coloured trousers. The registration number of the vehicle was clearly visible. At least they now had something concrete to work with. The picture corroborated Carol's statement.

The man may not have had anything to do with the attack on Alice Brennen but if not, he was a potential witness. He required to be traced. It was not all they had hoped for but at least it was another piece of the jigsaw in place.

The officers could only speculate as to why Carol had not mentioned the photograph when the police had taken her statement in relation to the incident in Harcourt Drive. There could be a number of reasons. It may have just been the case that because it was a new phone, she wasn't used to it and had accidentally taken the picture without realising.

While Audrey went away to make some enquiries about the taxi, Brian Wallace remembered that he had to contact The Black Watch again to enquire if they had anything for him. He got through to Major Pritchett in the personnel department who, after much argument, agreed to fax Captain Craig Hamilton's service record to Glasgow. The file arrived about twenty minutes later and was extensive but of no great interest, until the medical reports prior to Craig Hamilton resigning his commission.

The file showed that Craig Hamilton had enrolled as an officer cadet on leaving university in 1996. He was promoted to second lieutenant. His first posting was to Germany. He was then promoted to lieutenant and sent to Northern Ireland. In 2002 it was noted that he had applied for special leave to be best man at his brother James wedding. It was further noted he did not get the special leave as the day prior to returning to Scotland he was wounded whilst out on patrol. He'd been shot in the leg which required an operation and therefore a period in hospital.

He made a full recovery and in 2005 was again promoted to captain and posted to Iraq. Later that same year The Black Watch were involved, with others, in some very heavy fighting. Whilst moving up to the frontline Hamilton's vehicle was hit by an improvised explosive device (IED). Hamilton and two of his men were injured by the bomb, two others died.

Craig Hamilton seemed to be alright but, in fact, he was severely concussed and having managed to get himself out of the vehicle had wandered off. It was a miracle that he wasn't shot.

Unfortunately, a story went around at the time that he had left his men, which was completely untrue. He was, if you like, shell shocked. Later he began suffering from severe headaches. The doctors thought he may have had a fractured skull. After the conflict he was seen by doctors and diagnosed as suffering from severe stress and psychological problems. When seen by a specialist he kept repeating the same phrase, "my men, my men". It appeared from records that over time he had lost several men under his command.

In the last incident the two seriously injured men were evacuated back to the UK. One later died of his wounds. The second received a medical discharge. None of the losses or injuries were attributed to any misconduct on the part of Captain Hamilton.

The note from an army doctor at the end of the file noted read, 'Captain Hamilton, although not apparently injured or wounded in any way, is definitely not fit for active duty. He has serious psychological problems which will not, it is feared, be resolved in the short term. It is my opinion that Captain Hamilton be considered for medical discharge at the earliest opportunity.'

Wallace showed the file to DS Lynch who had returned with bad news. The taxi in Carol McVey's photograph had been bearing false plates. The one thing about that was the man walking towards the taxi was more than likely the culprit for the attack on Alice Brennen. All they had to do now was find him.

Audrey read the file and said, "Of course Craig Hamilton beat them to it boss, and resigned his commission."

"Exactly Audrey," Brian Wallace replied. "The poor sod was almost out of his mind worrying if it was his fault his men died or were wounded. I wonder who the soldier was who got a medical discharge? Do me a favour and get back on to Major Pritchett at Army Personnel will you, and see if you can find out. I'd phone myself, but after our earlier conversation, I don't think he likes me."

Audrey disappeared into the detective sergeants' office and phoned Pritchett. Ten minutes later she was back in the DI's office.

"Boss," she said, "I think we may have a breakthrough. The soldier we were looking for is one Private William McIntosh. He was badly wounded in Iraq and returned home where he has undergone numerous operations to remove shrapnel and repair his injured legs. In his record he complained that it was Captain Hamilton's fault and, realising he was to be discharged, swore he would sort Hamilton out if it was the last thing he did. "In fact, it does mention in McIntosh's file that Hamilton tried to visit him in Glasgow Royal Infirmary and McIntosh nearly shouted the place down. Oh, and I forgot to say McIntosh comes from the Gorbals."

"Really?" Wallace jumped to his feet in delight. "Ex-soldier, from Glasgow with a limp and a grudge against Craig Hamilton. It doesn't get better than that, does it? It also makes what was said more plausible as well. Remember what the shop assistant said, 'HURRY IT UP CAP'. If that was said by an ex-soldier couldn't it be short for 'HURRY IT UP CAPTAIN'? Do we know where McIntosh is at present?"

"I'll get right on to it," Audrey replied. "The last known address we have for him is the flats at Norfolk Court. Oh, by the way, in his unit he was known by the nickname 'BOSH', short for Billy McIntosh."

That night over dinner Audrey spoke to Gerry about the cases she and DI Wallace were working on. Because Gerry was ex job, he had great sympathy for them. He had noticed that Audrey seemed more upbeat. She told him about finding Carol McVey's phone and the photograph she had taken of the possible suspect and the taxi but she was so deflated that it had false plates.

Gerry told her to look on the bright side. If the taxi had false plates it was more likely to be the culprit than just a witness and he pointed out that perhaps if the vehicle drove onto Alexandra Parade then there was a possibility that it would've been picked up on one of the many businesses' CCTV.

"What good would that do?" Audrey asked.

"Well it might have had false plates but what about the taxi licence?" Gerry replied. "Maybe he forgot to change it or cover it up, you could trace the vehicle that way through the city licensing office."

Audrey realised that what her husband had said was true. It was a long shot but was worth a try.

"You know Lynch sometimes you surprise even me. I think that deserves a reward."

"Really," Gerry smiled, "and what might that be?"

"I'll do the dishes," she laughed, putting her plate in the dishwasher.

Her mind was racing, all joking aside, it was a brilliant idea Gerry had just come up with. It would be her first job in the morning.

Gerry spent the next hour giving Audrey a full update on the progress of their new home. The builders were making good progress and things were beginning to take shape. For what seemed like the first time in ages they both went to bed at the same time. They made love and fell into a deep sleep, secure in one another's arms.

It was not until the next morning when Gerry gave Audrey a small box that she realised they had been married for one year and she had not forgotten exactly, to get him a present, but she'd never found the time. Audrey understood that she was very lucky. Many a husband, wife or partner could never comprehend what being a police officer entailed. Audrey knew lots of colleagues whose marriages or relationships had broken up. Gerry had bought her a beautiful wristwatch. Sarcastically he remarked that she might look at it occasionally and it may remind her to come home early now and again.

Christmas was a very low key as Audrey was working. Gerry was invited along to Sandy and Jean's for lunch and a few drinks. It was early evening before Audrey caught up with them for a large glass of white wine. She had bought Gerry a new laptop to keep in the flat so that he could keep on top of his emails. Audrey promised to show him how it worked. For his part, Gerry bought Audrey a beautiful gold charm bracelet because she had always said she wanted one.

The following day, whilst the rest of the staff had another day off, Sandy and Gerry were back behind their desks.

# CHAPTER SIXTEEN

While Sandy had been busy with company business Gerry had also had his hands full. He had postponed his search for the bogus workmen for the time being. Gerry knew they only worked in an area for a short time before moving on. It had now been several months since Effie had been robbed and no doubt the culprits had enjoyed a nice holiday from their ill-gotten gains. When they did return Gerry intended to be ready but, in the meantime, the new house was top of his agenda.

The Buckingham Terrace Trust, or the BTT as it had now become known to the staff and clients alike, had opened its doors. Almost immediately it started making an impact with the working girls in the city centre. Word of mouth gave them the confidence to go there. They knew that it was a safe and secure environment. Also, they were able to seek help and advice on a variety of subjects. The qualified staff and volunteers were only too happy to help. The premises were not just a drop in for prostitutes. They were also a residence for several at risk or vulnerable women and their children.

One person who was really enjoying work at the BTT was Ann Marie Docherty. She herself had been one of a number of rape victims who Gerry had previously helped. There was no doubt that, with financial assistance from Gerry, she had been able to turn her life around. She was able to fund her own college education. So far, she had a diploma in counselling and theory and was now studying for her advanced diploma in psychotherapeutic counselling. Already she had helped numerous 'working girls', as well as women who were desperately trying to extricate themselves from abusive or violent relationships, looking for a place of safety in which to bring up their children in peace.

Ann Marie had been able, with others, to offer emotional support and advice on a number of subjects. Usually top of the list were problems with housing, the legal processes, personal safety, plus offering support for the children of such relationships.

Ann Marie loved her work. She attended college on Mondays, Tuesdays and Wednesdays and the rest of the week she could be found until all hours at the BTT helping in any way she could. She no longer bothered with waste of time relationships and was happily free and single. It had, however, come to her attention that lately she kept seeing the same strange man in various different places across the city. He was either a student or employee at the college she was attending and had been seen loitering for hours on end outside her home in Haghill and also at the Buckingham Terrace Trust.

At the start of 2008, one of the security staff at the BTT, Mike Woods, had confronted the man one night out in the street. He had taken to his heels and ran off. Ann Marie was worried that somehow, he may have found out about her previous occupation and looked on her as an easy target. She did the best thing she could do: she told Gerry Lynch.

Within the week Gerry had identified Ann Marie's stalker. He was a student at the same college as Ann Marie.

His name was Steven McIntyre and he was studying information technology. It turned out that he was a bit of an obsessive, compulsive character and a bit weird. He lived in a hovel of a bedsit and yet seemed to be financially sound. It was almost as though when concentrating on something or someone else, in this case Ann Marie, he didn't notice things like the fact his room was a stinking mess. McIntyre was not mad, strange was a better description. It took Gerry three days to track him down. He had followed Ann Marie home from college and was stood across the street from her flat peering up at her window, like a lovesick puppy dog, in the hope of catching a glimpse of her.

Gerry pulled up in his BMW and before McIntyre could run away, he had nabbed him. Ann Marie was just having her dinner when the doorbell rang. She opened the front door and got the fright of her life as there stood her stalker. For a second, she was going to let out a scream but stopped short when Gerry Lynch also appeared in the doorway.

"May we come in?" he asked, pushing McIntyre into the hallway.

All three went into the living room and Gerry pushed McIntyre into a chair. Steven McIntyre was so frightened it looked as though he might faint at any second. Gerry made the introductions and then proceeded to explain to the young man the error of his ways. How, by his bizarre behaviour, he had placed the lady in a state of fear and alarm. If she wished, she could contact the police and he would be jailed. By now McIntyre was sweating from every pore and shaking uncontrollably. Gerry ended the lecture by turning to Ann Marie and asking her if she wished the police involved. At that moment Gerry was sure McIntyre was about to wet himself.

Ann Marie said she didn't want to get the police, she just wanted him to stop following her.

McIntyre was nodding so vigorously his head seemed as though it would come off his shoulders. Gerry lifted him out of the chair and physically marched him out of the house, down the stairs to the street. He kicked McIntyre's backside and he ran off into the dark frosty night, with Gerry's warning ringing in his ears.

The following day Ann Marie contacted Gerry. McIntyre had withdrawn from his course at the college. Later Gerry found out he had also moved accommodation. Result and crisis over, so perhaps he could get back to his day job and help Sandy Morton out. Well that was the plan.

When Gerry left work that night, he headed straight home. He was going to prepare dinner and wondered what time his wife would be home. When his mobile rang, he expected it to be Audrey, but it turned out to be the last person he expected to hear from.

It was Richard Jonson calling from New York. He had just received the terrible news that his father had been found dead in his room at the Dorchester Hotel in London.

"The police say it looks like a drugs overdose, Gerry," Richard said. "That just can't be right!My father never took so much as an aspirin his whole life. I don't know anyone in London, do you think that you and Sandy could help me get to the bottom of this?"

Gerry told Richard how sorry he was to hear of his father's death and that he would speak to Sandy and get right back to him. Richard hung up.

# CHAPTER SEVENTEEN

Gerry and Audrey had first met Richard Jonson in August of 2006. They had known Aimi McLeod for some time before that. She had surprised them by introducing Richard as her fiancée at a party up in Perthshire saying that he worked for a pharmaceutical company. That had been a slight understatement. He was actually the multi-millionaire CEO of Jonson Pharmaceuticals, of which his father Sven was founder and president. It was one of the biggest companies of its kind in America. Gerry and Richard had hit it off right away and since then the couples had become firm friends. Indeed, Richard had recommended Gerry's company to a business friend, Ralph Steinberg. This had resulted in Gerry's firm obtaining their biggest ever contract to date, which had transformed the company.

Now Richard had received this terrible news from London and Gerry was flattered that he thought that he and Sandy were the only people in the world that could help him.

Gerry immediately phoned Sandy Morton and told him Richard's story. As always, he got a measured reply. There was no doubt that if the death had happened in Glasgow then they may well have been of some use. Given that it had occurred in London, Sandy couldn't see how they might help. They had no contacts down south.

What Sandy had to say was true: they needed someone who knew their way around London and who had contacts in the capital. Suddenly a thought came to Gerry. He told Sandy that he would need to hold the fort yet again. He was heading for London and would keep in touch. As soon as he had hung up Gerry went searching for his old holdall, the one he had brought to Glasgow when he had been released from hospital in Argyll back in 2005. This was not an easy task as the flat was now packed with stuff. It took some time but eventually he came across what he was looking for on the top shelf of a wardrobe in the spare bedroom. In the holdall he found a printed business card. On the card was a mobile phone number, the name Graham Cahill and COG. Although by now it was getting late Gerry phoned the number on the card. It was answered quickly by what sounded like an old lady. He asked for Graham. The woman asked how he had obtained the phone number. He had no reason to lie and explained he had got it from Graham when they were in the same hospital in Argyll. Moments later Gerry was speaking to Graham Cahill.

Audrey eventually arrived home from work thirty minutes later, expecting that her husband would have made one of his dinners which she so looked forward to. Not tonight. Gerry was on his mobile and asked her to phone for a takeaway. He spoke to Richard Jonson and told him he would see him in the morning in London and that he would not be alone. When the call ended he told Audrey the bad news and also what he had planned.

Bright and early the next morning Gerry had to forgo his usual run. He was on the first plane from Glasgow to London. On arrival he took a taxi straight to Mayfair and the Dorchester Hotel. As he entered the foyer Graham Cahill was the first person he saw. He looked to Gerry exactly the same as the last time they had been together in hospital in Argyll.

The two men shook hands warmly and moved to the lifts. They made their way to Richard Jonson's room on the second floor. He had flown in from America the previous night. The room was beautiful and afforded a nice view over Hyde Park.

After the introductions the three men got down to business. Richard looked awful, he was pale and drawn but then losing your father could do that. He explained a little about his father more for the benefit of Graham, rather than for Gerry who had met him.

Sven Jonson had graduated in chemistry from university in Stockholm back in the 1970s. After marrying his wife Netta, the couple moved to America. Sven had received an offer to work for a large pharmaceutical company there. Richard, their only child, was born there. Sven enjoyed his work but had a passion particularly for the research and development of drugs to combat cancer in all its forms. He had lost both his parents to the disease. It was his belief that the drugs should be accessible to everybody, no matter what their lot in life and should not have to be about the cost. By the mid1980s he decided to go out on his own and created Jonson Pharmaceuticals. Initially the company was based in Hawaii, but now some thirty-five years later it was amongst the largest and most successful companies in the USA. The headquarters were in New York however the family had retained a holiday compound in Hawaii. That was where Richard and Aimi had married. Sven and Netta had been perfect hosts for what Gerry thought was the experience of a lifetime.

Richard explained that once he had completed his studies, he joined the company. His father insisted that he start right at the bottom and work his way up to his present position. It was hard work but enjoyable. Sven wanted his son to do every job in the company. His motto was 'never ask someone to do something you can't do yourself'.

Medicine is one of the hardest businesses to be involved in. Like his father, Richard soon learned its main problem was costings. Everyone had their own ideas regarding what the cost of medicine should be. Some companies were certainly in the habit of selling drugs to different countries at exorbitant prices thereby making huge profits.

Jonson Pharmaceuticals had never been about that, believing that their pricing structure should be such that every country should and would be able to afford their drugs on the open market. It was in this way that Sven Jonson hoped to help all people, not just the ones who could afford to pay. This strategy had worked. The company sold drugs worldwide and Sven and Richard were millionaires several times over.

It was in pursuit of exactly those principles that, two days previously, Sven had jetted off, alone, to London for talks with representatives of the British Government. He had a plan to propose which would save the UK approximately one billion pounds per year. The plan was simple - allow Jonson Pharmaceuticals to supply all drugs to the NHS.

Sven was staying at the Dorchester and had met a government official over dinner the previous evening at the Carlton Club in St. James's Street in the city, where a general consensus was agreed. On returning to his room at the Dorchester, Sven had phoned Richard in New York to let him know that the meeting went well. However, before negotiations had been completed or any contracts signed Sven was found dead in his bed at the Dorchester.

A post mortem examination had determined that Sven had died of a massive overdose of cocaine. This was something which Richard just couldn't accept. His father had never so much as taken a tablet for a headache in his life, let alone recreational drugs. Not knowing many people in the UK who could help, Richard had phoned Gerry from New York.

Gerry spoke next, directing his remarks to Richard, "You know my partner, Sandy Morton, was the best detective I ever worked with. If this had happened in Glasgow, or even Scotland, we would have been only too happy to look at the matter for you. London is a different kettle of fish altogether. That's why I have brought Graham here with me today. I'll let him explain."

"Mr Jonson, the only reason I know Gerry is that we were both in hospital at the same time some time back. Let's just say, we both had issues. I liked Gerry and from the start we got on great. We were pretty much bored stupid sitting about all day and so we took to playing each other at chess, albeit badly, to pass the time and we became friends. Both of us knew that once we were released from hospital an uncertain future lay ahead. I gave Gerry my card and told him if ever he needed my help, I would be there for him, so here I am. It's only fair that I tell you a little bit about myself and once I've finished if you don't wish to hire me then I will understand."

Richard nodded to Graham, indicating he was in agreement with his suggestion. Graham continued.

"At the time I met Gerry I worked for a secret government department that answered only to the Prime Minister. We were known as COG or Covert Operations Group. It was our task to get involved in operations and deal with them with the minimum of fuss. These were matters which MI5 and MI6 were not to become involved in under any circumstances. They were definitely black operations. We were a small group, all ex-army and all born killers. In other words, we were paid assassins for the British government but because we did not officially exist, if we were caught, we would be disavowed.

"I no longer work for COG. as we were disbanded after a fiasco in South America. I now just do freelance work. If you want my help, I have many contacts in London and, more especially, in Whitehall that may help you find the truth regarding your father's death. I am available should you require my services. Finally, if you do wish me to make enquiries into the matter, all I need to know to begin with are the names of those present at the meeting with your father."

"Dad met two representatives of the British government, Sir Maurice Whitton who is apparently a top civil servant who has the ear of the Secretary of State for Health. He was accompanied by a second man, Charles Ludden, who intimated he was an aide to Sir Maurice."

The name Charles Ludden certainly peaked Graham's interest.

"Mr Jonson, if Charles Ludden has anything to do with this matter, then I am on board one hundred percent and it will not cost you a dime. Let me explain. I was sent to the hospital in Argyll to recuperate after being badly injured during an operation in South America. It later transpired that a certain person who was supposedly working on our side was feathering his own nest by also assisting the enemy. When I returned to London after my stay in hospital, I learned that the same person had unbelievably been promoted within government circles.

"That person was Charles Ludden and he is responsible for the death of God knows how many people, including friends of mine.

"I will be perfectly honest with you; he is the reason that COG no longer exists. The PM got wind of the fact that we were about to carry out an unsanctioned hit on Ludden. He was adamant that this would not happen and shut down the whole group. We were left in no doubt what would happen if Ludden should meet with some misadventure at a later date.

"At the time my immediate boss and his staff were way past retirement. They were institutions within the Institution. Given their advancing years possibly the PM thought it was long past time they were put out to grass. Perhaps he was right. I felt bad about them losing their jobs, the group had been everything to them, it was all they had left and to be fair to them, they were still bloody good at what they did. My colleague, Laura Reid and I remained operational but as I said previously, on a purely freelance basis. We created a company doing exactly what we had done previously, solving problems. Fortunately, I come from a fairly wealthy background, so Laura and I were able to employ our old boss and his staff. I like to think we are well respected globally."

Richard Jonson made it quite plain, he wanted Graham on board and anyone else who could assist. He wanted the culprits caught and wasn't too bothered about how Graham went about it. He was not happy that his father's death had been written off as just another drugs overdose. Some rich old guy dabbling in recreational drugs. Also, he had learned that missing from his father's room were his laptop and a diary into which he wrote notes daily. He had been given the rest of his father's possessions by the police and arrangements were being made the following morning to have his father's body flown back to Hawaii for burial.

Richard thanked both Gerry and Graham for coming. The three parted promising to keep in touch.

Graham headed over to Clapham Common to pick up his colleague Laura Reid. Their first job was to carry out some enquiries at the Carlton Club and find out a little bit more about who was supplying drugs to the UK and who worked with who.

Gerry headed to the airport. On the flight from London back to Glasgow he had time to reflect on matters. Just about two and a half years previously he had been in hospital being treated for a breakdown. He had taken over a small private investigation business when its owner died, and now he was involved in an investigation which he felt may have global implications.

Sven Jonson was a very big name in the pharmaceutical industry. Gerry knew that in some ways it was a cut-throat business. Companies could make vast fortunes if, for instance, they came up with a new drug or treatment. That was why billions of pounds were spent on research and development every year.

Even if you knew nothing about all this, it was on the news on an almost daily basis. A child or some other poor soul who was suffering from a curable illness, the drugs were available but only at an exorbitant price. It was as though countries were being held to ransom to pay for these drugs or lose face with the people.

He recalled what Richard had said about speaking to his father the night he had died. Sven had been very encouraged with his initial talks and believed that the company were on their way to a contract worth billions of dollars with the British to supply the NHS for the next ten years.

The final piece of the puzzle was why were there items missing from his father's personal affects? It seemed obvious the laptop and diary would probably contain information that competitors would rather get rid of than become public knowledge.

Richard had provided an extensive list of drugs which Jonson Pharmaceuticals proposed to supply to the NHS. None of them meant a thing to Gerry or Graham. The companies who currently provided these drugs were however much more interesting. Most were large, well known American based companies. There was one in particular which had stood out for Richard: Amporox.

It was the new kid on the block having only emerged onto the scene in the last couple of years. Richard knew that this company, although registered in the USA, had dealings in eastern Europe. He had been led to believe it was Russian owned and manufactured its drugs in either Romania or Poland. Of late this company had been muscling into the market in a big way.

It was common knowledge that there was a shortage in the supply of cancer drugs. Over one hundred different drugs were affected. Supply problems had forced health officials worldwide to approve temporary price rises of, in some cases, up to four thousand percent, to boost stocks. The NHS were overpaying millions per month and pharmacies were still running short. Basically, they were being ripped off. And one of the companies benefiting greatly from this was Amporox.

Richard's research confirmed it was indeed manufacturing a variety of drugs at a very low cost in either Romania or Poland or possibly both, and then exporting them to the parent company in America, where the prices were far greater. They were then exported across the world. Purporting to be made in the USA Amporox could charge top prices for its drugs and rake in a fortune. It was certainly a company which needed looking into.

There was one thing about the whole situation which Gerry understood. When his parents and colleagues had been killed and severely injured by members of the Graham crime family, he had sworn revenge against them. Someone else had got there before him. Now his friend Richard was in a similar position. The only difference was the suspects were scattered worldwide and he had no option but to hire help. Gerry had no doubt though that Richard's need to avenge his father's death was just as great as his own had been.

One thing the three men had agreed before parting was that Aimi and Audrey were to be told nothing of their enquiries. They may have had just the same desire to see Sven avenged but Richard didn't want Aimi to be involved in any way and Gerry felt the same about Audrey. Also, Audrey was a serving police officer and the situation could end up with her in all kinds of trouble if she became involved.

# CHAPTER EIGHTEEN

Once back in Glasgow, Gerry updated Audrey and Sandy on his visit to London, leaving out a great deal that they were better off not knowing. He then had to arrange things to enable him to travel to Hawaii for the funeral of Sven Jonson. There was no way Audrey could come with him as she was snowed under at work. She knew that Richard and Aimi would understand.

After a few days Graham Cahill was in touch as he and Laura Reid had already made some progress. With the aid of his old boss, Colonel Crichton, he had managed to obtain a copy of the initial report to the Secretary of State for Health, written by Sir Maurice Whitton. It seemed that Sir Maurice had been very impressed with the proposals which Sven Jonson had made and recommended that the Secretary look favourably on awarding a contract to Jonson Pharmaceuticals. It was a move that would save the country millions of pounds. The document showed that Charles Ludden had also attended the meeting. It appeared that he agreed completely with Sir Maurice's recommendations.

Using his vast network within government and city circles, Crichton had discovered that the meeting had taken place in the Wellington Room at the Carlton Club. He had somehow obtained the details of everyone who had dined in that room on the same day. Graham and Laura had spent the last few days checking each diner out. There was nobody of any great note apart from the table directly adjacent to where Richard's father and his hosts had sat.

At the next table were four men, William Hearst, Jakub Bielski, Andrei Dimitriu and Reece Parkinson. It turned out that Parkinson was an associate of Charles Ludden, which probably meant he was connected to MI6. The other three men all worked for Amporox, in fact they actually ran operations in their respective countries. Hearst in America, Bielski in Poland and Dimitriu in Romania. At that point they had not discovered any connections to Russia.

The possibility was there that they could have overheard directly what had been said or perhaps they recorded the meeting. Whichever, they knew the outcome of the meeting before Sir Maurice had time to write his report, probably thanks to Charles Ludden, and Sven Jonson had died that same night as a result. It was not difficult to reason that being fierce competitors with Sven Jonson's company, they may well have been involved in the killing of Richard's father.

Graham and Laura had checked the CCTV system at the Dorchester Hotel for the night Sven had died. At around 10pm there was a blip in the system on the same floor as his room, which seemed to right itself approximately ten minutes later. It was Graham's opinion that it was then that someone had entered Sven's room and killed him. The strange thing was it seemed he had known his killers and let them into his room as there was no sign of forced entry. Graham told Gerry that Laura was still trawling through the CCTV at the Dorchester to try and identify anyone, perhaps either earlier or later, in the foyer. Cahill had also arranged to attend Sven's funeral so he could update Richard on their progress in person.

There were hundreds of mourners at Sven Jonson's funeral. Gerry saw at least two former Presidents of the United States, along with the great and good from all across the country. Many were from charities which the Jonson family supported. After a beautiful outdoor ceremony, Sven was laid to rest in the family mausoleum which he himself had ordered to be built. It sat on a rocky promontory overlooking the beautiful blue seas of the Pacific Ocean below.

Gerry hardly saw Aimi as she was attending to Netta who had taken her husband's death very badly. He was, however, able to pass on his and Audrey's condolences.

The night before the funeral Laura had contacted Graham with an update. Approximately ten minutes before the CCTV malfunction at the Dorchester Hotel, Charles Ludden was caught on camera in the foyer. Laura had also identified another man who she recognised from her many trips to Russia. He was a known Russian Mafia enforcer called Ruslan Sokolov. A former member of Spetnaz, the Russian special forces, he was easily identified, with a lion head tattooed on the back of each hand. His first name, Ruslan, meant lion in Russian. The fact that he could be easily identified did not bother Sokolov. Usually he didn't leave any witnesses.

Reading between the lines it appeared that Sven's meeting had been overheard. It seemed reasonable to assume those working at Amporox wanted him out of the way. It was possible that Ludden was working in their employ. Perhaps he called on Sven at the Dorchester and was allowed entry to the room on the pretence of discussing further the proposed deal. An associate, probably Sokolov, also gained entry and killed Sven, thereafter stealing his laptop and diary. The fact that a Mafia enforcer was working with or for Amporox was quite disturbing. It suggested that Amporox was indeed a Russian Mafia led operation.

When they returned to New York, Netta was coming to live with Richard, Aimi and their son, young Sven. Richard would have them closely guarded around the clock.

After the funeral Gerry flew straight back to Scotland via Heathrow. Graham Cahill accompanied him that far. They discussed what was next. Graham had asked Richard if he could obtain as much information on Amporox as possible. He and Laura intended to do the same and gather what they could on the company in Europe. Once they had a clearer picture, they could arrange a meeting to decide the best way forward.

The priority for Richard was to ensure the safety of his family. Graham had given him the names of a couple of people he could trust in that regard. Richard had now been elevated to the job of President at Jonson Pharmaceuticals. He needed to appoint a new CEO and take care of business to show that the company was still in good hands. As far as he was concerned there was only one candidate: his friend Ralph Steinberg. Richard had approached Ralph almost immediately after his father's funeral and was delighted when he accepted. Richard also had to arrange another meeting with Sir Maurice Whitton to continue the work his father had started. This time, he would be arranging the venue.

# CHAPTER NINETEEN

Now Gerry was back in Glasgow, the weather wasn't too bad, so he got back out patrolling in search of the bogus workmen. He had again begun touring around Easterhouse, Baillieston and Riddrie in his unmarked van. When he was a police officer he had always hated thieves. He still did and these people robbing Aunt Effie had made it personal. As he drove about the streets Gerry could feel it in his bones. The bogus workmen would be back soon and when they returned, he would be waiting for them with open arms.

Floating around the area was handy for Gerry as it allowed him to visit the building site, which was slowly becoming his new home, on an almost daily basis. At the start of the project, Gerry had told the builder the job he wanted doing and trusted him to do just that. No expense was to be spared, no corner cutting. This was a home for him and his wife.

Every day the house was coming on in leaps and bounds. The builder was doing exactly as promised. This was now the fourth job he had carried out for Gerry, only this time he was building for the couple, their dream home. It bore no resemblance to the old house and was going to be a property to be proud of. It would certainly cost but would be well worth every penny spent on its creation.

Once completed they would have a beautiful four bedroomed detached house, with a huge open plan lounge leading into a state of the art kitchen area. The rear ground floor wall was going to be completely glass looking out onto a wonderfully manicured garden. A side door led directly to the double garage and gave access along a short corridor to an indoor swimming pool and gymnasium. Upstairs each of the four bedrooms would have its own en suite. The property sat on a corner plot leading to a quiet cul-de-sac occupied mostly by elderly residents.

The fact that Gerry was now visiting the site daily led to him eventually getting lucky. It had been many months since Aunt Effie had been robbed. Despite Gerry touring the area and staying vigilant on the lookout for likely culprits he had come up empty. In a way Effie wasn't that bothered because Gerry had reimbursed her. Gerry was desperate to trace those responsible as he knew the robbery at Effie's house was likely to be just the tip of the iceberg. These people needed to be caught and stopped, and for him it was almost a matter of pride.

One day, Gerry arrived on site as the men were trying to negotiate a troublesome delivery. A new septic tank had arrived and required to be manoeuvred into the back garden. The articulated lorry that was doing the delivery had to reverse into the street to make the load easier to put into place and was blocking part of the roadway. Gerry was assisting by guiding the driver back. It was whilst doing this he noticed something in the street which struck him as odd.

At first the penny didn't drop, he carried on with what he was doing. He had seen two men and a woman further down the cul-de-sac getting out of a small dark green Ford van which had squeezed past the lorry to gain access to the street. It wasn't possible to see the logo on the side of the van, it looked like one owned by the council. The three people were all wearing dark green coloured polo shirts, similar to those worn by Glasgow district council housing officers. The question was why would they be in this street where all the homes were owner occupied?

Suddenly as though hit by a bolt from above, Gerry realised something else that was wrong. It was still only February and yet all three were heavily suntanned as though they had been in very sunny climes for a few weeks. He supposed it was possible but what were the chances that all three work colleagues had been on holiday at the same time?

Gerry's nose was bothering him, he needed to investigate. He went out into the street and approached one of the men to have a word. On seeing Gerry, all three ran back to their van and sped out of the street. But not before colliding with the side of the lorry and ripping the front offside wing from their vehicle, nearly knocking down Gerry in the process.

He was unable to give chase as his own car was blocked in by the lorry and the suspects would be long gone by the time he could get out of the street. He had however managed to take the registration number. On examining the van's wing that had been left at the scene, Gerry noted that underneath the green coloured paint it appeared that the vehicle had originally been red in colour. He gathered up the wing and headed along to Baillieston Police Office to report his findings and suspicions to the local constabulary. Hopefully there would be a lookout broadcast for the vehicle and three suspects.

When he thought about the events of the day later that evening Gerry realised there was something else. He could have sworn he had seen the two men before. He wasn't sure as he'd only had a fleeting glimpse, but the more he thought about it the more convinced he was that he knew them from somewhere.

# CHAPTER TWENTY

In the early hours of the following morning DI Wallace and DS Lynch found themselves at Lightburn Hospital. A body, believed to be that of the missing care home worker, Irene Rooney, had been found at the gates of the hospital. In similar circumstances to the previous two bodies, it was frozen solid and wrapped in cling film. A subsequent post mortem later that morning would confirm her identity and the fact that she too had been strangled.

No stone had been left unturned in this investigation. Brian Wallace had even tasked a young detective constable to go out and discover where the cling film had come from. After many hours trawling though every outlet imaginable he had finally come to the conclusion. It was unremarkable and could have been purchased just about anywhere.

There next stop was obviously down to Gallowgate to speak with Joseph McGarvie. There was still no evidence against the former politician but he appeared to be the only person who'd known all three victims. They had to speak to him as a matter of course and perhaps something would finally come to light.

He lived in a flat on the second floor above a junk shop. It seemed he was the only occupant in the building. As they reached the second floor and stood outside the door both officers gave the other a knowing look. There was a very pungent odour. Wallace tried the door handle: it was locked. He forced open the door whilst Audrey used her mobile phone to contact the office for some assistance. Opening the door did not help, the smell jumped out of the flat to greet them. It was not one of the better things about the job, death. Joseph McGarvie was in the kitchenette, seated on a chair but slumped across the table. There was a hypodermic needle still stuck into a vein in his left arm with a tourniquet tied around the upper arm. He appeared to have been dead for some time. It seemed probable that having dumped the body of Irene Rooney he had returned to his flat and injected himself with an overdose, probably heroin. Whether by accident or in a fit of remorse was a matter for conjecture. Being the cautious types, Wallace and Lynch would wait for the results of the post mortems on both bodies.

The following morning DS Lynch spoke with McGarvie's family doctor. He stated that the only thing wrong with Joseph McGarvie was that he suffered from stress. As such, he had prescribed him with the appropriate medication in tablet form. The doctor stressed that it was in tablet form. To his knowledge, Joe McGarvie had never taken drugs of any kind, certainly not something like heroin, and definitely not by injection. He was most insistent, as Joseph suffered from a fear of needles and injections and would never stick one in his own arm. Later in the afternoon DI Wallace sent Audrey out with young DC Clarkson to snoop about and see what, if anything, they could come up with. One interesting thing about McGarvie's death, which was slightly strange, was that there were no fingerprints whatsoever on the hypodermic syringe, not even McGarvie's. This suggested only one thing - he had been murdered.

When Audrey and her young assistant returned to the office, they had a theory they wanted to run past the DI. When Moira Henderson had gone missing, Joseph McGarvie was the obvious suspect as he was having an affair with the woman. The same had happened twice again with Avril Paterson and Irene Rooney, only because of the first incident and the fact that McGarvie had worked with both these women. But someone they had overlooked was Kevin Reilly.

Audrey explained to DI Wallace.

"Enquiries with Labour Party members in the area revealed that Reilly and McGarvie had both applied to be candidates for the Party back in the day. Reilly was not best pleased when he was overlooked in favour of Joe McGarvie.

"DC Clarkson and I also spoke to a few of the two men's old school mates. It's surprising how many still lived locally. The opinion we got from them all was the same. Kevin Reilly and Joe McGarvie were the best of pals all the way through school days but they could remember Reilly being jealous, if not a little angry, when Joe won a school prize in a writing competition. According to our records, he was never interviewed when Moira Henderson went missing. Oddly enough he owned the estate agency and was the manager of the care home where McGarvie and the two other murdered women worked. Perhaps we should have a word, boss?"

The next morning after the team meeting, DI Wallace and DS Lynch headed first to Glasgow Sheriff Court to apply for a search warrant for the care home and, if necessary, Kevin Reilly's home. Both were eighty percent certain Reilly was somehow involved. The other twenty percent was what was known in the trade as a 'fishing expedition'. Thirty minutes later they were on their way to the care home with a search warrant, which the Sheriff had graciously granted.

On arrival they interviewed Kevin Reilly after first cautioning him. Reilly seemed quite unperturbed and without blinking and in a very matter of fact fashion, he told them all they wanted to know and more. He waived the right to legal representation and seemed happy to be at last unburdening himself.

He was taken to London Road Police Office so DI Wallace could get his confession on tape. Strangely it seemed that Reilly was revelling in being, for once, the centre of attention and not second best to Joseph McGarvie.

Once the procedure had begun and the tape switched on there was no stopping Reilly. Yes, he had killed Moira Henderson because he knew of her affair with Joe McGarvie and he was jealous. It was not just because of the affair but Joe McGarvie in general. Reilly resented the fact that he had been overlooked as a candidate and McGarvie had been selected instead.

Back in 2005 he had waited for Moira Henderson to leave her home. He had stopped in his car and offered her a lift to the campaign office, which she had excepted. Instead of driving her there Reilly had driven to a quiet street and had made advances towards Moira. On being rebuffed he had lost his temper and strangled her. In a panic he had then driven home. Having stripped her body naked, he later disposed of her clothing and other possessions by burning them. He had wrapped Moira in cling film and placed her in a chest freezer he had in the garage. At that point he had no idea what he was going to do with the body. Nor did he realise how long he would keep her in cold storage.

Quite calmly Reilly had stopped at this point and asked for a cup of tea. Once refreshed he continued as before as though confession was indeed good for his soul.

Why two years later had he left her body at the People's Palace? There was no special reason for the People's Palace, it was just as good a place as any. Why two years later? Quite simply, he needed the space.

Joe McGarvie was friendly with Avril Paterson and Reilly couldn't have it starting all over again.

He was jealous of Joe and so had to kill Avril in just the same way as Moira. He had waited to get her alone in the back shop of the estate agents one night. Just as Moira had done, she refused his advances and so he strangled her too.

He put Avril in his freezer and burnt all her clothing. To make room he had been forced to dispose of Moira's body and had dumped her at the People's Palace.

Then at the care home he saw it happening again. Irene Rooney smiling at Joe McGarvie as he loaded the patients onto his bus. So he killed her too and this time he had to dump Avril to make room. Why at the back gate of Shettleston police office? No reason, it was as good a place as any.

Reilly also admitted injecting McGarvie with an overdose of heroin. He knew Joe hated needles and was scared stiff by them, so he gave him a sedative in a drink. He'd gone around to the flat pretending to be worried about his old friend, all the time intending to do him in.

The thing was that in all their years together at school and right through their adult lives, McGarvie had thought Reilly was his best and closest friend. All the time Reilly had hated him with a vengeance, from initially being jealous of him winning a school prize he thought he should have won. Later his hatred resulted in more sinister consequences when he had killed three women. All the time poor Joe McGarvie never suspected his 'friend' of doing anything wrong.

Reilly ended his admissions by telling Wallace that if they were searching his house, they would find yet another woman in the freezer. He didn't know who she was but had picked her up in the centre of town a couple of weeks before. She hadn't done anything wrong, just the voice in his head had told him to kill her.

Later that day the team did indeed find the body of a fourth woman in Reilly's freezer. She turned out to be a prostitute, Jane Brady, missing from Govanhill for the past three weeks. Scenes of crime officers were also able to obtain the DNA of the previous three victims from the freezer.

Despite entering a plea of insanity at the time of the crime Kevin Reilly stood trial on five counts of murder. He was convicted of all five and sentenced to five life sentences. He was to spend the rest of his life behind bars.

At the end of that enquiry Brian Wallace ensured that the whole of his squad enjoyed a small celebration. For one night only, they let their hair down. The DI had reminded them that they still had a few more other crimes to solve before they could fully pat themselves on the back.

The next day they were all assembled at London Road Police Office for the morning meeting.

There was a lot still to do and they were all ready to go. It never ceased to amaze Brian Wallace what a bottle of beer and a decent night's kip could do for morale.

Later when they spoke about the case both Brian Wallace and Audrey Lynch agreed. Humans were a strange breed. What they did and how they perceived things in different ways never ceased to amaze. Neither could understand how such a simple thing as losing out on a school prize could escalate in Kevin Reilly's mind from annoyance, to jealousy and envy and finally to pure hatred of Joseph McGarvie. It had cost five people their lives and taken from start to finish almost three years to solve.

# CHAPTER TWENTY-ONE

James Hamilton sat in the office of his shop and watched as Grace McAuley served an elderly lady who was looking for a present for her daughter. She couldn't decide between a bracelet or a beautiful necklace. Eventually, after what seemed like an age, she went for the bracelet. Grace wrapped the gift for her, the old lady left the shop.

"Grace," James shouted, "put the closed sign on the door and come into my office immediately."

"Yes Mr Hamilton" she replied and thought, 'God what's wrong with him it's only 10 o'clock in the morning.'

Once more James had his way with the girl. It wasn't that he couldn't keep his hands off her - anyone else would have done just as well. It was that he could not contain himself until Wednesday when he went to Glasgow to see his special girl. Having satisfied his sexual appetite for another day he remained in his office whilst young Grace opened the shop up again. Once more he was lost in his thoughts.

James had married Christine Hamilton in 2002. They hadn't wanted a fuss and so the wedding took place at the Registry Office in Park Circus, Glasgow. That ceremony was followed by a second at the Garnethill Synagogue to appease James parents.

Craig Hamilton was supposed to be the best man although he was not James' choice. As it turned out he couldn't make it, having been wounded serving in Northern Ireland. For James, the excuse gave him another reason to hate his brother even more.

Christine's uncle Robbie Collins stepped in, and also insisted on paying for a lavish reception at Cameron House Hotel on the banks of Loch Lomond. The happy couple then jetted off on honeymoon to Tenerife.

They initially moved into James' house in Ayr and Christine commuted every day to Glasgow on the train. She still insisted on taking her gran, Annie and mum, Sandra to bingo on Wednesday nights and would stay over either at her mum's or uncle Robbie's house.

Because he had been in Northern Ireland at the time of their wedding, Craig only knew Christine - he had never met any of her family. For the next five years Christine worked harder than ever. She loved her husband and wanted nothing but the best for them.

In 2004 it had been Craig's turn to fall in love. He met Joanne Hanson, a twenty-five year old model, at a Christmas charity bash in one of Glasgow's posh hotels. It was, so they had thought, love at first sight. He was a dashing lieutenant in uniform, and she was just stunningly beautiful.

They married just a few months later in Glasgow Cathedral. Members of Craig's unit formed a guard of honour outside the cathedral. They looked fantastic in their dress uniforms.

The reception was held at the garden of Joanne's parents, George and Elizabeth Hanson, in a huge marquee at the rear of their home in Helensburgh. Anyone could see Joanne got her good looks from her mother. Her dad George was just a normal working man who had done well for himself. He had started off with his own lorry years ago and now had a fleet of forty vehicles. He never bothered much with counting his money but he was a very wealthy man indeed. His wife would get very angry with him because no matter how well she had dressed him, she could never get the grease and dirt out of his hands.

Craig and Joanne honeymooned in the Maldives before returning to Glasgow to live in a luxury apartment which Christine had found for them, and which Joanne, in her other guise as an interior designer, had decorated. The first few months of their marriage were fine, until Craig was ordered to return once again for another short tour of duty in Northern Ireland. Joanne, who had been spoiled by her parents, especially her mother, soon became disenchanted with marriage. She was lonely and craved attention. She began to sulk and fell into a depression. Matters got even worse when Craig was posted to Germany and then Iraq.

Enter the knight in shining armour or, more precisely, the lecherous brother-in-law.

When Christine stayed in Glasgow to take her grandmother and mother to the bingo, James Hamilton got in the habit of calling in on his new sister-in-law to offer a shoulder to cry on. This soon led to James and Joanne embarking on an affair which they fuelled with champagne and cocaine. By the time Craig had finished with Germany and been sent to Iraq he didn't know the woman he was married to anymore. She had turned into a monster.

When Craig eventually got back from Iraq, given his physical and mental state, the writing was on the wall for the marriage. They separated, she stayed in the apartment and he moved back in with his parents. He needed to be with someone who could give him love and whom he could trust. Joanne was neither.

After treatment, Craig settled down. He would never be the same man again, but he was better than he had been. Tablets prescribed by his doctor and a more sedate occupation working for his father helped greatly. He began managing the jewellers shop in Gallowgate. His father drove him to work and back home again at night as Craig wasn't ready to drive. His assistant at the shop was a very efficient employee who took a great weight off his shoulders. Sometimes he felt he should recommend her to his father as the manager. Craig appreciated her commitment and really liked her.

One day, some months after he had started in the shop, Craig had a visit from his brother James who was dropping off some new stock. Craig had heard that one of his old army unit was in Glasgow Royal Infirmary getting treatment for injuries he had received in Iraq. He asked if James would take him to visit the man. James couldn't think of a reason to refuse so took Craig to the hospital.

They parked down Wishart Street and walked up to the hospital. They entered the building and took the lift up to the correct floor. As they walked into the ward Craig spotted his old comrade and called to him. "Bosh, how are you getting on, old son?"

The man in the bed almost turned purple on seeing Craig and spewed forth a stream of expletives. He called Craig all the names under the sun and threatened to kill him. James feared the man was having a fit. The hospital staff had to restrain him as he attempted to get out of bed to attack Craig. The effect on Craig was startling, he ran from the ward, down the stairs and when James caught up with him, he was vomiting in the roadway.

James wondered at the time if this old comrade may be of use to him in the future. He learned from Craig, when he had calmed down, that the ex-soldier was called Billy McIntosh and had been injured when with Craig in Iraq.

Afterwards James had thought to himself that he was sure he knew McIntosh. Craig later confirmed he had been in the guard of honour at his wedding. That is where James had seen him before, over a few beers at the wedding reception.

# CHAPTER TWENTY- TWO

Christine Hamilton had worked hard to expand her business, making herself very wealthy in the process. She and James had lived near the racecourse in Ayr for a while and they had fancied a change. When the chance had come up for them to purchase one of the largest detached properties overlooking the sea in Dunure just south of Ayr, they jumped at it. The property cost in the region of one million pounds but Christine could afford it. Initially James wasn't so sure, then thought that it may go some way in raising him up the social ladder locally and he was happy to agree. After all it was Christine's money that was buying the property, not his.

While Christine worked hard at making money, James had been getting himself in a bit of a mess financially. He was now not only feeding his own, but also Joanne's, cocaine habit and she was costing him a fortune in presents. She was high maintenance, but definitely still worth it. Joanne was gorgeous and while her attention was on James, he felt he had got one over on Craig.

One day just before Easter 2008, James was in his shop when he got an unwelcome visitor, his local drug supplier, Hughie Grant. James sent Grace on an errand and invited Hughie into his office.

"How's it going, Hughie?" he said, trying to be pleasant.

"Never mind all that crap, Hamilton," Grant replied. "Where's my money?"

"Look Hugh, I'm a bit short of readies at the minute," James tried to placate him. "I'll have it soon."

"Okay, Jamie boy," Grant said, "this is your last chance. Either I get the nine thousand you owe by the end of the month or I pass you up the chain."

When Grace returned Grant had gone. James was gulping down a whisky and sweat was pouring from his brow. He opened his wall safe and, making no attempt to hide it from his assistant, James took out some cocaine which he snorted in front of her.

"Grace, find out the times of flights to Amsterdam from Prestwick next week," he ordered. "Oh! And then come here, naughty girl!"

The following Tuesday James flew from Prestwick to Amsterdam. He didn't bother visiting any relatives when he got there. He went straight to the diamond centre in the city, where he purchased a small amount of diamonds. He stayed in a hotel and that evening had a visit from one of his Dutch contacts. He sold James a much larger amount of diamonds at a reasonable price, which he intended to smuggle into the UK the next day.

The next morning James got a taxi to Schiphol Airport and flew back to Prestwick arriving back in his shop in Ayr before lunchtime. It was a trip he had been taking more and more to help sort out his financial problems. He always only declared the small amount of diamonds which he had purchased at the diamond centre. The rest he smuggled in to sell for his own gain.

After a quick fumble with Grace, he was off to Glasgow to sell the illegal diamonds to several different jewellers in and around the city. It was a win-win situation for all concerned. James had bought the stones at a reasonable price and wouldn't be paying tax as he had smuggled them into the country. He then made a profit selling to the jewellers. They in turn also made profit selling the diamonds at retail prices to customers. He could have paid off his drug debt there and then but decided to let Hughie Grant wait as long as possible. He was a wee weasel of a man and James hated him. It was nearly the end of the month when James finally paid Grant, who assured him that would be the end of the matter. What he didn't tell James was the feelings of hatred was mutual and he had already grassed him up for non-payment to the main dealer in Ayr, Donnie Cochrane.

The unfortunate thing for James was that Cochrane originally came from Glasgow and had been an associate of Robbie Collins for many years. When Robbie had been looking for a trustworthy lieutenant to help him expanded his drug empire into Ayrshire, who better than Donnie Cochrane.

Word eventually reached Robbie regarding James and it gave him a problem. He would do anything not to hurt his niece, so what could he do? He felt the only thing he could do was tell Malky, as Christine's dad. Malky would need to have a serious word and put an end to the drug taking, although Robbie knew he wouldn't really want to do that as Malky's reaction would be to go and beat the crap out of James. Robbie told Malky and after his old friend had calmed down, suggested that he warn James off and then watch him for a couple of months to see what he got up to. After that they would assess the best way forward.

The following Wednesday afternoon Malky drove down to Ayr. This was because he knew his Christine would be in Glasgow with Sandra and Annie. Malky watched as James closed the shop for the night and then followed him. He didn't go home to Dunure but drove to Glasgow. Malky followed him and was horrified to see him go to Joanne Hamilton's apartment block. She came outside to meet James and Malky saw them kissing at the front door of the building. Malky remained in his car all night and in the morning followed James back to his shop in Ayr.

To say Malky was angry would be putting it mildly. His first thought was that he wanted to either shoot his son-in-law or rip his head off - he was taking the piss out of his daughter. After a while Malky calmed down and decided he would be better going back to Glasgow to speak to Robbie about the situation. Robbie sympathised with Malky and in all honesty wanted to kill James too, but decided to err on the side of caution. He persuaded Malky to stick to the original plan and see what James got up to.

What neither man realised was that Christine wasn't happy either. She knew her husband was up to something. His recent behaviour had become increasingly erratic and he seemed to spend half his time visiting Holland. She had decided to employ someone to find out what was going on. To this end she visited QLM Investigations in Gordon Street and explained her problem to Pamela Gibson. She, in turn, had passed the file to Alex Burnett to look into the matter and report back.

For the following two months everyone got on with their lives and nothing seemed out of the ordinary. James made another couple of visits to see Joanne on Wednesdays. A couple of weeks when she was away elsewhere, James visited the casino and brothel at the Ardoch Hotel. He ran up quite a bill.

It seemed that he had taken quite a shine to a Russian girl called Natasha. James also bought a lot of cocaine and once more, to pay for this high living, had to travel to Amsterdam and obtain more gems which he sold on to his contacts in the industry.

Christine Hamilton had not wished to bother any members of her family with her problems. Little did she know that every step that James made he was followed by Robbie's men who reported back to their boss on a daily basis.

Realising what James was up to with his frequent visits to Holland, and ever the businessman, Robbie believed he could turn the situation to his advantage. His own drug empire was now massive. He had formed a business relationship with the Russian Mafia which he was already beginning to regret. They had filled his hotels with their own girls and their requirement for drugs was quite astounding. Robbie needed more outlets in which to launder his drug money. Why not jewellers shops? He explained his plans to Malky and swore that he would sort James out.

Malky wasn't pleased - he just wanted to physically hurt James for cheating on his wee girl. The only thing stopping him was loyalty to his boss, Robbie, who was not only his long standing friend but also his brother-in-law.

Robbie would deal with it.

That hadn't stopped Malky letting Robbie know in no uncertain terms his feelings on the matter. Robbie wasn't offended, although if it had been anyone else speaking to him like that, Robbie would have dealt with them, but he knew how much his old friend loved his family.

# CHAPTER TWENTY-THREE

As spring turned to summer, Malky Gourlay was a happier man, but it had nothing at all to do with the time of year. Robbie Collins had finally run out of patience with James Hamilton and was ready to act. What they didn't know that whilst they had kept an eye on James, Alex Burnett had also been watching him and updating Christine Hamilton on a weekly basis.

As far as Robbie Collins was concerned, enough was enough. He instructed that the next Wednesday James Hamilton came to visit Joanne Hanson would be the last. Malky's instructions were clear - to follow James and phone Robbie when he was on his way.

The following Wednesday, James Hamilton gave his assistant Grace the afternoon off. She didn't seem too pleased as she left the shop. Possibly because they had not yet had sex that week. James had seemed preoccupied to her and indeed he was. He was, for some unknown reason, really looking forward to seeing Joanne Hanson this evening, more so than ever before.

At the end of the day's business he quickly locked up and jumped into his car for the journey to Glasgow. He hadn't forgotten to take a large quantity of cocaine from his safe before leaving. James had no idea that he was being followed, nor that a welcoming committee was gathering in the city.

As he reached Glasgow he found the traffic was, for once, not too congested and he had made good time. Nothing seemed untoward as he parked outside the building and took the lift to the second floor and Joanne's apartment. He used the key she had given him to open the door and as he walked into the hallway he called her name. In reply all he heard was a scream.

Rushing into the living room he took in the scene. Joanne was sitting on the leather settee in some distress. Standing next to her were two huge, very menacing looking men. Both were over six feet in height, both wore long leather coats, dark glasses and both had shaven heads. James froze for a moment, then he heard the sound of a very familiar voice.

"Hello James, good of you to join us."

To Hamilton's horror he saw Robbie Collins sitting in one of the easy chairs by the window. He was just about to continue speaking when Joanne let out another scream.

"Get rid of that irritating bitch," Robbie instructed his two henchmen. James thought that perhaps they would put her in the bedroom but that didn't happen. One of the men pulled Joanne up from the settee and punched her in the face knocking her senseless. Both of them then carried her out of the apartment. James would never see her again.

Robbie then turned his attention to James.

"You sit, and keep your mouth shut."

Robbie explained to James the error of his ways. How cheating on his wife was not on. Christine was his family, his niece and Malky's daughter, and treating her the way he had was absolutely not on. How he was lucky to still be alive as Malky wanted to kill him. How owing the casino £200,000 meant owing Robbie. Then using some cheap whore. And all the time making a mug of Christine.

Collins really laid into James and reduced him to a quivering wreck who thought he was about to die. That didn't happen. Instead Robbie offered him a business deal.

Ever the one to take an opportunity, Robbie told James how he had been followed to Holland and was seen visiting jewellery shops in and around Glasgow. Robbie knew exactly what was happening and he wanted in. He saw it as a great chance to use these various premises to launder more of his drugs money whilst also making even more profit.

He told James his future.

"Firstly, you are finished with the whore and the casino. You will never see this tart again. You will never be unfaithful to Christine again. From now on you work for me. You can carry on with your shop and nothing we do will affect your family. Family is everything. When, in the future, you go to Holland, you will be going for me. You will visit all your jeweller friends and tell them that they will be required to sell you their shops or suffer the consequences."

Robbie wanted into the jewellery business.

"Do all this and your £200,000 debt will be written off. I'll give you thirty seconds to think about my offer. If you agree then we start with a clean slate and I'll keep Malky off your back. If you don't agree it ends here".

As if to emphasise the point Robbie took out a cut-throat razor which he opened and began cleaning his fingernails. As he did so he glanced at his wristwatch. Time was up.

James left the apartment and somehow drove home to Ayr. He was in a trance, numb. Robbie had scared him witless. He knew he could never see Joanne again. God knows what those two goons had done to her. Now he was at the beck and call of Robbie bloody Collins.

What he didn't realise was that he had been followed from Ayr to Glasgow and back by Alex Burnett from QLM. His latest report was due on Pamela Gibson's desk in the morning. It was all pretty much run of the mill stuff similar to other weeks recently, until today.

Alex had been a policeman in Glasgow for thirty years, with twenty of those working as a detective constable and had spending time working in the drug squad. He was obviously well acquainted with Robbie Collins and Malky Gourlay. Today he had seen a couple of other people he had also recognised and who may be of great interest. He had seen Joe Cassidy and Jock Henderson heading towards the river escorting, almost carrying, a woman. Alex had no idea who the she was. The two men were well known to be two of Robbie Collins associates. Alex lost sight of them and had no idea what they were up to. He had waited and, for once, James had not long afterwards returned to his car and drove home to Ayr.

When James got back home, he poured himself a whisky, downed it in one and poured another. By the time he had seen off the bottle his fear had turned to anger. Firstly, he was angry at himself for being so weak. Then he turned his ire towards Robbie and Malky Gourlay, who it turned out had been following his every move. Despite all the alcohol he had consumed James found it impossible to sleep. The more he thought about things and the way he had been ridiculed by Robbie Collins the angrier he got. As the night turned into dawn his anger turned to hatred and eventually in his mind he had hatched a plan which would hurt Robbie Collins and his precious 'family values'.

When Grace McAuley got to work on Thursday morning, she was shocked to see that her boss had already opened up. He usually did not appear until quite late after what-ever it was he got up to on Wednesday nights. Although he looked tired James was his normal self and kissed her as she entered the shop. James had realised that during Robbie's rant the previous day no mention had been made of Grace, therefore what they got up to was not common knowledge. They had gotten rid of Joanne and barred him from seeing the Russian girl, but he could still take pleasure from Grace. For the present time he would play along with Robbie's wishes.

# CHAPTER TWENTY- FOUR

The following morning at the offices of QLM in Gordon Street, Alex Burnett handed over his report on the surveillance of James Hamilton to Pamela Gibson.

Early on Alex had picked up on the fact that James was being watched by a team, who used a black SUV with blacked out windows. This week he had seen the vehicle, occupied by two shady looking characters he didn't recognise, parked along the street from James Hamilton's shop. Yesterday the same vehicle was in position but was occupied by none other than Malky Gourley.

Alarm bells were certainly ringing for Pamela. She knew that Malky Gourlay was their client's father and Robbie Collins' right hand man. That threw up numerous scenarios, none of which were good. It seemed that James Hamilton, given his trips to Holland, was probably dealing in either stolen diamonds or drugs. Neither of which Christine would want to hear. Somehow her father and uncle were also involved, as well as whoever lived in the apartment James had visited yesterday. Whatever the reasons Pamela was duty bound to update the client. She decided to consult Gerry and Sandy first.

Pamela and Sandy visited Christine Hamilton that afternoon in her office in Glasgow. They updated her on the surveillance on her husband including the events of yesterday. Christine sat quietly as they passed on the findings. Once they had finished, she thanked them and settled her bill with them. She no longer required their services.

That night Christine did not go home to Ayrshire. She visited her uncle's home where they had a long and frank discussion in his office. The two of them were there for over two hours. By then each had had their say and an agreement had been reached. Christine spent the night at Kirklee Avenue and went straight to her office the next morning.

The next day James Hamilton was too busy to notice that his wife had not come home the previous night. He had other things on his mind. He'd been ordered to Holland where he was to purchase a quantity of diamonds. At least this time it would be Robbie Collins' money he was using to buy the goods. On returning to Scotland he was to visit his various contacts in Glasgow and sell them each what they required. He was then to drop the bombshell that he required them to sell their businesses to him by the end of the month or they would suffer the consequences. Half of them thought he was joking, the other half told him exactly what he could do with his offer. Even when he explained it was not an offer but an ultimatum nobody took him seriously. Perhaps next time he would need to take some muscle with him to make the point.

All the time he was going about his business trying to act normally he couldn't get Joanne out of his mind. What had those brutes done to her? He got his answer later the very same evening.

As he drove through Glasgow, heading back to Ayrshire, all the newspaper stands had the same headlines:

*'MODEL FOUND DROWN IN CLYDE.' 'MODEL COMMITS SUICIDE AFTER DIVORCE.'*

In reality James had always known exactly what had happened to Joanne. He knew Robbie's men had killed her he just hadn't wanted to face the truth. He stopped and bought a newspaper. Once he reached home, he read the article. It seemed they had simply thrown her into the River Clyde where she had drowned. The truth was a slightly gorier tale. They had forced cocaine down her throat before handing out a severe beating. Many of her internal organs had been damaged either by the thugs or the punishment the river handed out, as the lifeless body, which they had indeed thrown into the water, was carried away in the current.

Something had compelled James to stop and purchase a newspaper. Once he had read the article a strange feeling came over him. He knew he had to act but before he could events took over and led him to consider his next move more carefully.

* * *

When Robbie Collins leased the Balgair and Ardoch Hotels to the Russian Mafia he expected that they would carry out their business in a proper manner. He had also got them the use of a house in Winton Drive to live in. He had rented this for them through Christine's company, without her knowledge.

In recent weeks Robbie's men, who ran the casino, had reported that a number of new members of staff had arrived at both the hotels, the old guard having gone back home to Russia. Some of the new arrivals seemed to be less level headed than their predecessors. A few heated arguments had taken place inside and outside the Ardoch Hotel and Casino. The situation was just simmering below boiling point. This was of great concern to Robbie as he had a certain standing in the criminal fraternity in Glasgow. He had to show that he had everything under control and was in total charge.

Things came to a head when Christine Hamilton was assaulted at the Balgair Hotel by Alexei Orlov. Members of her staff had called at the house in Winton Drive several times after complaints from neighbours regarding the conduct of the tenants within. They had, at different times, reported late night parties going on into the early hours, drugs being used and sold, scantily clad women running about the street apparently drunk. The employees from the estate agents had been sent on their way by the Russian tenant with a flea in their ear. That was when the problem was brought to the attention of Christine for the first time. She'd had no idea that her uncle had rented the property and was less than pleased when she found out.

She confronted Robbie regarding the property, he was forced to admit that he had rented the house for his Russian business associates from the Balgair and Ardoch Hotels to live in. Christine was furious with him and let him know in no uncertain manner. She wasn't stupid - she knew exactly what kind of business was being conducted and wanted no part of it. His sister Sandra was not too pleased either. Robbie should have known better, Christine was to be kept away from any criminal behaviour.

After the row with Robbie, Christine stormed out of his house and headed off on foot to the nearby Balgair Hotel to speak to Alexei Orlov. All she got for her trouble was a slap and a punch in the face. When she returned to her uncle's home about thirty minutes later, her left eye was beginning to swell shut and the bruising on her cheek was a nasty purple colour. She had, it was later discovered, suffered a fractured cheekbone.

Robbie was incandescent with rage. Since his childhood he had hated men who hurt women. Just as his father had hurt his mother. He quite simply lost the plot. With Noel and Malky in tow he went to the Balgair hotel himself to sort out Alexei Orlov. By the time the three men reached the hotel Robbie was ready to explode.

He found Orlov in the small office behind the reception desk, drinking from a bottle of vodka.

One of his henchmen sat on a small couch nearby. Robbie stormed into the room and without speaking, picked up the bottle of vodka and smashed it across Orlov's face. His man reached inside his jacket but Robbie was too quick for him. He produced a razor and slashed the man right across his face, opening it up from forehead to chin. The man fell, screaming to the floor.

Robbie, Malky and Noel then turned their attention back to Orlov. They were interrupted by the sound of police sirens approaching. This was the only thing that saved the Russian.

Just fifteen minute later the three had returned home. All of them had to change into fresh clothing and destroy the garments they had been wearing as they were covered in blood. By that time Alexei Orlov was on his way to the intensive care unit of the nearest hospital. He would not be assaulting any more women, not in Glasgow anyway.

Eventually, when he recovered sufficiently, he returned to Russia. All the time he was in hospital he was guarded by his compatriots for fear that the Collins gang may return and finish what they had started.

Christine went to stay at her mother's house to recover from her injuries. That did not stop her contacting her solicitor with a view to commencing divorce proceedings against her husband.

Word soon reached the Ardoch Hotel of the assault on Christine and the retribution Robbie had handed out, and an already heated situation was ignited. The result was that one of Robbie's men, Bernie McGlynn, was shot dead outside the casino by Yuri Denko, who was supposed to be in charge of running the hotel.

Perhaps it was fortunate for Denko that somebody phoned for the police and he was arrested before the Collins gang were able to get their hands on him. He was found at the house at Winton Drive stuffing a pile of cash and documents into a suitcase with the intention of obviously fleeing the country.

When James Hamilton heard of all that had taken place, he knew exactly what he must do.

He telephoned a mobile number in Spain. Three days later, travelling on a false passport from Spain via Dublin, William McIntosh landed at Prestwick Airport. He booked into a local hotel under the name on his passport, Sean O'Leary. Later that night he was visited by James Hamilton. By the end of the week McIntosh was back in Glasgow and making plans.

William McIntosh had served in the same battalion of the Black Watch as Craig Hamilton. They were in Northern Ireland together. McIntosh was delighted when he was selected to be part of the honour guard when Craig Hamilton married Joanne Hanson. Who wouldn't be happy? A wedding in Glasgow cathedral followed by free booze and then extended leave in his home city. The two men were then sent to different parts of the world.

In 2005 they were reunited in Iraq. Craig Hamilton was by then a lieutenant and had already been there for several months. He had the reputation in the camp of being a decent officer who cared about his troops, if somewhat unlucky. During his tour, through no fault of his own, he'd lost a lot of soldiers under his command, either killed or badly injured in action.

McIntosh was one of three others who were assigned to Hamilton's team. In the next few weeks they had many narrow escapes. Then one day their luck ran out when they were out on patrol in an armoured vehicle. It was blown up by a roadside improvised explosive device. Two soldiers were killed outright. McIntosh and a further man were badly injured. Later at the field hospital McIntosh picked up someone saying that Lieutenant Hamilton had been uninjured in the incident and had walked away leaving his men. In his badly injured state and pumped full of morphine this is the message that McIntosh's brain computed.

He was sent home to Scotland where he underwent numerous operations to his damaged legs. He was left with was a discharge from the Army, a permanent limp, constant pain and a diagnosis of post traumatic stress disorder. He swore vengeance on the man he blamed for his problems: Craig Hamilton. He couldn't believe that many months later, while in Glasgow Royal Infirmary, he'd had a visit from Craig. McIntosh had completely lost control and had to be physically restrained from attacking his old lieutenant.

Several weeks later whilst trying to get by on pills and alcohol, James Hamilton tracked him down to a pub he frequented on the south side of Glasgow. He remembered James from the wedding, and he had been with his brother at the hospital.

James offered him a job for which he was willing to pay £10,000. He wanted McIntosh to rob his brother's jewellers shop, and frighten the life out of Craig and his young assistant. He asked that all the items in the display cabinets be stolen. James had also stressed that the main objective was to empty the contents of the safe in order to cover his own tracks.

Being homeless and short of funds, McIntosh was only too pleased to agree. He would have done it for nothing just to get back at Craig Hamilton. James agreed to pay two of McIntosh's associates £1000 each for the robbery and had given him the combination to the safe should Craig give him any trouble.

Everything went according to plan with the robbery until Craig recognised McIntosh. When they had gone into the office Craig had attacked him and tried to disarm him of his knife. In the struggle McIntosh had stabbed him through the heart.

McIntosh was not that bothered that he had killed Craig Hamilton. It was what he had sworn to do.

Later that day he met with James Hamilton who paid him the agreed fee and took possession of all the jewellery that McIntosh and his two associates had stolen. What McIntosh found strange was James' attitude to the death of his brother. It hadn't bothered him in the slightest. In fact, he actually seemed pleased.

Now plans were rolling for the big one. James Hamilton had offered McIntosh £100,000 to carry out this new job. If it came off it would send a shock wave across the criminal fraternity of Glasgow and beyond. There was no rush. The longer they took over the preparations the less chance of any mistakes being made. If successful McIntosh would be very well paid, very well paid indeed.

On his first night back in Glasgow, McIntosh contacted a certain man in the Cranhill area of the city who he knew could supply just about any gun and ammunition for the right price. McIntosh placed an order and was to get back in touch in exactly seven days. He knew he was hardly sniper material but was proficient enough for what was required.

In the meantime, he contacted the West of Scotland Property Agency. They had a property to rent which would be perfect for the job in hand. It was rather strange how things were falling into place and hopefully would impact on members of the precious Collins clan.

The following day William McIntosh met two agents from the property agency, having altered his own appearance and using yet another false identity, he rented a second floor flat for an initial period of three months. He gave the name Gregori Kiroff and the agents got the impression that he may be Russian. The flat was situated on the second floor of a building on the corner of Saltmarket and Greendyke Street Looking straight out of the window he had an unrestricted view down the side of the city mortuary and across to the new entrance to the High Court building. It was a distance of approximately 220 to 230 feet. Less than one hundred yards, even he couldn't miss from there, could he?

McIntosh moved into his new 'home' and kept himself to himself. At the end of the first week he took delivery of an AK-105 assault rifle, which was manufactured in Russia. Also supplied was one thirty round detachable magazine of 5.45 x 39mm ammunition. They hadn't come cheap.

The idea of obtaining this type of weapon was obvious. It would throw suspicion immediately onto the Russians. Although manufactured by Kalashnikov in Russia, in actual fact, the weapon was more widely used and therefore more likely to have been sourced originally from Syria, Armenia or Namibia. McIntosh now had all that he required, it was just a matter of settling in for the long haul.

# CHAPTER TWENTY-FIVE

**D**espite the weather not being great over the past few months, Gerry's builder had been cracking on with the house. Gerry visited as often as he could to check on progress.

One day he stopped off on his way back to the office with Sandy Morton. They had been to a business meeting and Sandy asked to see how the house was coming along. Although he only lived around the corner, Sandy had been so busy he had never actually seen the site since the old house and jungle of a garden had been removed.

Gerry parked out on the roadway and he and Sandy strolled onto the site after each had donned a pair of Wellington boots from the back of Gerry's car. Gerry was having a word with the builder when Sandy heard someone shouting his name. He recognised Alex Bruce straight away but, goodness, he was a blast from the past.

Bruce was a joiner who lived in Maryhill Road, Glasgow. Sandy had come across him many years before when he had been a detective sergeant stationed at Maryhill Police Office. Alex Bruce had been a witness on a building site where a lot of expensive equipment was being stolen. Since those days he had put on a pound or two and his hair had all disappeared. A woollen tammie kept his bald head warm.

"How are you, Alex?" Sandy asked.

"Well in all honesty," Bruce replied, "I could be better."

Over the next half hour, he unburdened himself of his woes to Sandy. It was an all too familiar story to the ex-DCI.

Alex's daughter Sheila had married a local Maryhill crook who had got himself killed years ago in a dispute between gangs. He left Sheila with a wee lassie, Sharon. Now Sharon was twenty years old and history was repeating itself. She had a boyfriend, Paddy Boyle, who was a complete waste of space. She was pregnant at sixteen and had a smashing wee boy called Joe who was Alex's first great-grandchild. She was given her own council flat in Saracen Street as there was no room at her mother's or Alex's.

As soon as she had moved in than so had Boyle. He stole just about everything from the flat that wasn't screwed down to feed his drug habit. In between leaving young Sharon with a black eye here and there, and a couple of bruised ribs, she got pregnant once again. The social work department were also involved, because wee Joe had turned up at nursery school with unexplained bruising on his body. Alex Bruce suspected that Boyle was also hitting the young lad as well as his granddaughter.

Two years ago, Sharon had given birth to a wee girl, Kelly Ann. Boyle, in the meantime, was in and out of prison. Nothing spectacular: drugs, assault, theft. Like so many in her position Sharon borrowed money from the wrong people and was soon up to her neck in debt. Alex had bailed her out more than once. She lost her flat and was currently living temporarily with him while she found herself and the children new accommodation. The problem was Paddy Boyle would not leave her alone. He was constantly calling round to Alex's house causing trouble when either full of the drink or on drugs.

Alex told Sandy Morton he was afraid to do anything in case he got in trouble with the police. Sandy reassured Alex that this was his lucky day. The man whose house he was helping to build might just be the one to solve his problem. He introduced Alex to Gerry.

Sandy knew that Gerry kept a close eye on all things to do with the Buckingham Terrace Trust and if anyone there could help Gerry would know who to contact and he was right.

Alex repeated his problems to Gerry, who did indeed know the very person to help. He phoned Ann Marie Docherty who was still heavily involved at the BTT, giving counsel to those who needed it. It had not been long ago that Gerry had helped her out, perhaps she could return the favour. Gerry told her all about Sharon Crawford, her children and the problems they were having. She got straight onto the case and within the week Sharon, her son Joe and daughter Kelly Ann were all resident at the Buckingham Terrace Trust.

# CHAPTER TWENTY- SIX

**B**ack at London Road Police Office, the start of a new week saw Wallace's team redoubling their efforts. The weather had taken a turn for the better. It was nearly summer although not yet that warm. At least the sun was making an occasional appearance.

The first stop for DI Wallace and DS Lynch that Monday morning was Joanne Hanson's apartment by the River Clyde. They had been allocated this enquiry as someone at headquarters felt there may be some connection with the murder of her ex-husband, Craig Hamilton.

The SOCO team had finished their work that morning and so the two police officers had a free run of the place. It was a very nice apartment indeed and must have cost plenty. Wallace and Lynch looked about the place but saw nothing untoward. They knew that Joanne had been a model and there was plenty of evidence of that with photographs of her on just about every wall. The apartment was also very tastefully furnished, a testament to her abilities as an interior designer.

Wallace did however note that there was a small mirror and a razor blade in the bedside cabinet in the master bedroom. A sure indication of cocaine use, but was hardly top detective work, given that the lady had traces of cocaine in her bloodstream when her body was pulled out of the river. In the bedroom was also a wall safe which was empty. The contents had been catalogued and taken to the police office. Wallace had taken possession of the large amount of jewellery found in Miss Hanson's bedroom. His and Audrey's next port of call was to visit Joanne's parents.

The sea breeze was freshening as they drove into Helensburgh. They followed signs for the House on the Hill famous for having been designed by one of Scotland's greats, Charles Rennie Mackintosh. The Hanson family home was just half a mile up the Luss Road. Audrey drove up the gravel driveway to the front door. DI Wallace jumped out of the car and rang the front door bell. A few moments later the door was opened by George Hanson, the detectives identified themselves and he showed them through to a large conservatory at the rear of the building. He introduced his wife, Elizabeth Hanson. They recognised her immediately as she was a very beautiful woman and her daughter had looked just like her.

As usual Brian Wallace did the talking.

"Mr and Mrs Hanson, may I say that we are all saddened by your loss. I have a daughter myself and cannot imagine how you are both feeling just now. I am sorry to bother you at such a time but there are a few questions I should like to ask, if you don't mind?"

"No, just ask whatever you like, Detective Inspector," George Hanson replied.

"As you may know, your daughter's ex-husband, Craig Hamilton, was killed not long ago and now your daughter. Do you think their deaths could be connected in some way?"

"We have no idea," Elizabeth Hanson responded. "After they separated, they never saw each other as far as we were aware."

"Since their divorce was Joanne seeing anyone else?"

"Not to our knowledge," George answered, "although Joanne was always a law unto herself."

DI Wallace showed them the jewellery they had taken from Joanne's apartment. There were necklaces, bracelets, wristwatches and earrings, all diamond encrusted and worth a fortune.

"There are some beautiful pieces," Audrey exclaimed. "Do you know who gave them to your daughter?"

"We have no idea," Elizabeth again spoke. "We assumed Craig gave them to her when they were married."

"Well, thank you both for your time," Wallace said, heading for the door.

On a hunch in the afternoon DI Wallace and DS Lynch went to visit Joseph Hamilton at his shop in the Argyll Arcade. The police already had a list of the items which had been stolen from the Gallowgate shop. It amounted to £180,000. Pawnbrokers and known fences of stolen property all over the country were being checked. To date there had been no joy in tracking down any of the stolen goods. None of the items found in Joanne's apartment coincided with any on the list either.

Brian Wallace asked Joseph Hamilton if he would be kind enough to look over some jewellery and handed over the pieces found at Joanne's apartment. He did not say where they had come from.

Joseph examined the items for a long time using a large magnifying glass.

"All the stones in these pieces were cut by my son James and indeed made by him. I would say at retail they would be worth in the region of £150,000," Joseph said. "Where did you get them?"

I'm sorry, Mr Hamilton," Brian Wallace replied. "At the moment I can't tell you that, as they are part of our enquiries."

Joseph Hamilton accepted his answer without question.

"Just one other thing, Mr Hamilton," Wallace asked. "Do you know Robbie Collins?"

"Yes, of course, Detective Inspector" Joseph replied. "He is the uncle of Christine, James' wife. In fact, he somewhat saved the day when they were married. Craig was due to be the best man, at their wedding but couldn't make it as he had been wounded in Northern Ireland and Collins stepped in. He also paid for the reception at Cameron House Hotel. I knew he was a businessman but later I learned that he has the reputation of being a notorious criminal in the Glasgow area. My family have nothing to do with him now. I haven't seen him since James' wedding."

"Do you think Christine has anything to do with Mr Collins' businesses?" Wallace asked.

"I would doubt it," Joseph relied, "she is too busy with her own property business."

Wallace and Audrey thanked him and drove back to the office. Both officers had the same question on their mind. For a man who supposedly knew so little about jewellery either Craig Hamilton had a good eye, or somebody else had given Joanne the diamonds. The answer awaited them on their return to the office.

DC Charlie Ross had the results of the scenes of crime officer's examination of Joanne Hanson's apartment. Apart from Joanne's own fingerprints there were others all over the premises. Their owner was James Hamilton.

"How did we get his prints?" Willie Wilson asked.

"He was in the habit of visiting the Gallowgate shop, so I took his fingerprints down in Ayr purely for elimination purposes," DI Wallace replied. "Seems I did something right for a change."

Tomorrow they would have to visit James Hamilton. He had more questions to answer. The first being why were his fingerprints all over Joanne Hanson's apartment and what did he know regarding the jewellery found in her safe, all of which had apparently been made by him?

What neither Brian Wallace nor Audrey Lynch had expected was a gift, that would throw up more questions for James Hamilton to answer and go some way to solving the murder of his brother Craig.

That evening Brian Wallace got a phone call at home from his old friend Sandy Morton. It wasn't a social call, it was business, but business which cheered Brian up no end. Sandy told him that his company had been hired to carry out surveillance on a certain party. They had carried out their client's wishes. During this job, QLM's operative had seen some very unsavoury, well known characters down by the River Clyde acting suspiciously. Sandy felt that this may assist in relation to the death of Joanne Hanson. The two friends made arrangements for ex-DC Alex Burnett to call in at London Road Police Office the following morning to give a full statement.

# CHAPTER TWENTY- SEVEN

**D**uring the investigation into the shooting of Bernie McGlynn outside the Ardoch Casino, his killer Yuri Denko was subsequently arrested whilst attempting to flee the country. During the enquiry, searches were carried out at the house where he was living in Winton Drive, also at both hotels, the Balgair and Ardoch, as well as the casino itself.

It was learned that Christine Hamilton's company owned the house in Winton Drive and had rented it to her uncle Robbie Collins. Whether she knew he had got the premises for the use of his Russians acquaintances had still to be ascertained by the police. It also came to light that Robbie Collins owned both hotels and the casino, or at least CGH Company Limited owned them, which was the same thing, as CGH stood for Collins Glasgow Holdings.

The two hotels had been leased to Russian nationals, Alexei Orlov and Yuri Denko, both of whom were believed to be members of the Russian Mafia. One was presently in intensive care, the other on remand in HMP Barlinnie. From the Ardoch and Balgair Hotels, the police removed twenty women whose ages ranged from sixteen to twenty-five. All had been working as prostitutes. Thankfully they had taken interpreters and members of HMRC with them to assist.

Each hotel had an older woman acting as a madam, watching over the girls who were all under the charge of several Russian men. Six to be exact, who were all taken to Stewart Street Police Office. The women detained were split between Baird Street and London Road Police Offices. Firearms and a surprisingly very small amount of drugs were found in both hotels. That was enough to keep the Russians in custody until all the girls had been interviewed.

Before assisting their colleagues to interview the women at London Road, Audrey showed her DI some literature on the subject which she had been given on a newly promoted sergeants course at the force training centre at Jackton. It gave an insight into the possible problems which lay ahead. Human trafficking and slavery were growing industries. The profit which could potentially be made was beginning to rival that of weapon and drug trafficking. Those involved thought it to be a better business model. You could sell a sex slave as many times a night as you liked, whereas a weapon or a quantity of drugs could only be sold once. It was an easy way to make money, but the competition was tough.

The Russian Mafia were known to be heavily involved in many crimes including human trafficking and had long since moved from Mother Russia to many different countries across Europe, including Britain. It was known that women, and some men, were leaving Russia and the Baltic States. They were promised jobs in other European countries, many brought to the United Kingdom using false documents. These people thought they would be given good jobs in hotels or catering. The reality was they were in debt to the Mafia for huge amounts of money. They were beaten, often drugged and forced into prostitution. If they even thought of going to the police or some other authority they were told that members of their families back home would be killed. It is believed that, of the vast numbers involved in this trade, few people would last even three years. By then they would have repaid the cost of their purchase, transport and pitifully meagre upkeep a hundred times over. Nobody cared, certainly not the criminals who were earning phenomenal amounts of money. There was always someone to replace those who fell by the wayside. Brian Wallace found the pamphlet most informative.

Now after the girls had spent a night in the police office, it was time for them to be interviewed. It was going to take some time, as hardly any spoke much English. Thankfully the interpreters were once again on hand to assist. Progress was indeed slow and as the day wore on it became apparent that the girls all had a similar story. They came from all different parts of the old USSR and had paid for a chance to come to the west to make a better life for themselves. They had all been told the same thing. That they would be given jobs in hotels or catering. All had agreed to pay a large amount of cash from their future wages back to the Russians for the opportunity.

Without exception all the girls in Glasgow had first been taken to Holland where they were forced into prostitution and made to take drugs. Those who had refused were beaten or raped, in some cases just disappeared. Some had been in Glasgow for over a year, others had only arrived recently from Holland with Bogdan Volkov, one of the six men arrested the previous night.

One girl, whose English was better than most, gave the team a breakthrough in their investigations when she asked if the police could contact her boyfriend. Natasha Kuznova asked to speak to James Hamilton. DI Wallace and DS Lynch interviewed her, she was to prove the breakthrough they had been looking for.

Natasha was a twenty-four year old Ukrainian from Odessa. She told Wallace and Lynch that she had signed up with what she believed was an employment agency back home and had agreed to pay the equivalent of £10,000 from her future wages to come to Britain with the promise of a job as a receptionist in a top hotel. They had told her this was because she could speak English well. Natasha had believed them and left Ukraine two years before on a plane bound, she thought, for Britain. She was on board with three other girls and they stopped once in Krakow, Poland. Just over five hours later they landed, not in Britain, but in the Netherlands. They were taken to a house in what they later learned was the red light district. The next day it was made very clear to them what their futures entailed. Either they did as they were told, or they would suffer the consequences. Natasha explained that a few girls did rebel and try to break free but, as she had already said, they met different fates. They were beaten or raped, on at least two occasions, girls were simply never seen again. Everyone knew they had been disposed of. The girls were expected to work long hours and hand over all the money they earned to the house madam. They were fed enough to keep them alive but were locked up like prisoners when not at work in a house in Haarlemmerbuurt in Amsterdam. It was little wonder many turned to drugs.

After six months in Amsterdam it was decided that Natasha should be moved to Britain as she could speak the language and would probably make more money. She was taken to Newcastle by ferry and then in a minibus on to Glasgow, always accompanied by one of the Russian men.

There had been four other girls with her. Three were taken to the Balgair Hotel but Natasha and another girl went to the Ardoch.

She went on, "I had only been in Scotland one month when I met James Hamilton. He came to the Ardoch just one night a month at first and then more regularly. He always asks to see me. I was his favourite. He tells me he loves me. I am his girl. He gives me jewels. I asked him to take me away with him and he says he will get me out of hotel."

"Where is the jewellery he gave you, Natasha?" Audrey asked.

"I hide them in my room in hotel," she replied.

Natasha was taken back to the Ardoch Hotel where she gave the police a quantity of jewellery from under a loose floorboard. She was then returned to London Road to continue her interview.

The information that Brian and Audrey had gleaned from Natasha Kuznova was going to do more than just help their enquiry. The Russian and Dutch authorities would be passed the information. This would allow them to find out more about the set up in Holland and how people were being brought into the Netherlands by the Russian Mafia. Interpol would be more than interested. Later several premises in Amsterdam and indeed in Edinburgh would be raided and more Russian Mafia members taken into custody. More women would be rescued from a life of slavery.

Joseph Hamilton was again consulted regarding the origins of the jewellery which now belonged to Natasha Kuznova. He confirmed that this jewellery had also been made by his son James and was worth about £15,000. The big break for DI Wallace and his team was that this time, the items were on the list allegedly stolen from the shop in Gallowgate.

It was time to seek out James Hamilton again.

Wallace and Lynch went to his shop in Ayr to be told by Grace McAuley that he had not arrived at work that day. They went to the house in Dunure and again were unsuccessful in finding him. All the time he had been at Prestwick Airport. He was flying out on yet another trip to Holland, to purchase more diamonds with Robbie's money before selling them to his fellow jewellers. The perfect way for Robbie to launder his drug money and make a profit on the side.

When Wallace and Lynch finally tracked James down the following day, they took him back to London Road Police Office for questioning. By the time they arrived Charles Grayson, Robbie's solicitor, was there to represent Hamilton. After being given a short time to consult with his client the interview commenced. Apart from giving his details for the purpose of the taped interview James Hamilton answered each question put to him in the same way - "No comment." Even when confronted with the various pieces of jewellery, he made no comment. It was obvious that Grayson had instructed him to say nothing.

Wallace had no option but to release him, pending further enquiries. A frustrating state of affairs for him but with no further evidence there was nothing else he could do.

The very next morning James Hamilton left Prestwick Airport for another trip to Amsterdam. Each time he had gone to do business for Robbie he had been able to put aside for himself a small cut of the profits that he made. The differences were easily covered by the varying exchange rates and value of the Pound against the Euro.

James now needed money urgently, not to pay off Robbie, nor to pay Billy McIntosh. He was funding his own cocaine habit which was out of control.

# CHAPTER TWENTY-EIGHT

The day of Yuri Denko's trail at the High Court in Glasgow had at last arrived. It was a typical Glasgow morning - grey, overcast with the expectation of some rain later. Autumn was here.

Billy McIntosh was more than glad the day had arrived as he was at the end of his tether. In some ways his time in the flat had been like rehabilitation, but he'd had enough. He had kept away from people, only emerging to buy food. He had paid for the rental, three months in advance for the premises and would have been due to make another payment next week. Hopefully he wouldn't still be there.

Robbie Collins, Malky Gourlay and Noel Freeman would also be attending court that day. Robbie had been called as a witness, Malky and Noel were going to support him and, of course, the family of the deceased Bernie McGlynn. It had been decided that rather than mess about trying to park the car, the three men would go by taxi. One had been booked for 9.30am, they didn't want to be late.

Robbie, as usual, was dressed immaculately in a blue suit and crisp white shirt. His silk tie and the handkerchief in his top pocket matched perfectly. Malky wore a dark suit, white shirt and a tie which Sandra had bought for his last birthday. He didn't care for it much, but he would never tell his wife that. Noel looked like a male model. He was much slimmer and smaller in stature than his two colleagues. He still had a full head of dark hair and wore an Armani suit which was wine coloured.

They all knew that it was unlikely that Robbie would give evidence today. There was a lot to do before any evidence was heard, not least the swearing in of a jury. It was, however, essential that all three men attend every day of the proceedings to show solidarity with the McGlynn family and to remind other members of the gang just who was in charge.

James Hamilton had left his shop in the capable hands of Grace McAuley. He needed to be in Glasgow. As soon as the taxi had left Kirklees Road, carrying Robbie and his associates, James used a disposable mobile phone to let Billy McIntosh know they were on their way.

Everything was ready at the flat. When Billy had originally rented it, he had purposely used a Russian passport as identification and given the name Gregori Kiroff. He had kept the flat as clean as possible and in the kitchen were two beer glasses and several empty beer bottles. These had been removed from the Ardoch Hotel by James Hamilton during his many visits there before it was raided by the police. He had not been interested in seeing Natasha or anyone else nor did he visit the casino downstairs. His sole purpose was to lift glasses and bottles bearing the fingerprints of the members of the Russian Mafia. This was to throw the police off his and Billy's trail and lay the blame for what was about to happen squarely at the Russians' door.

That morning the taxi driver decided to take his fare to the High Court via the M8 motorway and onto High Street, as there were roadworks affecting alternative routes. Down the High Street and Saltmarket the traffic had thinned after the early morning rush. There were surprisingly few pedestrians as well. It took just twenty minutes from leaving Kirklees Road for the taxi to arrive at Jocelyn Square and come to a halt at the new entrance to the High Court.

Robbie Collins was first out of the car followed by Noel then Malky, who paid the driver.

The three men were standing on the wide paved area in front of the main entrance. Immediately there was the sound of gunfire and they were hit by a hail of bullets. Robbie looked in horror as he saw Noel fall face down onto the pavement, shot several times in the back and head. Dead before he hit the ground.

Malky turned and made an effort to grab Robbie, trying to shield him, and push him down onto the pavement out of the line of fire. The gunfire continued and Robbie felt a stinging sensation in his right shoulder. He had been hit. As Malky tried to shield him, he and Robbie looked straight into one another's faces. Suddenly Malky was thrown forward onto Robbie as he too was shot in the back of his head. His body careered into his old friend knocking Robbie to the ground but not before he took another bullet in the neck. Even the taxi driver was wounded in the arm and covered in glass from the shattered windows of his cab.

The firing stopped as quickly as it had started. People were rushing everywhere in the aftermath.

Noel Freeman and Malky Gormley were both dead at the scene. Robbie Collins had been more fortunate. He had a gunshot wound to his right shoulder and one in the neck. He was unable to speak for several weeks after the event. The taxi driver had been struck a glancing blow on the forearm but would be fine. He had a story to tell his grandchildren. After he told the tabloids, of course.

After carrying out the shooting, Billy McIntosh had left the magazine from the Russian made rifle in the flat together with the fingerprint evidence. He took the rifle with him. He folded it, placed it in a rucksack and hurriedly left the building. He ran across the back garden and climbed onto a Vespa scooter which he had parked at the rear of the flats in Steel Street. The parking at the rear of the flats had a controlled entry with a kiosk and crash barrier. Billy simply mounted the pavement and passed by the side of the kiosk. Then it was right onto Turnbull Street, and away before an ambulance had even arrived at the scene of the shooting.

Robbie Collins was taken to Glasgow Royal Infirmary. The bodies of Noel Freeman and Malky Gourlay were taken to the city mortuary. Seeing as they had died on the pavement at the back door to the premises, that was not a difficult task.

Witnesses at the scene soon pointed the police towards the second floor flat at the corner of Saltmarket and Greendyke Street. The first officers in attendance found it just as Billy McIntosh had left it.

The first question to be answered was if it was down to the Russians, why had they left so many easily found clues? And, secondly, given the premises were owned by Christine Hamilton's property company, did she know anything about the incident?

SOCO went over the flat in the usual professional manner. Fingerprints were obtained from the glasses and beer bottles in the kitchen area. The rest of the flat had been wiped clean. The empty Kalashnikov magazine was photographed in situ and seized as evidence.

Christine Hamilton was not hard to find as she was at the hospital with her grandmother and mother to see how Robbie was. Despite being in bits over the loss of Noel and her dad she was happy to answer any questions that would help the police catch those responsible. She admitted that there had been some animosity between Robbie's staff and the Russians at the Balgair and Ardoch Hotels. Due mainly to her having been assaulted and Bernie McGlynn being shot dead.

She told the police that she had no idea who had assaulted Alexei Orlov. Whilst not denying that the property at the corner of Saltmarket and Greendyke Street was owned by her company, she had no idea who was currently renting the premises. Christine promised the police that they would have the information first thing in the morning.

While all this was going on in Glasgow, Billy McIntosh had made his way back down to Ayrshire. He had disposed of the Vespa scooter and was now using an old blue coloured Ford transit van. He left it legally parked and walked to the hotel where he had originally stayed when he came home from Spain. Once more he booked in using the name Sean O'Leary. The hotel staff believed him to be an Irish businessman who travelled back and forth between Ireland and Scotland on a regular basis. The following day he had an appointment to meet James Hamilton again. He was due payment for this latest job, then he was heading back to Spain.

Over a few beers in the hotel bar he sat and watched the news on television about the shooting in Glasgow. He was annoyed to learn that he had only managed to kill two of his three targets. Perhaps James wouldn't be as happy as he had expected him to be. He would still need to pay up though. By 10pm Billy was shattered - it had been a long day and he was looking forward to a long lie in bed the next morning. He had ordered room service to bring his breakfast up for him.

He wasn't due to see Hamilton until late in the afternoon.

# CHAPTER TWENTY- NINE

**B**right and early the next morning Christine Hamilton and one of her female employees were waiting to speak to DI Brian Wallace when he arrived for work. The woman was one of the two agents who three months earlier had rented out the flat at Saltmarket. She was able to tell Wallace that the man had given his name as Gregori Kiroff and had shown her his Russian passport.

While he looked about the flat with her colleague, the woman had taken the opportunity to use her mobile phone to photograph the passport. She showed Wallace the photograph. Although the photograph showed a man with blonde hair, Wallace recognised him immediately.

The agent said that the man didn't say much but offered three months rent in advance, producing a bundle of cash. He signed the agreement and she handed over the keys. That was the last she'd seen of him. One thing she did recall about their meeting which she thought was strange was that even though he was Russian, he had the letters B,O,S and H tattooed on the fingers of his left hand.

Wallace thanked both ladies for their information and they left.

The DI called a meeting of his team. The latest development had now opened up a new direction for the whole enquiry. Once the team gathered, he issued them all with a copy of the photograph which the letting agent had shown him, together with a similar photograph of a slightly younger man with dark hair.

"This is the man who is the main suspect in the murder of Craig Hamilton. It is now also believed that yesterday he was involved in the shooting incident outside the High Court. His name is William McIntosh, former soldier in the Black Watch, formerly resident of Norfolk Court in the Gorbals, his present whereabouts are unknown. He is armed and must be considered dangerous. He has a nickname 'BOSH', the letters of which are tattooed on the fingers of his left hand. Given that he appears to have at least two different passports, let's get some help from HMRC and upgrade the vigilance at all ports and airports. I have no doubt our man will attempt to leave the country soon."

As the team made off to get on with the tasks at hand Brian took Audrey to one side.

"Audrey, can you get on to the television people and see if we can get a piece on the early evening news. I'm going to publish both photographs and ask the public for help in tracking him down."

"I'm on it, gaffer," Audrey replied.

Ten minutes later Audrey found Brian back in his office staring into a mug of lukewarm coffee.

"Penny for them?" she said.

"Oh, I was just trying to put things in some kind of order, Audrey. Hopefully we will capture McIntosh and that will go some way to clearing the books, but we still have the murders of Carol McVey, Tracy Reagan and Joanne Hanson to solve, as well as the armed attacks and rapes. We could do with a break like we got today to help in those investigations as well. I also need to speak to James Hamilton again."

# CHAPTER THIRTY

Once more the police were unable to track down James Hamilton. He was not at home or the shop in Ayr. Neither was he at the house in Kirklees Road or visiting Robbie in hospital.

James was in Ayrshire, keeping himself hidden out of sight, until his appointment with Billy McIntosh. They had arranged to meet at an old abandoned farmhouse a few miles outside of Ayr. James arrived at the location two hours before the meeting time. He had come in his Jaguar, but it was well hidden behind what was left of the barn. He also had a holdall full of money for McIntosh, as well as a celebratory carry out consisting of half a bottle of whisky and six cans of stout. Twenty minutes before the meeting was due, James saw an old Ford van slowly making its way along the badly rutted road. It was McIntosh. As the van stopped James emerged from his hiding place. He carried the holdall in one hand and the drink in the other.

"You're early," James said.

"You too," McIntosh replied.

James opened the front passenger door of the van and placed the holdall containing the money on the seat.

"There's your money," James said. "One hundred thousand, as we agreed."

"But I didn't kill Robbie," McIntosh replied.

"That's okay, two out of three is not bad and I'll be able to handle Robbie from now on."

McIntosh opened the holdall and held a bundle of cash up.

"I'll trust you it's all there," he said.

James lifted the bag containing the drink. "Fancy a wee snifter to celebrate?" he asked.

"Why not," McIntosh replied, pulling the holdall towards him, making room on the seat for James.

James handed the half bottle of whisky to McIntosh who opened it and took a long drink before smacking his lips and wiping his mouth with the sleeve of his jacket. "That's better," he said whilst taking one of the cans of stout James had offered him. It didn't take too long before the whisky was finished. And there were only two cans of stout left.

James asked Billy how the hit had gone. McIntosh took great delight in explaining every detail of what had happened. Hamilton sat there sipping his stout listening intently.

After about thirty minutes or so, McIntosh suddenly felt very lethargic and nauseous. He was unable to move or speak as though paralysed. He watched in horror as Hamilton took back the holdall. James took out a bundle of money and held it up to McIntosh's face who saw it was actually just pieces of paper. Then James went into Billy's rucksack and retrieved the Kalashnikov rifle. He opened it to its full length and loaded a round into the breech. He placed the weapon under McIntosh's chin.

"Sorry about all this, Billy," he said. "I had to drug you with Rohypnol and make up the holdall to look as though it was full of cash. I don't have that kind of money, so I had no other option."

With that, he callously pulled the trigger and Billy McIntosh's brains splattered the roof of the van. James didn't give it a second thought. He gathered up the empty whisky bottle and cans, placed them in the holdall, full mostly of paper and headed for his car. He drove calmly and slowly down the farm track away from the buildings and back towards Ayr.

The next flight to Amsterdam left Prestwick at 7pm.

The next morning James concluded his business in Holland and flew back to Scotland before lunchtime. He drove to Glasgow to visit Robbie and assure him that he was on top of the job.

Robbie had been told he should not try to speak and so on a piece of paper wrote 'Jewellers - get it sorted'.

James told him that was his very next job. He left the hospital and for once did exactly as he was told. He visited all the outlets for his illegal diamonds, warned them that if they didn't sell up to him by the end of the following week, the wrath of Robbie Collins would be upon them.

By late afternoon James was shattered. He had been running on cocaine and adrenaline all day and needed to rest. Still he had no idea that he was being sought by the police. He drove to Ayr but didn't go home but instead went to his shop, which was now closed for the day.

He went straight to the wall safe and took out a quantity of cocaine which he proceeded to cut into lines and snort. He opened a bottle of whisky and began drinking. By around 10pm he had gotten himself into a state, shaking uncontrollably, ranting and raving, making no sense at all. One minute he was full of bravado, the next petrified that Robbie Collins would find out he was responsible for the deaths of Malky and Noel.

This was how Grace McAuley eventually found him at almost midnight. She had been walking home after visiting friends and had seen the lights on in the shop. By this time James was well into a second bottle of whisky and had lost count of the lines of coke he'd snorted. Grace had been trying to track him down all day to let him know that the police were looking for him. Not just the local police but also a team down from Glasgow.

Because of the state he was in she had to stay and try to calm him down. There was no way she would be able to get him home like that. Grace went to make coffee and when she came back James was snorting yet another line of cocaine. He seemed to calm down and fell asleep, due more to exhaustion than anything else.

When sometime later he awakened he appeared to have shaken off all his demons and almost seemed serene.

"Grace," he said, his voice croaking from too much whisky. "Grace, I'm in terrible trouble. I've done some awful things."

"Is that why the police wanted to speak to you?" she asked.

"Yes," he replied tearfully. "I need to tell you my story as you're the only one I can trust."

He then proceeded to tell Grace the whole story.

He told her how he had resented his parents for adopting another child, how he'd hated that boy and eventually arranged to have him killed. Everything to do with smuggling diamonds into the country. How he'd tried to upset Robbie Collins' apple cart by having him and his close associates murdered because he had ordered his men to kill the only woman he had truly loved, Joanne Hanson. The fact that she had once been married to his brother had nothing to do with it. Finally, he told her about the killing of Billy McIntosh to cover his own tracks. Having unburdened himself he fell asleep once more with his head resting on Grace's lap. She sat like this for a while, tears streaming down her face, horrified. She'd had no idea.

The diamond smuggling and murders were awful, but worst of all in her eyes he had been cheating on his wife. Obviously, she knew that but had thought it was just with her. He had just used her like a common whore, taking his pleasure when he chose, whilst keeping a woman in Glasgow. Grace sat for several hours, not moving in case she woke him. All she could think about was what James had said. She'd worked for him for over two years and from the start he had teased her. He had always been suggestive in his remarks and she had been flattered when he began showing her some attention. Then the petting had started and finally the sex. What a fool she had been. Drawn in by his silver tongue, she had believed that he actually loved her the way she loved him. What a fool she had been.

As dawn approached and daylight was just creeping over the rooftops, she stirred herself. She gently moved James head and put on her coat. Grace took the contents from the till and glanced back at him one more time, sleeping like a baby, before she walked out into the deserted street.

At the taxi stance the driver of the only cab in the rank was resting his eyes. Grace tapped on the window and he sat up.

"Good morning," she said, sliding into the back seat.

"Morning love," the taxi driver replied sleepily. "Where to?"

"London Road Police Office, Glasgow," she replied.

# CHAPTER THIRTY-ONE

At about 6.15 am, Brian Wallace arrived at work that morning with a renewed spring in his step.

He was in even before the CID clerk and as he was emptying the mail from the CID dookit in the front bar the desk sergeant had a surprise for him.

"Mornin' sir," he said. "There's a young lassie been here for the last hour waitin' on you". He pointed to the public seating area near the front door. There was Grace McAuley.

By the time the rest of the squad came in to start the early shift Grace had told Wallace the full story. When Audrey Lynch arrived in the office Brian spoke to her.

"Audrey, please can you look after Grace? Take her up to the canteen and get her some breakfast and take a full statement from her. She has just given me her story. I'll have to act on it immediately."

"No problem, sir," Audrey replied. She walked over to a very sleepy looking Grace McAuley. "Come with me, Grace. You look as though you could do with a cup of coffee and some breakfast."

DI Wallace was straight on the telephone to the police in Ayr. He expected that James Hamilton would still be at the shop premises in the High Street. Wallace wanted officers there immediately to arrest him. He was now the main suspect in a number of murder enquiries as well as having committed numerous HMRC offences. Wallace asked that they let him know the minute Hamilton was in custody and he would send a couple of his team down to Ayr to pick him up. There was no doubt that this new turn of events was another massive breakthrough.

An hour later the duty officer at Ayr phoned back to say they had James Hamilton in custody. He apologised for the delay but said Hamilton was in some state due to drink and drugs and he felt that he had to have him examined by the police casualty surgeon to make sure he was fit to be detained. That examination was now complete, so they could come and collect him as soon as they liked.

DI Wallace told the duty officer that two officers were on their way. The same officers took Grace McAuley back home to Ayr once she had given her statement.

It was early afternoon when DCs Wilson and Grant returned with their prisoner. The duty inspector at Ayr hadn't been kidding - James Hamilton was in an awful state. He was unshaven, his clothing was dishevelled and his eyes red and sore. At the charge bar the allegations against him were read out and he was asked if he required a solicitor. He asked that Charles Grayson be informed and also his wife. Once booked in he was placed in an observation cell, so as not to cause any harm to himself and a uniform officer was delegated with the task of keeping an eye on him. Hamilton lay on the mattress provided and fell into a deep sleep.

That same morning Robbie Collins was allowed home from hospital. The wound in his shoulder was healing well, as was his throat. The doctors had told him he could speak but to keep it to a minimum until his vocal cords had fully recovered.

It was a very sad house that he came home to. Annie, Sandra and Christine were all devastated by what had happened to Malky and Noel. They also worried that if it was the Russians who had been responsible for the attack then it could happen again anytime.

Robbie gathered the three women together in the lounge. It was time for a few home truths.

Firstly, in a croaky voice, Robbie expressed his deep regret at the loss of Malky and Noel. He then went on to tell Christine all about her husband, his love affair, gambling, drug abuse and diamond smuggling. From a source close to the investigation he had received information that James was suspected of arranging not only the shooting incident but also the murder of his own brother.

All three women were stunned by these revelations. Robbie apologised to Christine and told her that as far as he was concerned, he was washing his hands of anything to do with James. She told her uncle it was okay, she had already instigated divorce proceedings against James, as she knew about his infidelity. Her lawyer was just awaiting her instructions. She'd had no idea about the rest of it.

The room was quiet for a time until eventually it was Sandra who spoke.

"Robbie, Christine," Sandra began. "Seeing as we are getting everything off our chests and out in the open, there is something I need to tell you both to know, something only me and Mum know. I've waited all these years so as not to upset Malky. I know that he loved me, I was thankful for that. I loved him too, more than I can tell you."

She turned to her brother and daughter before continuing, "Robbie do you remember just after me and Malky were married, you and he got put away for eighteen months? Well that Valentine's Day some of my mates took me out to the dancing to try and cheer me up. All they did was get me drunk and I stupidly went with a fella I'd met there.

"The result was I fell pregnant and Mum arranged for me to go to Atholl House in Partick. I was in there for six weeks and had a beautiful baby boy. I had to give him up for adoption. It really broke my heart but there was nothing else I could do. Malky and, for that matter, you Robbie would have gone mental when you got out. Anyway, I gave the boy up and when Malky got out we had our Christine. You all know that I love each and every one of you but there has always been something missing. All these years I've wondered what happened to my lovely wee boy. I didn't want to do anything about finding him while Malky was alive. I have been so happy all these years being Malky's wife and bringing up my daughter, who has made us all proud and is a joy to me. But now Malky has gone I want to try and find my boy."

Sandra burst into tears. They all did. Soon they were in a group hug. Robbie promised he would do anything he could to help his wee sister. Christine was the same. Old Annie sat in the corner of the room and wondered what her husband Archie would have thought of all this outward show of affection. Whilst the others remained in the lounge, Christine went through to the kitchen area as she had phone calls to make. Firstly, she phoned her lawyer to arrange an afternoon appointment for herself and her mother. She also instructed him to commence her divorce proceedings. Then she phoned her office and told them that with immediate effect she was taking leave for an undetermined length of time. Only in extreme emergencies was she to be contacted. Christine then returned to the lounge and told her mother to get her coat on. If she wanted to start looking for her son there was no time like the present.

During the next few hours after the arrest of James Hamilton, numerous attempts were made to try and inform Christine that her husband was in custody at London Road police office. She was not in Dunure, or at her mother's home, or Robbie's house. Even her office didn't know her whereabouts and her mobile phone was switched off. There were no sinister reasons for this just that Sandra and Christine had been busy all that day.

They had made a start in an attempt to find the baby boy Sandra had given up for adoption. They'd had little success. Atholl House had no records of baby births and the Registrar at Martha Street could not help. Their initial enquiries had not been fruitful but there were other agencies they could try. Christine had spoken with her own lawyer and through him had made an appointment to see a solicitor in Glasgow who specialised in tracing adopted children. They had however also been told not to expect too much as back then it was not uncommon for doctors to arrange adoptions without leaving a paper trail. Both women had however remained upbeat.

Christine said to Sandra, "Don't get too downhearted, Mum, this all happened thirty-four years ago. We can't expect things just to fall into our lap."

Sandra was just relieved that at long last a burden had been lifted from her shoulders. Now, at last, with the help of her daughter, she was now looking for her wee boy.

When later they returned to Robbie's house, they found a message for Christine to telephone London Road Police Office regarding James. Never having dealt with anything like this before, Christine did not know what to do.

"Just leave it to Robbie," her mother had said, "he'll know what to do".

# CHAPTER THIRTY- TWO

The following morning DI Wallace decided that James Hamilton would perhaps be a little more responsive to questioning. He had some bad news for Hamilton before they began the interview. Wallace and Audrey entered the interview room. Hamilton looked much better than he had the previous day. He had washed, shaved and eaten breakfast.

"Morning, Mr Hamilton," Wallace said. "Before we make a start, I have some news for you. Your wife has finally been contacted regarding your arrest and I have this for you." Wallace handed over an envelope which Hamilton hurriedly opened. Christine had sent word that it was her intention to commence divorce proceedings.

James Hamilton broke down and began to weep. After some minutes he composed himself and asked about his solicitor. Once again Wallace had bad news. Charles Grayson had intimated that he would no longer be representing James Hamilton.

"It looks as though Robbie has cut you adrift, James," Wallace commented. "Do you want me to contact a duty solicitor for you?"

Hamilton couldn't speak but managed to nod, so Wallace and Audrey left his interview until a solicitor could be found to represent him.

They resumed thirty minutes later once the duty solicitor arrived. Wallace reminded James Hamilton that this was the second time he had been interviewed regarding a number of matters. At the last interview he had, on the advice of his legal counsel, chosen to answer each question with 'no comment.' He then went on to outline to Hamilton that the police had now obtained more evidence which corroborated certain matters.

"There is no doubt you frequented Joanne Hanson's apartment on a regular basis and gifted her rather large amounts of jewellery, James. At my request, your father examined the jewellery. He confirmed it was all made by you and was worth in the region of £150,000. What do you have to say to that?"

Hamilton simply replied, "Yes."

"Now I understand that you have been having sexual relations with three separate women: Joanne Hanson, Grace McAuley and a prostitute at the Ardoch Hotel. Is that correct, James?"

"No," Hamilton replied. "It was four women. You forgot about my wife Christine, but now she's divorcing me."

James Hamilton sat with his head slumped onto his chest, crying like a baby. After a while he was silent and then spoke very softly.

"Whatever Grace told you is true. I told her everything."

Over the next ninety minutes or so James Hamilton told Wallace and Audrey everything. He admitted smuggling diamonds illegally into the country from Holland. That was why he had set up the robbery at the Gallowgate shop. His brother Craig had found out about his wrongdoing and was going to speak to their father. James thought he would steal all the jewellery so it couldn't be checked. He had arranged for Billy McIntosh to carry out the robbery. He lied and said he was not aware that the man was suffering from post traumatic stress disorder and had ended up killing his brother because of a grudge he had against him from his army days.

James denied all knowledge of the shooting incident at the High Court. In both cases he said Grace must have misunderstood what he had said. When speaking about the Ardoch Hotel he gave them the name of the prostitute he had been seeing as Natasha. He admitted that he had given Joanne Hanson jewellery, but it was all legitimate and had been presents from him to her. The jewellery he gave to the prostitute Natasha was stolen from the Gallowgate shop. The rest of the haul was in a large vault, which he'd had built without his wife's knowledge, at the rear of his garage under the house in Dunure.

As to the death of Joanne Hanson, James laid the blame squarely at the feet of Robbie Collins and his two henchmen. He later gave a full statement to that effect.

At the conclusion of the interview Hamilton was charged with the murder of his brother Craig Hamilton as well as various crimes and offences relating to the robbery at Gallowgate, drug offences and the smuggling of diamonds. He appeared at court the following day and was remanded in custody. For his own safety he was sent not to HMP Barlinnie but to HMP Saughton in Edinburgh where he was placed in solitary confinement. Both DI Wallace and DS Lynch knew that there was very little evidence to support the murder charge, only the statement of Grace McAuley and the admissions James Hamilton had made to her, which he had since retracted.

A search warrant was obtained for Hamilton's home in Ayrshire and the stolen jewellery from the shop in Gallowgate was all recovered.

Now that the pressure was off slightly, Brian Wallace told Audrey to take a long weekend off. As he'd reminded her on the day they'd had lunch in Dunure, sometimes it's good to take a step back and come back refocused and refreshed. She needed no prompting. She and Gerry needed some time together. They'd hardly seen each other in the past few months. They headed straight for one of their favourite places, a log cabin in the Perthshire countryside. Gerry certainly knew Audrey had been really busy from the first day of her promotion, and she now needed to relax and perhaps they could get their relationship back on track. They had been like passing ships in the night for the past few months.

On Thursday afternoon Gerry loaded his BMW and he and Audrey drove up to the Perthshire countryside for their long overdue beak. Gerry had liked the log cabin since the first time he had seen it, many years before. He had brought his parents there for a holiday on numerous occasions. Eventually he had bought it as the place was ideal. Being all on one level in stunning scenery on the loch side, it was perfect for his disabled father. Over the years the family, including Audrey, had been here many times. They had added to the cabin bit by bit and only the previous year had bought a jacuzzi. Both Gerry and Audrey were really looking forward to the break.

# CHAPTER THIRTY- THREE

The weekend away was just what Gerry and Audrey had needed, unfortunately, as was always the case, it was over all too soon. On Tuesday morning, Audrey was back at work to prepare for the upcoming raft of trials as well as picking up on the many enquiries still outstanding.

One thing had happened in her absence. The body of William 'Bosh' McIntosh had been found in a van parked on a derelict farm in Ayrshire. At first glance, it looked as if he had committed suicide, shooting himself with a Kalashnikov rifle. This had been seized for ballistic and forensic analysis. But DI Brian Wallace had been in touch with the investigating officers looking into the death and sent them a copy of the statement made by Grace McAuley in which she had stated James Hamilton had admitted the crime. Because of this blood and hair samples were taken from the body for examination.

Rohypnol was usually untraceable after a maximum of sixty hours. That is if someone was given a normal dose. In the case of Billy McIntosh, James Hamilton had crushed a massive amount of the drug into the half bottle of whisky which McIntosh had drank. Although the tests on blood samples taken came back negative, traces were found in the samples of the deceased hair. It seemed that when someone was given a huge dose, as was the case with McIntosh, traces linger much longer in the hair than in a person's blood. This corroborated Grace's statement. As a result, James Hamilton was charged with the murder of William McIntosh.

Subsequent tests on the Kalashnikov A-150 rifle proved that it was the weapon used in the murders of both Malky Gourlay and Noel Freeman and the attempted murder of Robbie Collins. There was insufficient evidence to add charges related to this incident against James Hamilton. Of course, that didn't mean he wasn't involved, and Robbie Collins knew that. James Hamilton's life wasn't worth a button. All Robbie had to do was say the word and Hamilton would be attacked. But he preferred to see how long Hamilton was likely to be imprisoned for after his trial. The longer he was in prison, the longer the torment would last. This meant that for the time being he would be unharmed.

Before the trials commenced certain other matters were concluded. More through fear than any sense of doing the right thing, a couple of jewellers who had dealt with James Hamilton had come forward. Enquiries then revealed several more. There was no option but to charge them all with defrauding Her Majesty's Revenue and Customs. All pled guilty and were each fined £10,000. No doubt they all rued the day they ever had any dealings with James Hamilton. At least they now had a clear conscience.

For his part in the dealings Hamilton was sentenced to two years imprisonment and fined £50,000. But that was the least of his worries. He still had to stand trial for the murders of his brother Craig and Billy McIntosh.

In a separate trial at the High Court in Glasgow, the six members of the Russian Mafia all stood trial on charges relating to the Ardoch and Balgair Hotels.

They all pled not guilty in relation to possession of drugs and this was accepted. They were found guilty on charges of being involved in human trafficking and possession of illegal firearms and ammunition. They received sentences totalling sixty years imprisonment. The Russian government arranged their extradition and they would be serving their sentences in a Gulag back home. The madams at the Ardoch Hotel and the Balgair Hotel were each fined £2,000 for their part in running brothels.

Robbie Collins had been called as a witness only to confirm what his niece had already told the police. He merely arranged for the Russians to rent the house in Winton Drive from his niece, Christine Hamilton's company. He denied any knowledge of the Russians' business in relation to his two hotels.

All in all, the whole police operation had been a great success. Six members of the Russian Mafia had been given stiff sentences and nineteen of the twenty girls found in Glasgow had been repatriated to their homeland.

The one exception was Natasha Kuznova as she was required as a witness in the forthcoming trial of James Hamilton and for her testimony and the information she had passed on, arrangements had been made for her to remain in Britain.

The next trial was that of Yuri Denko. As was expected, he pled not guilty to the murder of Bernie McGlynn. The weight of evidence against him, however, was massive. Just about every criminal who had been there that night was queuing up to give evidence against him. Probably to glean favour with Robbie Collins. Denko was subsequently found guilty and sentenced to twenty years imprisonment. He too, like his colleagues, was extradited back to Russia to serve his sentence.

The High Court in Glasgow, in May 2010, was the venue for the trail of James Hamilton. He was accused of the murder of his brother Craig Hamilton and that of William McIntosh. It began on a lovely summer day. James Hamilton pled not guilty to both charges.

Joseph Hamilton and his wife Magda attended the trial as did James' estranged wife Christine and her mother, Sandra. During the evidence, several photographs were shown to the jury of Craig Hamilton. As a baby, at primary and secondary schools, on his graduation from university, at his passing out parade when he had joined the Army, also on his wedding day, resplendent in his army uniform. The photographs were shown by the prosecution, merely to show a happy boy and man, until he was wounded whilst serving his country.

Of all the different images shown Sandra Gourlay was transfixed by just one. It was a coloured print of a baby dressed in a beautiful new blue coloured suit with a teddy bear on the front. The child had piercing blue eyes. She had to rush from the court before she was sick. Christine followed her outside.

"What's wrong, Mum?" she asked when she caught up with Sandra.

"That photograph of the baby," Sandra managed to reply before bursting into tears. Christine hailed a taxi and they went back to Kirklees Road. Once there, over a cup of tea and a stiff drink, Sandra showed her daughter a photograph she had taken of her son, before she had given him away. It had been against the rules, but she had taken it anyway. Christine saw immediately that it was the same child in the same suit.

"As soon as I saw that photograph, I knew it was my boy. They even kept his Christian name. His father was called

Craig. That's all I knew about him, so that is why I called the baby Craig."

Christine was horrified. What a bloody mess. Her husband had her half brother, her mum's son murdered. What was Robbie going to say about this?

They would soon know as Robbie was due home any minute. He'd been for a final check up at the hospital. His throat had now fully recovered.

Sandra could not wait to speak to the Hamiltons and so asked Christine to phone and arrange for a meeting with them that evening. The Hamiltons were surprised when Christine called and asked to come and see them with her mother. They were having a very hard time coming to terms with what James had done and had disowned him. They wondered why Christine wanted to see them, she had just said it was a family matter.

When the two women arrived, Sandra explained the reason for their visit. She showed Joseph and Magda her photograph of Craig as a baby in his suit with the teddy bear on. Immediately the Hamiltons knew Sandra was Craig's birth mother. There was not a lot said after that, just a lot of tears. Magda and Sandra embraced and consoled one another. They had both lost a son.

Christine could feel the sorrow in her mother. She would never get over this. Finding her son after all those years to discover he had been murdered by her daughter's husband. All this and the agony was still not over.

A few days later, whilst James Hamilton's trial was still ongoing Robbie Collins was contacted by his solicitor Charles Grayson. He had received word from the Crown Office that James Hamilton was not to face any charges relating to the deaths of Malky Gourlay and Noel Freeman.

There was plenty of evidence that Billy McIntosh had been responsible. The rifle had been tested and found to be the murder weapon and the property agent had been able to identify him as the person who had rented the flat from which the shots had been fired. There was nothing to tie James Hamilton to the murders, other than he was a known associate of McIntosh.

Robbie Collins was furious. He knew damn well Hamilton had set the whole thing up and that was why he'd drugged McIntosh, then tried to make it look like he had committed suicide in his van.

After a lengthy trial it seemed that the jury agreed in part with Robbie's thoughts on the matter.

James Hamilton was found guilty of the murder of Billy McIntosh and would be sentenced in a few weeks time. Then just as Brian Wallace and Audrey Lynch had thought might be the case, he was found not guilty of murdering his brother Craig. The evidence simply wasn't there. At the conclusion of the proceedings he was returned to HMP Saughton to continue his two years sentence.

# CHAPTER THIRTY- FOUR

**H**uge progress had been made in erecting Gerry and Audrey's new home in Baillieston. It wouldn't be long before it was finished. It had been a monumental task but hopefully worth it in the end. Not wishing to waste any time, the couple had already been on a couple of scouting expeditions into the city centre, looking for furniture.

On that particular day, Audrey had arranged to finish at 2pm, leaving her car at the office. Gerry would be driving into town. Typically, he'd left his wallet and bank cards at the office in Dennistoun and so had to first make a detour there. Eventually as Gerry drove his BMW along Alexandra Parade, he spotted a van up ahead that looked suspiciously like one he had seen before. The one used by the bogus workers he had encountered in Baillieston. He got nearer and noted that although it was displaying a different vehicle registration plate, the front offside wing had been replaced. It was a different colour to the rest of the vehicle.

The van turned off right into the front forecourt of a garage and MOT station called Brady Bros.

Gerry told Audrey of his suspicions. He now knew why he had thought he'd recognised the two men in Baillieston. When he was just a young officer he and Paul Corrigan had, on more than one occasion, jailed two young brothers, Noel and Keith Brady, for housebreaking.

That had been many years ago and the boys, like himself, had obviously grown up but leopards can't change their spots. When the van stopped Audrey was surprised to see it was driven by Derek McVey, the father of the murdered girl Carol McVey.

She questioned him regarding the vehicle, and he told her and Gerry it was one that his bosses used. He worked for the Brady brothers but knew nothing of their criminal activities either in the past or now.

He told the couple that the brothers and Charlene Crainey were currently next door in the second unit. He'd gone to collect the van which had been involved in an accident a while back. It had been left off the road for months but this week he'd been told to have a new wing fitted. Having got the van back it had been Derek's intention to repaint it later that afternoon.

Audrey phoned for assistance and within minutes a marked police vehicle attended. The two uniform officers accompanied Audrey next door and arrested both Noel and Keith Brady together with Charlene Crainey.

They were going to put up a fight and try and make a run for it but thought better of it on seeing Gerry standing in the doorway. The brothers had recognised him in Baillieston and cursed their luck. They were sure he had known who they were and had been resigned to a visit from the police. Little did they know that Gerry and Audrey had only come upon them as a matter of pure luck.

The three suspects were taken to London Road police office as, in the first instance, was Derek McVey. After being questioned he was later released as, it soon became obvious, he had no knowledge of the criminal activities of the brothers and Crainey. He was, however, sick as a pig as this would probably mean he would need to try and find a new job. Given that not too long ago he had buried his only child, his life had now reached its lowest point. Gerry on the other hand was cock-a-hoop at catching the three thieves. He hadn't had that feeling for such a long time and it felt good.

Audrey was less chuffed, and with good reason. She was pleased that her husband was happy and that they had caught three prolific criminals. But on the downside, searching their premises was going to be a nightmare. Not only did it contain several vehicles but dozens of vehicle registration plates, all of which would require to be catalogued and checked on the police national computer. No doubt there would be something of note on several plates.

Unless the culprits were helpful when interviewed this enquiry could grow arms and legs. Audrey also had a feeling that she would be the one lumbered with the case. She was right. Her first job was to send out a message to all stations that the three had been apprehended and asking for any stations with similar crimes to contact her. Almost immediately the replies piled up. Audrey knew she would be there for hours. It had also not escaped her notice that she had not been to look at one single stick of furniture, which caused her no end of annoyance.

Prior to interviewing the suspects, she telephoned Gerry and told him not to wait up as this was going to be a very, very long night. Gerry had simply given his statement and then gone home for his tea. Perhaps not being a policeman anymore did have its advantages.

\* \* \*

From his bedroom window, John Sinclair had earlier happened to see Audrey and the two uniform officers bringing the Brady brothers, Charlene Crainey and Derek McVey into the back yard at London Road Police Office. He had noted they were all handcuffed and he knew that was where the charge bar and cell block were located.

John hadn't been out to work much lately. There had been a major change in his life. The previous month his mother had been admitted to hospital unable to breathe, she would not or could not stop smoking. The hospital staff could do little for her but try to make her as comfortable as possible. Five days later his mother had passed away.

Only one week had passed since her funeral. John was lost and alone now, in an empty house, just full of ghosts and memories. He withdrew into a world of his own. That night he sat looking through his binoculars. Audrey was at her desk obviously trying to write a long report of some kind. John had been watching her for many months now: he was obsessed by her. Her hair, the way she walked, the clothes she wore, everything about her. He had to have her. He didn't want to kill her or rape her, he simply wanted to own her, to have her as his. To live with her and keep her. He had fanta-sised various scenarios in the past. As he now sat watching, the urge inside him grew. He must act and act now.

It was shortly after 1am when Audrey finished up for the night. She was dog tired after a very, very long day. Earlier when she had taken a short break to get some air, Audrey had moved her Vauxhall Corsa to the small car park at the front of the building.

She had moved her car for two reasons; to take her mind off the case she was trying to prepare for a few short minutes and for a quick getaway once she was finished. Now she found it wouldn't start. Typical. It had never given her any trouble before. There was little point in phoning to disturb Gerry, he'd have been in bed long ago. She was just about to go back into the office in the hope there was someone to give her a lift home when a taxi pulled up. Audrey recognised the driver and knew him as Little John. He lived locally and his grandfather had been a cop. Audrey had seen him in the office a few times. He asked her if she was in need of a lift home. Audrey had no reason to suspect anything untoward and was desperately tired. She asked if he could take her up to Dennistoun.

Audrey flopped into the back seat of the cab. Almost immediately she felt something cold spray her face. In moments she was unconscious. When she awoke it was still dark outside. She felt strangely refreshed after being unconscious, if a little dehydrated. As her senses returned, she saw that she was handcuffed to the headboard of a bed. Her clothing was intact, but her shoes had been removed. Then she remembered Little John. What did he think he was playing at? Infuriatingly, Audrey couldn't recall his real name.

Looking around the bedroom she saw a unit against the side wall. On it, displayed like trophies, were several items of women's clothing, purses and handbags. On the bottom shelf, next to what looked like a large scrapbook, was a knife which had a very long blade and looked very sharp.

Immediately. Audrey knew exactly who she was dealing with. Little John was the rapist and murderer that she and Brian Wallace had been seeking for over a year and here he was right under their noses, across the street from the police office. Finally, Audrey turned her attention to the tripod near the window which held what looked like a set of high powered binoculars.

Audrey called out and immediately the man she knew as Little John entered the room. He made no attempt to hide his identity and told her his name was John. 'That's right,' Audrey thought, 'John Sinclair'.

John smiled at her and looked pleased with himself. He gave Audrey a drink of water and then sat next to her on the bed. He told her all about himself and about all the crimes he had committed, even pointing out the different trophies he had taken from his victims and stored neatly on the shelves along with his scrapbook.

Audrey realised she had a lot to thank her university lecturers for. It appeared that Sinclair had no intention of raping or murdering her. He had entered a fantasy world where Audrey was his woman. Someone to be loved and cherished. Audrey had no idea how long this situation would remain but for the time being she knew she had to play along. His demeanour could change at any time, after all he was an unhinged killer.

As it was, even if Audrey had telephoned Gerry, she wouldn't have managed to get in touch with him. He had been urgently called to the Buckingham Terrace Trust.

# CHAPTER THIRTY- FIVE

There is an old saying - 'Once a polis, always a polis'. What it means exactly is up for debate. Some would say it refers to the fact that just because you are no longer in the police force doesn't mean you would stand idly by while a crime was committed, or someone needed help. That you would automatically always step in and do something.

When Gerry Lynch and Sandy Morton selected the four security guards for the Buckingham Terrace Trust, that was, no doubt, one of the qualities they had seen in their latest recruits. Another was that all four were fit and certainly capable of taking care of themselves. They had all previously been uniform police officers working in the city centre.

From the start, to make things easy, it was decided that they would work a three-shift system, seven day roster, just the same as in the police force. One guard day shift, one late and one on nights. The fourth would be on a day off. If anyone phoned in sick it was understood that those on duty would remain to cover until Gerry or Sandy could have them relieved with a staff member from elsewhere. The four men had a small office at the front door with strict instructions about who was and was not allowed in the building.

All incidents had to be recorded in a big ledger, similar to the old police first report books.

Sharon Crawford and her two children had now been at the BTT for almost a month. They occupied a small apartment on the first floor. There was a living room which incorporated a small kitchen unit, a bathroom and one bedroom. There was a single bed for Sandra and a set of bunk beds for the children to sleep in. Kelly Ann was taking time to settle into her new environment and invariably ended up sleeping in the single bed with Sharon. Young Joe loved sleeping in the top bunk because it meant he could climb up and down the ladder. He also attended a new nursery school locally, into which he had settled well.

All main meals at the trust were taken in the canteen, with the other residents and staff. There was little doubt that the family were thriving away from Saracen Street and the clutches of Paddy Boyle. The staff at the BTT had been a great help. Sharon had realised that any future they had together as a family had to be without Boyle. But just when things were falling into place disaster struck.

Over in Maryhill someone had slipped up badly. It was unknown whether it was a member of staff at Joe's old nursery, or someone in the social work or housing departments. Paddy Boyle had been released from his latest prison sentence and had called at Alex Bruce's house to see Sharon and the kids only to be told they no longer lived there. He knew Alex would never tell him where they were. After a week or so snooping about, somebody had let slip the name of young Joe's new nursery school. It was then just a simple matter of watching and waiting.

Boyle had borrowed a car from one of his mates and spent the last few days parked near Sunny Days nursery school.

He saw Sharon walking Joe to the school and then later walking him home. They were staying in some posh house in Buckingham Terrace, that looked like a hotel. Paddy had walked past the building and seen the sign Buckingham Terrace Trust.

Once more Paddy had watched from the borrowed car which he had parked across the other side of Great Western Road. He had seen several other women with kids coming and going. It was some sort of women's refuge but they also had security. Paddy had seen a couple of big guys who were obviously ex-coppers inside the front door. A few days later after sitting and watching for a whole day he had sussed out their shifts.

That weekend Paddy Boyle and two of his pals returned to Buckingham Terrace. Around 11.30pm Bob Sewell was on security duty at the BTT. There was a disturbance out in the street, right outside the front door. One man was down on the pavement and a second man appeared to be kicking him about the head and body. Bob didn't think twice, he opened the main outer door and went down to the street to break the fight up.

Paddy took the opportunity to enter the building, unnoticed, though the door which was ajar and now unattended. He quickly made his way through the building and on to the first floor.

Sharon had put her children to bed some time ago and after just checking that they were still alright, was just making herself a cup of coffee. It was her intention to have a quiet five minutes before retiring for the night herself.

Just then her grandfather, Alex, had called her on her mobile phone to see how she was getting on. Unfortunately, Paddy heard her voice and crashed through her front door. He began shouting and swearing at her, waking the kids who came through to the living room to see what all the shouting was about. At this point Bob Sewell was making his way back into the building after realising he'd been set up and the two young lads had run off together laughing. As soon as he heard the disturbance Bob had pressed the panic button to alert Cranstonhill Police Office. He then ran up the stairs two at a time. As he approached Sharon's flat, he saw that the door was hanging from its hinges. Without another thought he ran into the room.

It was just at this point that Paddy Boyle launched the kettle of boiling water in the direction of Sharon, who was trying to protect her children who were cowering behind her. The kettle hit Bob in the face and the lid opened causing scalding water to splash onto both his hands and face.

He let out a shriek of pain, but it did not stop him. His old instincts were at work, someone needed help. There was one difference from the old days. Bob had no hesitation and punched Paddy Boyle square on the jaw and knocked him unconscious. He then ran to the sink and poured cold water over both his hands and soaked his face. As the adrenaline subsided the pain worsened. Blisters appeared on his hands and face and they were bloody sore.

Thankfully the system worked and police officers were soon on the scene. Boyle had regained consciousness and was shouting the house down claiming he had been the one assaulted and shouting about police brutality. He was swiftly removed.

Karen McInnes, the live in manager, had called for an ambulance and despite the hour had also phoned Gerry Lynch to let him know what had happened.

Gerry attended immediately and went with Bob to hospital to have his wounds treated. His hands were placed in a saline solution which eased the pain and reduced the blisters. He was given a huge tub of cream to sooth his face. After treatment Gerry ensured that he got home okay, before he returned to the BTT.

By then it was after 2am, hardly worth trying to get out another guard. Gerry remained at the Trust for the night to cover for Bob Sewell. John Donnelly would be in around 7am to start early shift and then Gerry just needed to arrange cover for Bob whilst he was off sick.

But there was also something else. There was no doubt that Paddy Boyle would be charged regarding this evening's events but that was not Gerry's concern. Boyle now knew where Sharon and her children were. Gerry spoke to Karen McInnes and arrangements were made to have the family moved elsewhere for their safety. Hopefully this time they could stay hidden and live in peace.

# CHAPTER THIRTY- SIX

I t was around 7.45am when Gerry got home. There was no sign of Audrey and no message on his phone. He didn't think anything was wrong, having been a detective himself he knew anything could happen. He knew that Audrey was going to be late anyway after they had caught the Brady brothers, perhaps something else had come up. For all he knew she may even have been home for a couple of hours and now be back at work. Gerry went for a shower to waken himself up. For once he skipped his morning run and after breakfast he headed for the office. He would wait until after 10am to phone London Road Police Office as the enquiry team briefing would be over by then.

Sandy Morton popped his head around the door.

"Gerry, can you come to my office for a minute?" There was an urgency in his voice that had Gerry moving immediately. As he entered Sandy's office, he saw he was on the telephone.

"...yes, he's here now Brian."

Sandy handed the receiver to Gerry. Brian Wallace was on the other end of the line.

Audrey was missing!

In a matter of minutes, at the request of Brian Wallace, Sandy and Gerry were down at the police office. Gerry was frantic with worry. Sandy calmed him down, so they could hear what Brian had to say.

"Thanks for coming," he began. "Now, as you know, Audrey was working late last night, she signed out at 1am. Her car is still out in the front car park and a search of the building has failed to trace her."

Before Gerry or Sandy could say anything, he continued, "Sandy, I was going to be phoning you anyway this morning as I want you to view some CCTV for me to see if you can identify a couple of suspects."

"What has that to do with Audrey?" Gerry asked.

"Well," the DI said, "nothing, but I asked at the briefing this morning if anyone had seen Audrey leaving the office last night."

Brian Wilson then pointed to one of his detective constables, Craig Meek.

"This young lad may have the answer. He was working late last night and saw Audrey speaking to a taxi driver outside the office. He thinks she may have left in the taxi but couldn't be sure."

"Oh my God!" Gerry exclaimed. "Don't tell me she has been lifted by the killer?"

He was already tired from the previous night, now all his energy left him, and he slumped into a chair. DI Wallace assured him that everything else had been put on hold and finding Audrey was the priority. Checks had already been made on her mobile phone but there was nothing of use. It appeared to be switched off, which was less than reassuring.

Efforts were also being made to try and trace DC Paul Grant. He was on his days off and had told colleagues that he and his girlfriend were going hill walking. So far, they had been unable to contact him. Brian explained that he may hold the key to getting Audrey back quickly. He had, for the last few weeks, been tracing and viewing CCTV images. Firstly, on Gerry's suggestion that the taxi, or at least its driver, might be involved in the rape in Harcourt Drive last November.

He had also found CCTV images in the Joanne Hanson murder case and that is why DI Wallace had been going to call Sandy, to view the footage to see if he could identify anyone. Sandy viewed the images taken from a warehouse down by the River Clyde. When he saw the two men almost carrying a woman along the side of the river, he had no doubt who they were as he and Brian had dealt with them many times before in the past. Sandy identified them both without hesitation as Joe Cassidy and John 'Jock' Henderson, both associates of Robbie Collins. This was just as Brian had thought and corroborated the statement Alex Burnett had given. They were now in the frame for the murder of Joanne Hanson.

Meanwhile as Sandy was viewing the CCTV images, Gerry didn't know what to do with himself. He went out into the car park and examined Audrey's car. He had her spare ignition key with him. He tried to start the car, it wasn't for starting and on lifting the bonnet he saw the reason why. Amongst other things the battery leads were disconnected. Gerry realised that Audrey knew nothing about cars but it seemed to him that somebody had disabled the vehicle on purpose. This did nothing to calm his apprehension. He was afraid that Audrey had been abducted by a killer and all because she had become involved with the bogus workmen.

Gerry blamed himself to a degree as he had been obsessed with catching the Brady brothers. But there was no way that this was going to cause him to backslide again into self pity. He had been there and done that. His priority was Audrey. He must remain strong and alert.

Brian Wallace had ensured Gerry that on a regular basis someone was calling Paul Grant's mobile telephone. Each time they did it transferred to voicemail. Unbeknown to everyone at London Road Police Office, Paul Grant and his girlfriend Morag Barr were in the Cairngorms National Park. Morag had recently inherited a cottage a few miles from Braemar at the side of the River Dee heading towards Ben Macdui. She and Paul had spent the weekend walking in the Cairngorms and returning to the cottage at night. Morag had her mobile telephone with her but in the rush to get away Paul had left his on the coffee table in their flat. The following morning they would be driving home after a very relaxing couple of days. There was something about the air in this part of the world, it was invigorating. The only problem was the signal for mobile phones in that area wasn't good.

Back in his flat in Fielden Street, John Sinclair was watching all the activity in the police office through his binoculars and giving Audrey a running commentary. It was now many hours since she had been taken. So far Sinclair had treated her well enough. He had even allowed her to go to the bathroom and wash herself. Also, he had fed her and kept her well hydrated.

Audrey was in no doubt the guy was crazy. She was still handcuffed to the headboard in the bedroom and Sinclair had used an implement similar to a dog catcher's pole to keep her under his control when allowing her to go to the bathroom. She had no idea how long this fantasy would last. Audrey was wise enough to know that she had to humour him for as long as she could to give her colleagues a chance to find her. For his part, Sinclair was beyond happiness at having captured his dream girl.

The following morning Paul Grant and Morag Barr set off back to Glasgow. It was a drive of some 125 miles, which would take around two and a half hours. They were in no rush and stopped for lunch at Perth. They arrived back at their flat in Summerston about 3pm. Morag ran to open the door whilst Paul emptied their suitcase and gear from the boot of his car. Almost immediately Morag was back, handing him a note which had been pushed through the letter box while they were away. It read 'PAUL URGENT! CONTACT LRPO IMMEDIATELY. DI WALLACE.'

Paul saw that it was dated two days previous. He bounded up the outside stairs and into his flat.

He found his mobile phone and saw there was numerous voice messages for him and phoned his office immediately. Thirty minutes later he was in Brian Wallace's office outlining his findings. Gerry and Sandy were also present.

Paul had viewed hours and hours of CCTV footage from numerous business premises along Alexandra Parade for the day in November 2007 when Alice Brennen had been attacked and stabbed. He had sent Audrey an email with the results of his findings, but she had possibly been too busy with the Brady brothers and Charlene Crainey to open it. After all his hard work he had finally come up trumps and identified the taxi bearing what they already knew were false plates. Gerry's instincts had been correct as although displaying false plates, the vehicle was indeed displaying a valid licence. It was issued to John Sinclair who lived in Fielden Street.

"Isn't that just around the corner?" Gerry screamed, running out of the front door. Wallace sent two of his fittest detectives to chase after him.

Less than two minutes later Gerry was in the lift travelling to the second floor of the building. He knocked on the front door of John Sinclair's flat, when nobody replied he kicked the door off its hinges. The flat was empty.

A quick look around and Gerry and the two detectives soon realised they were on the right track.

They found the tripod and binoculars as well as all the 'trophies' from previous attacks and the large scrapbook. More worryingly, they also found a handbag which Gerry identified as being Audrey's. The flat had now become a crime scene.

Down in the car park the garage owned by Sinclair was searched and his taxi found. He had obviously fled in another vehicle with Audrey. Nobody had any idea what kind of vehicle he had. Even the neighbours were unaware he had anything but the taxi. More to the point, where had he taken Audrey? Gerry was beside himself.

When John Sinclair had taken a shine to Audrey Lynch he'd made it his purpose in life to find out everything he could about her. He soon learned that she was married, where she lived in Dennistoun and even where her new home was being constructed in Baillieston. More frighteningly he had even followed Audrey and Gerry up to the log cabin in Perthshire when they'd had their weekend away.

When they were out, he had used his expertise to unlock the cabin and have a good look around the place. He knew where everything was and had committed it all to memory. He was good at what he did, so neither Gerry nor Audrey had any idea that he'd had them under close surveillance all weekend. That last visit had been three months ago. Sinclair had also made discrete enquiries and learned that the cabin had been owned by Gerry Lynch and his family for some years.

Now, the day after he had abducted Audrey, Sinclair decided that it might be better to move her to somewhere no one would think of looking. The log cabin was perfect. He drugged Audrey before taking her down to the car park in his mother's old wheelchair. He had a Volvo estate parked in the garage. He placed Audrey in the back and the luggage he was also taking. Sinclair parked his taxi in the garage before driving off unseen. In his mind he was driving away with the woman he loved, to start a new life together. Nobody would ever find them. It was only just over eighty miles away. Ninety minutes of driving and they would be invisible to the outside world.

* * *

It was now three days since Audrey's disappearance, three long days during which time Gerry was demented with worry. Sandy did his best to console his old friend and keep his spirits up. He didn't want him to slip back to the bad old days when he had been hospitalised after suffering a breakdown.

Brian Wallace and his team had made finding Audrey their priority, not only because it seemed she may have been abducted by a killer and rapist, whom they had been searching for since Linda Coyne had been attacked in Carlton, but also because she was one of their own.

The staff at QLM were also on high alert. Pamela Gibson was coordinating the operation. It was something she was good at. Four of the team: John Johnstone, Barbara Rice, Alex Burnett and Ann Black, were paired up and were systematically searching everywhere looking for any sign of Audrey or John Sinclair. They interviewed other taxi drivers, neighbours, anyone who might be able to help.

Everybody drew a blank. Gerry was beginning to fear the worst.

In Perthshire it seemed that the novelty of having Audrey with him was wearing off. Sinclair talked incessantly and it was fairly obvious that he lived in a fantasy world. Audrey tried to answer all the questions he asked her, while attempting to appear calm. There was no doubt she was beginning to fear for her own safety, as Sinclair's mood swings became more erratic. It also seemed that the other cabins were presently unoccupied. Where help was to come from was a worry.

Strangely it was John Sinclair who provided the solution. Audrey knew that he liked her, loved her even, in his own warped mind. He was not worried that she was already married. But during a lengthy exchange between them, on day five of Audrey's incarceration, Audrey said something to make Sinclair stop and think.

Outside it was pitch black, there was not one single light visible from the holiday camp. Sinclair had been speaking to her for what seemed like hours and she was weary. At some point in the course of the conversation, Audrey let slip that she was pregnant. Sinclair suddenly went very quiet. He dragged Audrey into the bedroom and secured her hand-cuffs to the bed. She heard him outside the cabin, pacing up and down on the wooden patio, talking to himself. Then it went quiet for some time. It was so long that Audrey fell asleep.

When she awakened it was beginning to get light outside. Audrey got the fright of her life as Sinclair was sitting, silently at the end of the bed, just watching her. He said nothing to her but got up and walked into the kitchen area. He made them both a coffee. Still he had said nothing. He brought Audrey her coffee and asked, "Would you like to go home?"

Audrey did not need to think about that. "Yes please," she answered.

Sinclair went into his pocket and brought out a throw away mobile phone. He dialled a number. Gerry Lynch was asleep on the sofa in his office. He was exhausted having been up half the night with Sandy and other members of the staff, trying to work out what their next move should be. He was lucky if he'd managed two hours sleep. His phone was ringing. On answering it he found he was speaking to his wife's kidnapper. Miraculously he managed to remain cool. He wanted to rip the guy's head off but didn't want him harming Audrey.

"Mr Lynch," Sinclair began. "I've decided to let you have your wife back. I shall, of course, require payment for this service. Do you agree to pay a ransom for your darling wife?"

"Yes of course," Gerry replied. "Anything."

"I want you to know that the only reason I am giving her back is because she is pregnant," Sinclair said. "You have tainted her."

Gerry didn't know what to reply to that, so said nothing. Only he and Audrey had known that she was expecting. How had Sinclair found out?

"Anyway, Mr Lynch, I want £200,000 before I hand back your wife. I will give you a couple of days to get the money together and then I'll let you know where to drop the money off."

"The money is no problem," Gerry replied. "But I need to know Audrey is alright or you'll get nothing."

Sinclair looked at Audrey and whispered to her, "If you tell him where you are, I'll kill you."

He handed the phone to Audrey.

"Hello Gerry," she said.

"Hello darling," Gerry replied. "How are you?"

"I'm okay," she sobbed.

"And the baby?" he asked

"He's fine," Audrey said. "Just you remember how he got his name, don't you dare forget."

Sinclair grabbed the mobile back from her. "Okay, Lynch, you have two days." Then he hung up and ended the conversation.

Having made the phone call Sinclair was in a much happier frame of mind. He even made some breakfast. All he had to do now was sit back for two days and relax.

In Glasgow, Gerry was anything but relaxed. He knew exactly where Sinclair had taken Audrey. He phoned Sandy at home although it was only around six o'clock in the morning. Gerry told him where he was going and asked that he inform Brian Wallace.

After quickly swilling his face with cold water, Gerry went into the wardrobe in the office and dressed in a dark tee shirt, black jeans and grabbed the old overalls he had worn whilst looking for the bogus workmen who had robbed Aunt Effie. He left a note on Jenny Galloway's desk.

Five minutes later he was gunning his BMW along Alexandra Parade heading for the A80 and northwards to Perthshire. Gerry knew Audrey was at the log cabin. He knew this because when Audrey had first told him she was pregnant, they had shared a joke. Obviously, they were both delighted with the news. They then went on to speak about likely names. Audrey had said she wanted to be just like all the celebrities. Why not call their child after the place where he or she was conceived? They didn't take long to realise where this had happened.

Gerry had said, "No way is any child of mine going to be called Log Cabin Lynch!"

It had been a joke, but it could end up saving her life. Audrey had told him exactly where she was.

It only took Gerry just under an hour to reach the holiday village. His senses were on fire, he had never felt so alive. It was still early and nothing much was moving as he approached the campsite. He parked at the side of the site office facing back out onto the main road next to an old Volvo. Donning the overalls, he then walked down to the old walled garden area, which was where the log cabins were situated. It was normally a quiet secluded spot but all hell was just about to break out.

Using the other cabins for cover, Gerry managed to reach the last cabin before his own. Then to his dismay, he heard sirens in the distance which seemed to be heading his way. He knew that Sandy would have let Brian Wallace know what was happening and in turn he would have been obliged to let the local police know, but sirens! Any element of surprise had now gone and who knew what was going through Sinclair's mind. Gerry's primary concern was Audrey. He quickly covered the ground to his own cabin and sneaked a look through the window.

Audrey was sitting at the breakfast bar handcuffed to the metal towel rail. Gerry couldn't see John Sinclair. He moved to the patio doors and saw that Sinclair was sitting on the sofa at the back of the living room. Audrey was between the two men. It was now or never, Sinclair would soon hear the approaching sirens. Gerry had to act now. He took a deep breath and then leapt into action. The only weapon he had was the tyre lever from the car.

He burst through the patio doors and headed straight for his wife. Using the tyre lever like a jemmy, he forced the towel rail off the side of the unit, freeing Audrey and pushing her out towards the patio.

Sinclair was already up and out of his seat, with a knife in his hand. The anger of almost a week of worry was behind

Gerry's first punch. He struck Sinclair square in the face. All that was heard was the sound of breaking bone as he shattered Sinclair's nose and cheekbone. The punch was so ferocious that Gerry had broken his hand. Remarkably neither seemed to feel any pain, the adrenaline levels of both men must have been through the roof. It did however cause Sinclair to drop his weapon.

They were evenly matched in stature, both well built, six footers. Where Gerry was trained in boxing and taekwondo, Sinclair was no slouch when it came to a fight having inherited skills from his grandfather. It was a brief yet brutal battle with both men landing some telling blows.

Sinclair then took the fight to a different level when he managed to retrieve his knife, slashing Gerry on the arm and stabbing him in the left thigh. The police sirens were much nearer now. As Gerry tried to stir himself to renew his attack, Sinclair made a dash for the front doors. He ran down towards the edge of the loch, before turning along a pathway which was well worn and led into the forest.

Gerry paused for just a few moments to ensure Audrey was alright. She was sitting on the ground slightly dazed but was otherwise well. Ripping his overalls apart, Gerry hurriedly made a bandage for his arm and a tourniquet for his leg wound, from which the blood was pumping.

He hobbled off into the forest after Sinclair. Thankfully, having been to the place on so many occasions, he knew the woods like back of his hand. What he didn't realise was that Sinclair had also learned a bit about the place.

Gerry followed the blood trail for a good fifteen minutes and realised that Sinclair seemed to be going by a circuitous route back towards the main road. Despite his leg injury Gerry was running at speed and just before the roadway he caught sight of Sinclair. He obviously wasn't as physically fit as Gerry and was struggling to keep up the pace.

Now, thankful that he had reached the main road, he turned and smiled at Gerry, who was about fifteen yards behind him. Sinclair then disappeared in a blur as a vehicle flashed past. All Gerry heard was the screech of brakes followed by a thud. As he reached the roadway Gerry looked left and saw Sinclair laying in a pool of blood in front of a works van. Gerry had no idea whether he was alive or dead.

A short time later a marked police vehicle arrived and the officers took charge of the situation. All Gerry wanted to do was return to the log cabin and make sure Audrey was well. He hobbled back to the holiday camp. By now he had calmed down and the pain of his injuries was kicking in. It was then he noticed that blood was still pumping from his left leg and his makeshift bandage was saturated. The slash wound to his arm was just stinging and an irritation. His broken hand hurt like hell.

Gerry approached the cabin and saw Audrey sitting in the rear of an ambulance, being checked over by a paramedic. She looked up as he came towards the vehicle and said, "You took your time, Lynch."

Gerry knew she was just trying to be brave but was so overcome he could not reply. They held each other tightly and both burst into tears of relief. They were taken to the nearest hospital for treatment.

Apart from being emotionally exhausted Audrey was fine and everything was okay with their baby.

Gerry was not so lucky. He had shattered numerous bones in his right hand which would need surgery to try and repair the damage. His left hand was also broken. These injuries alone would keep him off work for months. He required twenty stitches in the wound to his arm. Another problem was the knife wound to his thigh. It had not severed an artery but had damaged one. This too required surgery and he needed a few pints of blood to stabilise him after losing so much chasing after John Sinclair.

As for Sinclair, he had survived, but no one knew how. He had been hit head on by a van travelling around fifty miles per hour. It was probably easier to list what was not broken or damaged. He too had to remain in hospital for many months, his broken body held together by numerous screws, bolts and plaster casts.

Eventually he would heal sufficiently to be released but he would never be the same physically again. There were also great concerns as to his mental capacity having also sustained brain damage in the accident. After all that he had suffered he was now deemed to be mentally unstable and unfit to enter a plea. He would be sent to Carstairs Secure Mental Institution where he would be detained at Her Majesty's pleasure. At least DI Wallace and DS Lynch could breathe a collective sigh of relief that at last a dangerous killer's reign of terror had finally been brought to an end. Perhaps things might calm down in the east end of Glasgow for a while at least.

# CHAPTER THIRTY- SEVEN

**W**ith two broken hands and his other injuries Gerry knew he would be laid up for some considerable time. It couldn't have come at a worse time. He consoled himself knowing that Audrey would eventually be stopping work before giving birth. Gerry was supposed to be making all the arrangements to move to their newly built home in Baillieston. He could hardly lift a phone. His only release was regular visits to his GP and the hospital. How he missed Matty not being around to give him a lift whenever he needed one.

Although he was unable to work this didn't stop him doing a lot of thinking and the thought of Matty had given him an idea.

Since the Brady brothers had been arrested it had left Derek McVey out of work. Gerry sent a message asking to speak with him. Just to get out of the house, Gerry arranged that they meet in Angelo's café. Over coffee or, in Gerry's case, a milkshake using a straw, he offered Derek a business proposition which he had already cleared with Sandy.

QLM would fund his purchasing and running the garage, with certain conditions. They would park their fleet of vehicles in the unit which the Bradys had used. It was handy for the office. It was the intention to employ an attendant working there during the day and a watchman at night. To kick start the business, Gerry also offered Derek the contract for servicing all QLM vehicles. He was delighted to accept. It was like an early Christmas present.

Yet again Matty's money would be going to help a local project, just as he had wished. Gerry was in a great mood as he made the short walk home, but it didn't last very long. He was back at the flat for no more than five minutes before he had visitors. His nemesis, DI Samson, nicknamed 'Delilah' on account of being completely bald, and a younger officer he did not recognise.

"Well, Detective Inspector," Gerry laughed. "What am I supposed to have done this time?"

"Let's go inside and I'll tell you," Samson replied.

Once inside Gerry's flat Samson introduced his colleague, DC Malcolm Scott, whose area of expertise was internet crime, especially the grooming of young children online.

"What the hell has that got to do with me?" a bemused Gerry asked.

"Do you own a computer or laptop, Mr Lynch?" DC Scott asked.

"Yes, I do," Gerry replied. "My wife bought me one last Christmas or the one before but don't ask me where it is because I hardly use it."

"We'll be the judge of that," Samson said, producing a search warrant from his pocket.

It took the two officers about ten minutes to find what they were looking for. Gerry's laptop was under a pile of clothing which was ready to be boxed for the big move. Unfortunately, the only place Gerry was going just then was to Baird Street Police Office.

As Samson assisted him into the back of the unmarked police car he whispered in Gerry's ear,

"Got you this time, Lynch."

Once they had arrived at Baird Street Police Office Gerry was placed in the detention cell. But not before he had requested that his solicitor Sam Bryson be informed.

Twenty minutes later DI Samson, DC Scott, Gerry and Sam Bryson were all seated in an interview room along the CID corridor. It was then that Gerry learned the full extent of the allegations against him.

DC Scott had made an initial search of Gerry's laptop and found on a social media site a page apparently in Gerry's name. There were several photographs attached to this page where, from the text, it seemed he was posing as a fourteen year old boy. Also, Gerry appeared to have posted pictures, supposedly of himself and his family. He had made contact with a ten year old local girl and had arranged to meet her in Alexandra Park.

He was informed that the meeting had taken place three days previously and the allegation was that he had attempted to entice the girl to go into the bushes with him and that he had given the girl a bracelet and promised her more jewellery if she was good to him. The girl had become afraid and run off but not before Gerry had allegedly groped her.

Gerry was astounded.

"When was this supposed to have begun?" he asked Samson.

"It's been going on for a period of three months," Samson replied.

Gerry lifted his bandaged hands and said, "And the attack was three days ago, really!"

Samson produced a gold charm bracelet and showed it to Gerry and Sam.

"Really," he replied sarcastically.

Gerry said nothing but knew it was the very bracelet he had bought for Audrey.

The police needed time to further examine the laptop and so Gerry was released pending further enquiries. It also meant Sam had time to build a case to refute all the police allegations. Gerry agreed that he would return voluntarily to Baird Street a week later to take part in an identification parade. There was much work to be done.

Gerry called a council of war in his office at QLM the very next afternoon. Present were Gerry and Sandy as senior partners. Jenny Galloway, who had been promoted in recent weeks to junior partner, Sam Bryson and Audrey. There was only one item on the agenda.

Gerry had told Audrey all of what had taken place and the previous night had got no sleep whatsoever as he mulled things over in his mind. The more he thought about it, the more he returned to the same conclusion each time and it didn't sit well with him. Apart from himself and Audrey the only other person who had access to the flat was Jenny Galloway's mum, Brenda. It seemed inconceivable that somehow Brenda was involved in all of this. Why would she be?

Brenda still cleaned the offices of QLM in Alexandra Parade, only now that they were larger it had become almost a full-time job. Gerry had put her on the payroll and she too had become a member of the QLM family. Despite the fact that Gerry was now married, Brenda continued to also clean his flat. Audrey had no time to do it due to her work commitments. Once Jenny and Sophie had moved across the hall from Gerry, Brenda also did some of her daughter's housework and collected Sophie from school each day. All this necessitated Brenda having keys for all three premises.

Gerry and Audrey both knew that their flat was over-loaded with clothing and various other items since they had married. They could never find anything. Last Christmas Gerry had bought Audrey something which she had always wanted, a gold charm bracelet. For the past few weeks Audrey had been unable to find it and on the odd occasion she'd had a chance to pack some things for the imminent move, she'd noticed other items of jewellery were also missing.

Gerry would have to speak to Jenny as Brenda was the only other person to have access to the flat. He told Audrey that he didn't believe for a minute that Brenda would do such a thing but still the question had to be asked. So that afternoon, despite feeling that the Galloways were almost family, Gerry got it out in the open at the meeting and did ask the question.

For a time Jenny sat very quietly and appeared composed, you could have heard a pin drop. Finally, she spoke.

"You know, all my life the one constant on whom I could always rely was my mother. She raised me on her own and when I had Sophie, she was my rock. She even persuaded Jimmy Quinn to give me a job which, incidentally, I love. Her only weakness is men. She's certainly had a few."

She paused for a moment and looked at Gerry. He sat looking at the floor. All this was very awkward.

"There was a time that I thought she'd found a keeper in you, Gerry, but that was not to be. In retrospect it was probably for the best. Now, when you offered me Matty's old flat I was over the moon because, as I've already said, Mum has had more than a few men but this latest bloke I don't like at all. I felt it was time to move into my own place. Not long after the move, I too couldn't find jewellery that I was sure I'd brought with me. Then I thought that perhaps it had been misplaced during the hurried move. Eventually I realised that it had either been lost or someone had stolen it. My first thought was to who had access to my flat apart from me. The only person was my mother. Personally, I can't believe she is responsible but if she is, then she has to be reported to the police and sacked from her job here. All I would say is that I, for one, would be much happier if we knew more about this latest fella before we confront my mum. He certainly has his feet under the table, but I just don't trust him."

The meeting broke up with each knowing they had work to do. Jenny would compile all the information she had on Brenda's boyfriend. Sandy would then make enquiries as only he could. In the meantime, Gerry and Audrey would be going through the diary to see exactly where Gerry was on crucial times and dates. Sam Bryson had assured them that this would be a great help. There were also statements to be taken from members of staff as to Gerry's abilities with the equipment in the office. He wasn't a technophobe, after all he did have a mobile phone, but he was useless when it came to anything such as computers.

One week later, as he had agreed to do, Gerry took part in an identification parade at Baird Street Police Office. He stood in a line up with five other men of similar height and description in the identification suite. It had been specially constructed with a one-way mirror so that witnesses could see those standing in the parade, but they couldn't see the witnesses. Everyone was however able to hear anything which was said. Sam Bryson was there to represent Gerry. The parade was run by two detective constables not connected to the case. A female DC took the lead and brought the young girl into the room. She asked her to take her time and if she knew or recognised any of the men who were behind the screen. Immediately she pointed to Gerry who was stood in position number five of the six men.

"I know him" the girl said.

Gerry's heart was in his mouth, this was a nightmare.

"Is he the man who attacked you?" the female DC asked.

"No," the girl replied.

"Then how do you know him?" the DC asked.

"That's Sophie Galloway's Uncle Gerry. Everybody in Alexandra Parade knows him."

Before leaving the police office, Sam Bryson left DI Samson with a comprehensive report which showed several times when entries were made on the internet, which it was impossible for Gerry to have made. Many involved him attending hospital visits to consultants and one when he was actually having an operation on his hand.

The following day Sandy called another meeting. He had a file for all those attending.

"With the information I was given by Jenny I was able to build up a picture of our man. Jenny's instincts about him were correct. Please take time to read your file and I will continue once you are all finished."

The rest opened their files and there before them was a photograph. They then read the report which was a comprehensive dossier on Brenda's boyfriend, Terence Banks. Apart from having many aliases, he had a hat full of previous convictions for theft, fraud, indecent assault and rape. There were currently six outstanding warrants for his arrest for failing to appear at court in various locations in England.

Sandy Morton had been busy doing what he was best at. He had ensured that Banks, or whatever his name was, had been at Brenda's flat prior to convening this meeting. One of QLM's operatives had him under surveillance should he leave before the arrival of his visitors. This had not been the case, and when DI Samson attended with his team they had taken him into custody. He was presently being interviewed at Baird Street Police Office and was to stand in an identification parade that afternoon.

Thankfully Brenda hadn't been at home when the police called. Jenny would go and explain everything to her mother later. There was no doubt Brenda would be upset but Jenny knew that she only needed another man in her life to get over it. Knowing her mother, she would be very upset to have hurt her friends. Most of all she would be livid that Banks had lied about his age. She thought she was dating a man who was younger than her.

As for Terence Banks, he made a full and frank confession. He had borrowed the keys for Jenny's and Gerry's flats without Brenda knowing. He had stolen various items of jewellery from both. He'd even stolen some from Brenda and she hadn't noticed. It was he who had set up the internet account in the name of Gerry Lynch. He had used this method several times in the past to entice young girls to meet him believing he was only thirteen or fourteen years old. He'd never worked a day in his life. The story that he told about being a salesman was totally bogus.

There were now several police forces throughout England waiting to interview him. They would have to wait until he had faced justice in Scotland. He wouldn't be getting out of prison any time soon.

# CHAPTER THIRTY- EIGHT

At the conclusion of the trial of James Hamilton, the Crown office had released the remains of Malky Gourlay and Noel Freeman for burial.

The family were able to hold their funerals. Both were lovely ceremonies. Robbie spared no expense. Their coffins had been carried in horse drawn carriages to Linn Crematorium. Sandra had scattered Malky's ashes through the streets of Possilpark where he had been happiest.

Robbie had Noel's ashes on his desk in a ceramic urn. He had made it known to the family that when his turn came, he too wanted to be cremated and have his and Noel's ashes mixed together.

As Robbie said, "We lived life together, so we will be together in death."

He had left instructions in his will where the ashes were to be scattered. It was a special place that both he and Noel had held dear.

It had been a hard time for all the family. Not only had they lost Malky and Noel, but Sandra had discovered Craig was her son and he too was dead.

Christine was still trying to come to terms with her divorce and how her husband had turned into a monster. She still took Annie and Sandra to the bingo in Possilpark every Wednesday and her property business was still going from strength to strength. The recession was biting as far as house sales were concerned, but more and more people had to rent property and her company had lots.

Soon, however, the family would unfortunately have to bear more pain.

Annie was now over eighty years old and one Wednesday as the women were returning from the bingo, she sat as usual in the back seat of the car. Christine was driving with Sandra in the front passenger seat. They were as usual talking excitedly about just missing out on this house and that house. They were laughing at something one of their friends had said. Sandra turned to speak to Annie and saw her eyes were shut, and thought she was asleep. She had in fact slipped away peacefully.

It was the final straw for Robbie, he was inconsolable. He remembered the times his mother had taken the beatings from his father to save him. He had tried all his life to some-how repay her but he knew in his heart that it was a debt which could never be repaid.

Once more Robbie made sure that the funeral ceremony was perfect. Sandra thought the whole of Possilpark turned out to say goodbye to one of their own.

Since the deaths of Malky and Noel and despite his own injuries, Robbie Collins had carried on with his business dealings, but something was missing. It just didn't feel the same without his two friends. His heart wasn't in it anymore but he had no one to whom he could pass the business on.

He certainly didn't miss the Russians, he wanted nothing more to do with them. Perhaps the time was right for him to go into retirement. With the passing of his mother his mind was made up. In truth it was not a hard decision. There was just one thing standing in the way.

The Crown Office had decided that the evidence of James Hamilton, Sandy Morton and Alex Burnett was sufficient to charge John Henderson, Joseph Cassidy and Robbie Collins with the murder of Joanne Hanson. The media were publicising it as the trial of the century. The last of the Glasgow hard men. The trial was set for the beginning of 2010.

It would be the last for Brian Wallace. He was soon to retire and, after a short break, would be taking up a new position with QLM Investigations. Gerry and Sandy had appointed him as their new office manager at Alexandra Parade. The company was growing so fast, Brian's experience would be essential. It would also be Audrey's last court appearance for a while. She was now heavily pregnant and would be restricted to light duties indoors until she took her maternity leave.

When the day arrived, Robbie Collins had left nothing to chance. Three top Queens Councillors had been engaged to defend himself and his two associates. Billy Henderson, who was John's brother and another of those closest to Robbie was also in the building for a most important job, should he be required. If things appeared to be going badly then he had been tasked with tampering with the jury.

This basically took three forms: threats of violence, actual violence and bribery. The way it worked was to study the members of the jury and decide who was most likely to give in to temptation. They were then offered a substantial amount of money to vote in favour of the accused. If they refused, then the juror or a member of their family was threatened with violence. Usually the money did the trick no matter how law abiding a juror considered himself to be, Nobody wanted a beating or possibly even worse.

On the first day, as always in Scotland, fifteen jurors were sworn in. Opening statements would begin the next morning. Already Billy Henderson had a full list of the jurors and he and his team had begun looking carefully at each one in turn. The press and television were all over the proceedings, even describing what Robbie Collins was wearing as he alighted from the prison van to enter the court building. As always he was immaculate but, given his previous experience at almost the same spot, he had been allowed to wear a Kevlar bulletproof vest.

Robbie was not a small man but he looked it, stood in the dock next to Joe Cassidy and Jock Henderson. The prosecution began its case and soon it was time for their star witness, James Hamilton, to give evidence. You could have heard a pin drop as Hamilton entered the witness box and took the oath. Everybody knew he had nothing to lose as he was already serving a life sentence but surely he would not give evidence against Robbie and his men.

But that was exactly what James did as, word for word, he reiterated the statement he had given to the police. He was then questioned at length by each defence QC. Whilst giving evidence James had noticed that Christine and her mother Sandra were sitting in the public gallery and smiled at them. Both looked right through him. On the conclusion of his evidence he was returned to HMP Saughton to continue his sentence. No doubt there would already be a book running to see how long he lasted after giving evidence against Robbie Collins - the clock was ticking.

Back at the High Court, Brian Wallace, Audrey Lynch, Sandy Morton and Alex Burnett all gave their evidence as did the officer in charge of the SOCO team. At the end of the day everything boiled down to evidence of identification. Only James Hamilton could place Robbie at the scene and in Robbie's defence Sandra and Christine had given evidence that on that day he had been at home with them. The jury were in no doubt that Joe Cassidy and Jock Henderson had been there as they believed the evidence given by Sandy and Alex. But being there did not prove they had killed her.

In the end Billy Henderson was not required to intervene. Robbie was found not guilty and Joe and Jock not proven. All three were free to go. While Joe and Jock were swept away by associates to one of their favourite pubs to celebrate, Robbie got Christine to drive him and Sandra home.

For once the media left with their tails between their legs. They had hoped for a more dramatic ending after talking the trial up. The reality was that it ended up a bit of a damp squid.

# CHAPTER THIRTY-NINE

**R**obbie had made arrangements to offload his drugs operation to several rivals across the city. If they wanted to get involved in a war for full control, that was up to them. He still had fingers in a few pies but he handed the whole operation over to his most trusted henchmen, as a thank you for their loyalty over the years.

Robbie would be alright as he had amassed a fortune over the years, enough to keep him for the rest of his life. The very next day he sat Sandra and Christine down in his office.

"I've decided that I'm going to retire to Spain so, Christine, I'll want you to find me a nice villa out there. I don't know if you want to keep this place? If not just sell it."

Robbie's decision was not altogether unexpected. Christine was thinking along the same lines herself. She wanted to keep her business but sell her house in Dunure and move nearer Glasgow.

After discussing it with her mother she decided to sell all three homes; her own, Robbie's and Sandra's. Given the recession and downturn in the market she was amazed when the properties sold so quickly. Before they knew it, the deals were all done.

Christine and her mum would be moving to a beautiful new house in the Lenzie area with easy access to the motorway and Glasgow city centre. It wasn't that far from Possilpark and the bingo either.

The house in Dunure was hardly advertised when someone snapped it up for three times the price Christine had paid for it. It just went to show that there was still money out there somewhere. She also had a buyer for Robbie's house. Joe Henderson bought Sandra's house in Bilsland Drive. He had always liked the place.

One afternoon, about a month later, Robbie sat in the office of his home in Kirklees Road. It was empty with the exception of a couple of wooden chairs. Sandra and Christine had moved to Lenzie earlier in the week. The following day he would be on an early morning flight to Spain. Christine had found him a beautiful villa just on the outskirts of Alicante on the Costa Blanca.

He had only one thing on his mind. Apart from Sandra and Christine, everything he had was worthless. Now it was time for payback and then to put an end to his evil ways. He had promised Sandra and Christine that if they gave him an alibi at his trial then he would, just one last time, bring all his influence to bear to give them revenge for the loss of a son and brother. They all knew that although James Hamilton had not been convicted of Craig's death he was responsible.

As he sat thinking, Robbie could not help smiling. He thought back to his own father and grandfather and the fearsome reputations they had enjoyed back in their day. Even he had a certain reputation and yet felt he was nothing like them. The funny thing was he'd only just realised that it was the women in the family who had the strength. They had been the real hard nuts, not the men. They had stood by him, giving him an alibi for the Joanne Hanson murder. Now it was his turn to repay his part of the bargain.

He picked up the phone. "Billy Henderson," he said.

That night James Hamilton lay on his bed in a single cell within HMP Saughton. He hadn't had an easy time settling into prison life. He'd been in jail for a while now, and the threat of revenge upon him for giving evidence against Robbie Collins and his gang had still not materialised. He'd had a number of close calls but so far had managed to escape uninjured. He did wonder how long he could survive. Perhaps Robbie had decided to call his dogs off for Christine's sake. He fell asleep thinking of his ex-wife.

The next morning when the prison guards opened James Hamilton's cell door, they found him dead. It would have looked like suicide by hanging, using a bed sheet, except that someone had cut out his tongue. Nobody liked a grass.

About the time Hamilton's body was found, at Glasgow Airport Robbie Collins sat drinking coffee when his phone rang. Robbie answered the call and recognised the voice.

"Hello Boss, problem sorted."

Robbie thanked the caller and hung up just as the address system came alive.

"Would passengers for flight MN3582 to Alicante please board at Gate 27."

He dropped his phone into a waste bin and walked towards departures.

# CHAPTER FORTY

It had been a very hectic year or so for all concerned, it seemed now all everyone wanted to do was just to go away on holiday and find a beach to lay on. Gerry and Audrey had settled down to marital bliss in their wonderful new home in Baillieston. There was to be no holiday for them.

Audrey had given birth to a beautiful baby daughter, who they named Ann after Gerry's mother. She would keep them both busy as they adjusted to a new routine. Not that Gerry was much use as his hands seemed to be taking forever to heal.

During his latest enforced lay off, and what with all the serious injuries he had sustained over the past couple of years, Gerry had been mulling over his plans for the future. He would still continue his daily run, business and family permitting. It did, however, seem that his days participating in boxing and taekwondo were over. Still he couldn't give up altogether and having spoken to Jim Kennedy about this, he had been persuaded to become an instructor in taekwondo. It was now Gerry's intention to open a class, hopefully for kids up close to where he had grown up in Easterhouse. He wanted to give something back to the local community. A plus was that his new home was not too far to travel up to Easterhouse and therefore handy should the family need him in an emergency.

He had been in to work but only for the odd day here and there. Gerry continued to mostly delegate work to Sandy Morton who now had their new associate and office manager Brian Wallace to assist. Jenny Galloway had been promoted for a while now and she took her new responsibilities as company director in charge of human resources very seriously.

Gerry was proud of the strides the company had made. He was especially happy that secretary, Sarah McCarty had also dedicated her future to the firm. She'd bought Gerry's old flat. It was the final chapter in laying her ghosts to rest. A lovely new home to go with the new start that Gerry had given her after finding her in a poor state trying to cope with having been raped and beaten. She enjoyed working at QLM as the people were nice, so nice that she'd even found herself a boyfriend.

All was well with the world and QLM. But it didn't stay that way for long.

Right from the start of their partnership Gerry and Sandy had agreed that the majority of the people they employed would come from a police background. The thinking behind this was that apart from knowing what they were getting, the background of any candidate was easily checked. This didn't apply to their clerical staff, Jenny, Sarah and Louise nor, in fact, to any family or friends.

For several weeks Pamela Gibson had become worried about Louise Cadden. Initially she had been an outstanding choice as a secretary and receptionist whilst working in the Alexandra Parade office. Once she had moved with Pamela and others to the Gordon Street office, she was even better.

Recently though, Pamela had noticed that Louise seemed distracted at her work and had begun making silly mistakes. Nothing that couldn't be easily rectified or would cost the firm anything. It was just she'd become shoddy and didn't have her mind on her work. Previously always punctual, her timekeeping had suddenly become erratic and some days she never showed up at all.

At first Pamela thought she may be having boyfriend trouble but when questioned Louise said not. Then one day Pamela came upon Louise in the small room they used as a staff canteen. She was sat at a table holding her phone in a flood of tears. Before Pamela could say anything Louise rushed from the room. Gathering her bag and coat she ran from the building. It seemed as though something was seriously wrong.

Pamela contacted the office at Alexandra Parade. Typically, Sandy Morton, Brian Wallace and Jenny Galloway were all out of the office on business. By luck she managed to speak to Gerry who had just dropped in for five minutes to see how everything was ticking over without him. She updated him on the situation regarding Louise.

There was one thing Gerry had learned during his time in the police and which he transferred to his business. Your colleagues become like family and so you must look after one another. As such, Louise was part of the QLM family and obviously in need of help. He told Pamela to pick him up from the Alexandra Parade office.

A short time later Pamela arrived and she and Gerry drove to Louise's address in Shettleston. Both knew that she lived in Gatehouse Street with her mother. There was no reply when they knocked at the door. A neighbour told them that Mrs Cadden had been taken away in an ambulance earlier that day.

Their next stop was Glasgow Royal Infirmary. After some time and a few enquiries, they tracked down Louise and her mother, Jessie. Mrs Cadden was suffering from a fractured right arm and a broken nose. It seemed that she had been attacked in her home by a couple of thugs who had been looking for her son Stuart.

Once Mrs Cadden had been released from hospital, Pamela drove the women back to Gatehouse Street. Louise insisted that her mother go to bed and rest. Louise got her settled before joining Gerry and Pamela in the living room. She managed to compose herself and tell them the full story.

It seemed that her younger brother Stuart had problems. He had lost his job as a lorry driver and despite all his best efforts he couldn't find alternative employment. This had led to depression and it appeared that he'd become addicted to gambling. Sadly, it cost him his wife, his family and his home. He had been forced to return to live with his mother.

This caused them great disruption as Stuart was also drinking heavily and taking some sort of medication supposed to help him sleep. Louise and her mother had known he had problems but hadn't realised the extent.

Stuart was in debt to the tune of several thousand pounds to a local bookmaker, Bobby Smith. He wasn't the nicest of people and had some very dodgy friends. Smith had assured Stuart that he would get a chance to pay back what he owed by undertaking some jobs for him and his shady pals.

Stuck between a rock and a hard place, Stuart had no option but to agree to Smith's demands. This had caused all kinds of trouble between him, Louise and their mother. They wanted him to tell the police, but it wasn't that easy. Bobby Smith had a reputation locally for handing out violent beatings for anyone who crossed him.

At first Jessie had been glad he was doing something to try and reduce his debt, then she found out what they were making him do. Stuart was delivering drugs all over Glasgow for Smith and his cronies and had even driven down to England delivering guns and ammunition to a gang in the north west, Liverpool or Manchester way.

Stuart's latest trip was to go down to the Newcastle area with a delivery and returning with some illegal immigrants he had been told to pick up. He hadn't returned as he should have by now and had failed to make contact, so Smith and his henchmen had come looking for him. But Jessie Cadden was ready for them. She had been raised in the east end of Glasgow and wasn't afraid of the likes of Bobby Smith and she told him so in no uncertain terms. It cost her a punch in the face, which caused her injuries. Smith had left her semi-conscious on the kitchen floor with his words ringing in her ears, "Tell your boy to get in touch or else."

Louise explained to Gerry and Pamela that all this unpleasantness had really affected both her and her mother. She knew that her timekeeping had been all over the place and her standard of work had dropped off. All she could do was apologise. Both she and her mother were terrified what was to happen next.

Gerry had known nothing about Louise having problems at work. Pamela ran the office and she dealt with any problems there, which was why Gerry had employed her. He couldn't deal with everything himself. He had to delegate and neither he nor Sandy had any complaints about the staff they employed. When it came to the likes of Bobby Smith and his friends, though, that was something to do with Gerry. The QLM staff were now his family and no one bullied his family, end of story.

He also had great sympathy, not just for Stuart but for the whole family. It hadn't been that long ago that Gerry himself was in the same state and had treated his then girlfriend Audrey terribly. He had suffered from popping tablets and drinking far too much. Thankfully he'd received the best of help, something for which he would be eternally grateful.

The first thing was to keep Louise and her mother safe and so he proposed that they move temporarily into Buckingham Terrace where there was someone to keep an eye on them. The next thing was to try and find out what had happened to Stuart. Why wasn't he answering his phone and why hadn't he at least called home?

A visit to the premises of Smith's Bookmakers in Shettleston Road was also called for.

Having taken Louise and her mother to Buckingham Terrace, Pamela and Gerry headed back to the Gordon Street office. Gerry borrowed a couple of Pamela's staff, namely Alex Burnett and John Johnstone. Both had been DCs in and around Glasgow and, having been around the block, were very capable of looking after themselves.

Gerry had Alex drive him and John to Smith's Bookmakers. On arrival Gerry asked the girl at the desk if he could speak to Bobby Smith. He lied, saying he had information regarding Stuart Cadden. The woman on duty in the shop lifted the telephone and called through to the back office. She didn't look old enough to work in a bookie's shop but that's not why Gerry and his friends were there. Having spoken to somebody she directed Gerry and his two pals towards the rear of the building.

The office door was closed, so Gerry knocked. It was opened by a man who more closely resembled a gorilla. Short, stocky, dark hair but going bald, earrings in both ears and as far as Gerry could tell, carrying a gun in a holster under his jacket. As Gerry walked into the office, he saw a second helper standing against the far wall poised for action. He was a taller man who looked older but also seemed to be quite well built. Gerry assumed, correctly, that he too was armed. The man he believed to be Bobby Smith sat in a chair behind a large oak desk. He was around forty years of age, very well dressed in a nice suit. He looked the quintessential business-man, only one thing let him down: bad attitude.

Gerry began the conversation. "I believe you've lost Stuart Cadden?" he said, reaching into his inside pocket for his cheque book. As he did so both Smith's hired helpers reached inside their jackets for their weapons. They were persuaded not to draw their guns by Alex and John who beat them to the draw. Neither of the two heavies had any way of knowing that the opposition were only in possession of replica handguns. The trick, however, served its purpose and both heavies were disarmed.

"Now," Gerry continued, withdrawing his cheque book, "I think Stuart owes you a few pounds. How much?" he asked Smith.

"A few pounds!" Smith snarled "The wee bastard owes me over five thousand."

"Can you prove it?" Gerry asked.

"Aye, nae bother," Smith replied, reaching into his wall safe and pulling out a thick ledger.

He opened it at a page which was headed with Stuart's name. Gerry could see that Smith had been correct. Stuart owed £5,245.76. Borrowing a pen from the desk, Gerry wrote a cheque for the exact amount and handed it to Bobby Smith.

"Now he owes you nothing," Gerry said, closing and lift-ing the ledger. "Just one thing before I go, if you or either of these goons here go anywhere near Stuart or his family again, I'll be back. If I have to return, I won't be so nice the next time."

With that Gerry swung the ledger and struck Bobby Smith right across his nose. The impact knocked him out of his chair and onto the floor. Smith scrambled to his feet looking pleadingly at his two henchmen, but they were not for moving or intervening on his behalf.

"Oh, I nearly forgot," Gerry said. "I hate wee rats like you, who think they can barge into the homes of other people terrifying them and assaulting women when they feel like it. If nothing else, it was a total overreaction and simply bad manners and that's just not on."

With that Gerry grabbed Bobby Smith's left arm and snapped it like a twig. He could see tears welling up in the bookmaker's eyes and he was biting his bottom lip to prevent himself from screaming in pain. Gerry left the office with Alex and John at the door he turned and said,

"Have a good day."

Finding Stuart Cadden proved harder than Gerry had hoped. It was well over a week since he had last been seen in Glasgow. Eventually they tracked him down to the Royal Hallamshire hospital in Sheffield. He had been admitted there several days earlier in a poor state mentally and physically. Gerry had Alex Burnett drive Louise down to Yorkshire to see her brother.

Either because of his condition or fear of the police Stuart had refused to tell anyone what had happened to him. But he told Louise. Alex left her at his bedside in order that she could get the full story.

Stuart had left Glasgow in his Ford transit van and delivered a quantity of drugs to an address in Newcastle. Having done that, he was directed to go just down the coast to a bed and breakfast in the town of Whitley Bay. He stayed there for the night, and the following day as it was getting dark, he picked up four eastern European men. They had been brought over from mainland Europe in a small boat and left in an old derelict fisherman's cottage. They were to be brought back to Glasgow by Stuart. From what her brother said, Louise assumed that they may have been enticed over to Britain with the promise of a job, only to be sold as slaves to a gang run by other eastern Europeans in the city.

Unfortunately for Stuart the men understood English and on arrival in the north east were well aware of their future prospects. They acted dumb and when Stuart came to uplift them, they hijacked him and his van, forcing him to show them the way to Birmingham. They had connections in the city. Stuart had been forced to drive them and they had taken his phone from him fearing he might summon help. That was why Stuart couldn't get in touch with anyone in Glasgow and they couldn't reach him.

To make matters worse the men stopped at a supermarket on route where they bought something to eat and drink. They purchased a case of beer and several bottles of spirits. The temptation for Stuart was too great, he was under severe stress and when he was offered a drink, he took far more vodka than was good for him. It wasn't too long before his driving became erratic. He'd had nothing to eat since breakfast and before he knew it, he was drunk. His east European captors had a simple solution. One of their number took over the driving and they put Stuart in the rear of the van to sleep it off. He had immediately fallen into a drunken sleep and couldn't remember anything after that, until he found himself in an ambulance being taken to hospital.

He had no way of knowing that his captors had decided to dispose of him and as they travelled at speed down the M1 motorway, they threw open the rear doors of the vehicle and pushed Stuart out. Doctors believed that it was because he was unconscious and in a relaxed state that had probably saved him in the end. That, and a huge slice of luck. By that time of night, the road was fairly quiet traffic wise. Fortunately, Stuart had rolled onto the hard shoulder where the driver of one of the few vehicles on the road had spotted him. He had still sustained some damage and was in a poor condition when the ambulance arrived.

For the first few days in hospital he found he was too weak to even get out of bed. Eventually he managed and telephoned Louise to tell her where he was. When she arrived with Alex, Stuart had at first thought he might be one of Bobby Smith's men. He was so relieved to learn that he wasn't and that in fact Gerry had paid off his gambling debt.

A few days later Louise took Stuart home to Glasgow on the train. Gerry had ensured that Mrs Cadden be there to greet them. Later Gerry had the chance to speak to the whole Cadden family. He was able to explain to Stuart how he himself had faced similar problems in his past in relation to drinking too much and taking far too many prescribed drugs. He offered to get Stuart into rehabilitation and to get back on his feet.

Being able to help people gave Gerry a great feeling of satisfaction. There was no doubt that it wouldn't have been possible had he not inherited the money from his late friend Matty The cash had been put to very good use and had helped numerous different people.

He had assured the whole family that Bobby Smith and his cronies would no longer be a problem. And if they did appear, all the family had to do was let him know. Louise took a few more days off to be with her family. She then returned to work where everything soon got back to normal.

# CHAPTER FORTY- ONE

Robbie Collins was loving his retirement in Spain. His only regret was that he hadn't done it years ago. He had a beautiful villa just outside Alicante which Christine had found for him. Usually he spent quiet days by his pool soaking up the sun and either reading or listening to music. He also enjoyed the odd glass of wine.

A local woman called Marie had been cleaning his home since he had arrived in Spain. It was a good job for her and there wasn't anything she would not do for Señor Robbie as she called him, he paid well.

At night he liked nothing more than taking a taxi into Alicante for dinner and usually ended up in a little bar he had found on the sea front called 'El Hombre Torcido' or 'The Crooked Man.' Unbelievably, it was owned and run by none other than Margaret Graham, the sole survivor of the infamous Glasgow crime family. She was now very settled in Spain and had a new Spanish boyfriend. All old rivalries from Scotland were forgotten. Here they were all ex-pats together. They enjoyed each other's company and hearing the Glasgow accent reminded them of home.

Robbie was really looking forward to a visit from Sandra and Christine. They now lived in their lovely new home in Lenzie. They both kept in touch on a regular basis and the following week were due out to Spain for a few weeks in the sun. He also had a surprise for them. After Noel, Robbie had never expected to find anyone else in his life but in recent weeks he had been seeing a young Spaniard called Miguel, who came originally from Barcelona. Life was good.

That didn't mean that Robbie was fully in relaxed mode. He still kept his eye out for any hint of trouble. He wasn't stupid. Over the years he had been involved in many shady deals and been responsible for the deaths of countless men. Somehow, he had survived relatively unscathed.

The problems with the Russian Mafia which had begun in Scotland had spread half way across Europe and had cost them many thousands of pounds and much inconvenience. Operatives had been lost and it would take a lot of reorganisation and the recruiting of many more girls to get back on track. Those in charge wanted their pound of flesh. Someone had to pay. Robbie Collins had enough sense to know he may well be a target given it had all started because of his association with the Russians. He was enjoying life while it lasted.

\* \* \*

Back in London Graham Cahill was annoyed. He had picked up the trail of Ruslan Solokov, the Russian assassin responsible for the murder of Sven Jonson. He and Laura had been tracking him back and forth across Europe for weeks. Unfortunately, Solokov had managed to give Cahill the slip in the gridlock which was central London. There was no doubt the Russian was a very classy operator.

Cahill called Laura's mobile to update her. She told him she had an idea that Sokolov may be heading for the airport and she would check it out. All Graham could do was wish her luck.

At Heathrow airport Ruslan Solokov was boarding a flight on his way home to Moscow. He had just dealt with a

Soviet dissident who had been causing embarrassment to the Russian government. He was sure his bosses would be delighted with him for a job well done.

He knew that for some time now someone had been shadowing him across Europe. In the centre of London, he had managed to shake them off. Now, as was his custom, he sat right at the back of the aircraft so the only people who had a good look at him were the hostesses and people visiting the toilets. Ruslan figured that meant the majority of fellow passengers never even knew he was there.

The flight took off on time and as soon as everything had settled, the air hostesses came offering the passengers sandwiches and coffee or alcohol. Sokolov may have been a hardened killer but he did have two weaknesses. He loved vodka and had an eye for a pretty girl. Already he had noticed the very pretty air hostess. She had short blonde hair, beautiful green eyes and a wonderful smile.

He asked her for a vodka and she obliged. Throughout the flight the air hostess kept Solokov well supplied with the miniature bottles of vodka. At some point he asked if he could see her once they had landed. She hadn't said no.

Just as the plane was preparing to land the air hostess approached Solokov to clear away all the small vodka bottles. She learned across the outer seat and placed her hand on his. He felt a slight prick as the hypodermic needle pierced his skin and she whispered into his ear.

"Sven Jonson sends his regards."

Ruslan Solokov was dead before the aircraft landed. Laura had injected the Russian with a toxic nerve agent known as VX or Purple Possum. It had been banned since 1993. The USA were known to have dumped their supply and Russia was following suite. It was similar to the nerve agent Sarin which, coincidentally, Solokov had just used on his latest victim in London. Laura could thank Bert Williams for her supply of VX. Bert never threw anything away, as he never knew when it might come in handy.

Laura Reid managed to discard the wig she had been wearing as well as the uniform of a stewardess, in a bin in the public toilets, before slipping away and out of the airport undetected.

Somewhere in London a Russian air hostess would have reported to the authorities that she had been attacked in the toilets at Heathrow and had her uniform stolen. It had been an easy matter to replace her on the flight and explain to the flight crew how Svetlana had called in sick.

Once in the centre of Moscow Laura met one of her many contacts who took her to a safe house. Only then did she telephone Graham Cahill's mobile. He was back at the flat in Camden awaiting her call. Given it had been several hours since their last contact he had assumed she was successful. Laura took great pleasure in updating him on Solokov and told him she would be home in a day or two.

Once Laura ended the call, Graham phoned Richard Johnson in New York. He was very happy to learn that his father's death had been partly avenged.

# CHAPTER FORTY-TWO

Since the death of his father Richard Jonson had been driven by one overriding emotion; revenge. He was very happy indeed to hear of the demise of the Russian assassin, Ruslan Solokov. He did, however, have a conscience, and worried that by employing Graham Cahill and Laura Reid he had perhaps overreacted. He contacted Gerry to ask his advice and what his thoughts were on the matter.

Richard flew to Britain. He was due to have another meeting with the UK government representative, Sir Malcolm Whitton, regarding the contracts his father had been negotiating prior to his death. They had already met a couple of times over the past few months. Richard had always been most insistent that they meet without Charles Ludden being present. This meeting, which was due to take place in three days time in London, was going to be at the offices of Richard's company.

Before it took place, Richard flew up to Glasgow to visit Gerry and Audrey and their baby daughter. After making a fuss over little Annie for a while and updating Audrey on all that was happening with his own family back in New York, the two men adjourned to the games room where they helped themselves to a couple of bottles of cold beer from the fridge.

Richard had not been idle since they had last met in London. He updated Gerry on what had been happening since they had last met. He had been very busy in America gathering as much information as possible on the company Amporox. The more digging he did the more dirt he was finding. The evidence of wrongdoing was overwhelming. He had put it all into a very thorough and lengthy report together with all the information which Graham and Laura had collated from Europe on the dealings of the company. It had been a long process checking the movement of drugs across continents, getting hold of hundreds of shipping manifests, collating information, following up on leads and gathering statements.

Lawyers acting on behalf of Jonson Pharmaceuticals had submitted the findings to the Food and Drugs Agency. They fast tracked their response and all Amporox operations within the USA were suspended with immediate effect. It was the FDA's intention to call the owners to book as soon as possible. It was, however, Wall Street which dealt the company the killer blow. Once the financial markets got wind of what was happening, the price of Amporox shares plummeted. Soon after the opening of business the following day the company was worthless.

Amporox ceased trading completely one week later. It disappeared just as quickly as it had first appeared upon the scene. The Russian owners let it disappear without trace, possibly to avoid any investigations being made at their end. What with one thing and another, Britain had not been the best place for their business this year.

"I've no doubt that the company was a front for the Russian Mafia," Richard said, "but I don't think we'll ever find out who it is that is actually in charge. That was why I needed to talk to you, Gerry. Graham and Laura have done a brilliant job uncovering some very shady dealings in Europe and the names of those responsible. My problem now is what to do about these people."

"What do you mean?" Gerry asked. "Don't you want to avenge your father's death?"

"Of course I do," Richard replied, "but am I doing the right thing?"

If Richard was expecting Gerry to tell him back down, then he was in for a surprise. His wife Aimi had explained some of Gerry's back story but not all. He was about to find out the truth. Gerry explained everything to Richard, how he'd lost his parents, best friend and other colleagues. All murdered by a family of Glasgow criminals. How it had affected him physically and mentally. The one thing that had kept him going was the thought of revenge. He had wanted so badly to punish those responsible but in the end was frustrated in his efforts.

"If it's my advice you are looking for, Richard, let me say this. If it had been my father who had been murdered on the orders of these people, would I want to kill them? Hell yes. They are like a disease and if the law cannot stop them then it is up to the likes of you and me to put an end to them and their evil ways."

The two friends finished their beers and returned indoors. They had agreed that neither would say anything to their wives regarding the matter they had discussed. After a lovely dinner Richard retired to bed as he had an early flight the following morning.

The following day in London he and Sir Malcolm had a very amicable meeting where it was agreed that Jonson Pharmaceuticals would become the main supplier of numerous drugs to the British Government. Both parties were delighted. Richard as it was a multi-million pound contract for his company, and Sir Malcolm as the government had replaced Amporex quietly and without any embarrassment or controversy.

Over the next few months the three former top executives with Amporox all died mysteriously in what appeared to be tragic accidents. Certainly, no blame could be attributed to Richard Jonson nor anyone at his company.

In March, William Hearst was killed whilst skiing in Aspen, Colorado. He apparently broke his neck in a fall. Accidents can happen, but Hearst was such an accomplished skier that his friends and family were shocked. There was some talk in certain quarters that the Russian Mafia may have been responsible.

In July, Jakub Bielski was holidaying in Gdynia on the Baltic Sea. He loved fishing and was out alone one day when there was, what the authorities later declared to be, a terrible accident involving his yacht. An explosion on board had ripped the vessel apart and it sank immediately. Bielski's body was never recovered.

Just a few short weeks later, in August, Andrei Dimitrio was holidaying at his villa on the Black Sea. Despite the fact he was a strong swimmer, he drowned after apparently getting into difficulties whilst swimming in the sea, not far from the shore. Markings on his skin indicated that he may have been stung by a jellyfish which possibly caused some allergic reaction.

Despite the various authorities looking into each death no evidence of criminality was found.

When Graham Cahill and Laura Reid returned to London, they found that their bank account had received a huge cash injection. A thank you from Richard Jonson.

# CHAPTER FORTY-THREE

It seemed to Gerry that in the last couple of years or so he had broken, bruised or damaged in some way or another every part of his body. At last he'd got the all clear from his doctor, it was all systems go.

He had been back behind his desk at QLM for some months and everything in that regard was perfect. In his prolonged absence Sandy, Brian, Jenny and all the rest of the staff had been brilliant.

The two Glasgow offices were always busy but the satellite offices all around the country had also reported a large increase in business.

When Gerry had been a young cop with his best mate, Paul Corrigan, they had dreamed of one day owning their own gym or martial arts club. During his long enforced lay off he'd had lots of time to think and plan for the future. Perhaps now was the time for Gerry to make his dream a reality.

At the time Audrey had been abducted, he had ended up breaking both his hands. This made him realise that perhaps teaching, and not fighting, was the way forward. His old mentor Jim Kennedy encouraged him to go ahead and try instructing. Jim had himself been an instructor for more years than maybe even he realised. As he pointed out, Gerry had the skill and ability to be a great coach and he would be doing what he did best; helping people. Gerry couldn't argue with that.

The main problem was Gerry himself as he had very little patience. When he wanted to do anything, it had to be done now. His first obstacle was to become an instructor. This required him to undergo around nine months training. It was in three parts, firstly online, then two classroom days and finally Gerry would be required to make a presentation to the Association to show he was capable of taking and instructing a class.

Somehow the time flew by and he muddled his way through the online bit of the course. Given his lack of skill in such matters, that in itself was an accomplishment. He then endured the classroom days and finally excelled in showing his ability to teach and become a coach. He passed with flying colours.

It had always been Gerry's hope to open a club in Easterhouse and give back to the community in which he himself had grown up. It hadn't been easy back then being a kid and he had no doubt that the kids of today faced many of the same pressures and problems as he had. He was sure that Matty wouldn't mind if he dipped into the fund to bankroll his new venture.

He knew it would take a few quid for the rental of a hall. Usually it was the student's responsibility to provide their own uniforms and any equipment they might need. But it was Gerry's intention to initially provide all they needed free. If the group was a success, then perhaps in the future that might change. All he wanted was to give the kids the best chance possible.

Gerry had always been proud of where he'd come from. Since then so much energy had been put into making a change. There was a whole new programme of regeneration being carried out all over the area. Properties were being renovated, new houses and schools built. They even had a fabulous, massive shopping complex serving the whole area and beyond.

Once he had everything in place Gerry made arrangements to hire a large room in the community centre in Easterhouse not far from where he used to live. He had hundreds of flyers printed and posted through as many letterboxes as possible. The class would run between 7pm and 9 pm each Tuesday night and was open to boys and girls, men and women, from five years of age upwards.

The club was to be called Chung-Yong or Blue Dragon. This was the same name as Jim Kennedy's club in Kirkintilloch. It was a small way Gerry could do something by way of homage to his mentor. Gerry's club would, similarly to Jim's, be affiliated to World Taekwondo which was Olympic recognised. Not that Gerry expected anyone of Olympic standard to turn up at his classes.

The first Tuesday night Gerry turned up to start the club half a dozen young boys came to see what it was all about. Within a couple of months, the club had come on in leaps and bounds. So much so that Gerry had to take on an assistant as the numbers grew.

All those who initially attended were beginners and as such wore white belts. Gerry knew that in a couple of months a few would be ready for advancement to the yellow stripe belt. All had a long way to go if they wished to attain the coveted black belt.

One boy who had showed great promise from the start and had made great strides was James Gormley, aged ten. He was the eldest son of Lynne Gormley, the woman who helped Gerry's Auntie Effie. His younger brother Luke, who was eight, also came to the class. Lynne had a third child, four year old Michelle, who suffered from heart failure. Times had been hard for Lynne as a single mother.

After six months James Gormley's attendance started dropping off and eventually he didn't come at all. His brother Luke still attended. When he was asked about his brother's poor attendance, he just shrugged his shoulders and said he didn't know why he wasn't coming.

One Friday night Gerry and Audrey had just returned with a large shopping from the local supermarket. Gerry was in the process of emptying the numerous bags from the car as Audrey carried Annie into the house. Just as he was finishing, Gerry's mobile rang. At first he didn't know who it was screaming down the line, then realised it was, in fact, Lynne Gormley, who was in a terrible state. It took Gerry all his time to try to understand what she was saying. Something was definitely wrong. Lynne was at Glasgow Royal Infirmary and asked if he would come as she needed his help.

Not knowing if it was Aunt Effie or not Gerry took off for the hospital.

He found Lynne in Accident and Emergency and soon realised what was wrong. Aunt Effie was okay, it was her son James. He'd been attacked on the football pitches near to their home and been given a severe going over. Gerry told Lynne he hadn't seen James for some time, since he stopped coming to his club. Lynne had no idea. From what she said, she thought he still went every Tuesday night with his younger brother. Neither of the boys had said a word to her about not attending.

After his examination, the news wasn't great. The young lad was undergoing surgery to ease swelling on his brain.

He had several broken ribs as well as a broken left leg. Doctors had decided that he should be placed in an induced coma in an effort to aid his recovery. Once out of surgery he would be taken to the Intensive Care Unit.

Lynne was beside herself. Eventually Gerry persuaded her that she would be better going home and trying to get some rest. She couldn't do anything staying at the hospital and she needed to see Luke and Michelle who were being looked after by a neighbour. Gerry dropped her off at her home promising to return in the morning to take her back to see James.

At 9am the next morning Gerry returned to take Lynne to Glasgow Royal Infirmary. Instead of coming out to his car, Lynne asked him to come into her house. She said they needed to talk.

Once inside Lynne directed Gerry into the kitchen where Luke was sitting having his breakfast.

"Tell Mr Lynch what you told me last night, Luke," she said.

Luke looked up sheepishly from his corn flakes and mumbled something.

"Luke Gormley," his mother chided, "sit up properly and tell Mr Lynch."

Reluctantly the young lad looked at Gerry and almost apologetically said,

"Our James was running drugs for Charlie Rice."

Gerry realised that it must have taken a lot for the lad to tell him what he just had. It was the law of the jungle in these parts. Nobody grassed on anyone else. He could see the lad was squirming and so he told him to get himself out in the fresh air. Luke bolted for the front door and ran off down the street.

Gerry and Lynne then had a conversation about what had happened when she had returned from the hospital the previous night. It seemed that fearing the worst for James, young Luke had come clean to his mother about what had been happening.

Unbeknown to his mum or, at that time, any other member of his family, James had begun running drugs for a local gang. The head of this gang was Charlie Rice.

This was a name known to Gerry. He and Rice were both around the same age and their paths had crossed a couple of times in the past. Rice had always been a bully and, like many of his contemporaries, had been involved in criminal activity from an early age. Whether disorder and the numerous gang fights which occurred back then or petty theft. He had long ago moved into and become heavily involved in the sale and supply of controlled drugs. Over the years he had steadily climbed the ladder and now ran his own operation.

What Lynne told him next saddened Gerry and set alarm bells ringing. It seemed that James had only become involved with Rice and his crew to earn money to help the family. He saw how hard Lynne worked to try and keep the family together. He thought if he could bring in some money, she wouldn't have to work herself into the ground. James knew it was bad enough for his mum trying to keep two boys going on her own without the added worry and problems with Michelle. She had been born with a heart defect which had been diagnosed as heart failure. The prognosis wasn't good as half of those diagnosed with the problem had a life expectancy of just five years.

Now this had happened to James. Luke had told his mum that it was his fault. Rice now also wanted Luke to work for the him as well. He had asked James to help persuade him of the benefits. James refused because he didn't want his little brother involved. After several times of asking nicely Charlie Rice decided that he should make an example of James, just to show the other kids he was exploiting what would happen if they didn't behave. James had never mentioned any of this to his family. Luke had been told to keep his mouth shut or he and the rest of his family would get the same treatment.

Lynne had arranged for the neighbour next door to watch Michelle and Luke while she visited the hospital. Gerry drove her down there. Overnight there was no change in James' condition. The staff told Lynne he'd had a good night and hopefully after a time he would be back to normal. It was hoped that in a few days she would see a vast improvement in her son.

She appeared to be heartened by what she had been told and seemed more positive as Gerry drove her back to Easterhouse once more. Having dropped her off he went straight to the local police office to speak to them about the attack on James Gormley and if they could throw any light on the involvement of Charlie Rice. He also enlightened them regarding what appeared to the grooming of younger boys to carry out their dirty work for them and, in the process, make them very rich indeed.

Rice was, of course, well known to the local police, many of whom had dealt with him over the years. The grooming of young kids was news to them though, they had no intelligence regarding this. It seemed that this was a new ploy used by the gangs to transport drugs from one place to another with less danger to themselves. Usually the families of the boys knew nothing about what was going on.

If young kids were caught with controlled drugs the likelihood was that they would get off much lighter than an adult in the same situation. Gerry let the police know that he had real concerns about this. Numerous other kids, James Gormley's age and younger, had stopped going to his taekwondo club on Tuesday nights. He put the question to the police. Did this have anything to do with Charlie Rice? Perhaps. It wasn't beyond the realms of possibility that the kids were working for him and he didn't want them associating themselves with an ex-cop.

Gerry left the police and drove home to Baillieston. He was glad to see Audrey and his beautiful wee daughter Annie. He held the wee girl in his arms and looked at her lovely smile, thankful his family were safe. Gerry felt so sorry for the predicament which Lynne Gormley and her family found themselves in. Her eldest son was in a coma, the youngest boy had been scared shitless by a bunch of drug-dealing scum and her daughter's life hung by a thread.

# CHAPTER FORTY-FOUR

The next morning, Gerry was in at his office much earlier than usual. He changed into his running gear and headed out into Alexandra Park. He loved running at that time of the morning when the air seemed crisp and clean. As he ran, he found himself formulating a plan in his head. Once back at the office he had showered and changed into his suit. He had only one thing on his mind this morning.

Charlie Rice had always thought he was a hard man and now it seemed he fancied himself as a player.... no way. Gerry was going to fight him all the way. He was not fighting for himself, or even the Gormleys, he was fighting for the whole community.

The old days were gone and in the past. There was no doubt where he was raised had once suffered from a bad reputation, some of it was deserved but not all. Things were changing, no longer should people have their lives ruined by criminals who just sat back and counted their ill gotten gains. It was time for a new attitude and about looking towards the future.

Gerry had never told Audrey about what had gone on with Richard Jonson and Graham Cahill. Aside from the fact that what they had done was illegal, Audrey would have gone ballistic had she known. At the very least if the authorities had even had any idea her job would have been out of the window. But Gerry knew Audrey wasn't stupid, she had known something underhand had happened. They'd agreed not to speak about it but, in her own way, Audrey had let him know she wasn't too keen on his friend Mr Cahill.

Now Gerry had come up with a plan which included once more seeking the help of Graham Cahill. He phoned Graham in London and explained his plan. Later that morning Gerry called into the Gordon Street office and spoke to both John Johnstone and Alex Burnett. He tasked them with carrying out surveillance on Charlie Rice. He wanted to know all about him.

After that everything was quiet for a couple of weeks. Gerry made sure arrangements were made for Lynne Gormley to be taken down to the hospital to see her son. As the doctors had hoped, being a strong, fit lad, James was on the mend. It was hoped that he would be able to go home soon.

Gerry continued the taekwondo class although the numbers had dropped off. Despite this more than twelve people were attending and this meant Gerry still required to have an assistant present. He wasn't allowed to take a class on his own. He was convinced that people were afraid to come because Charlie Rice had warned them off. He hoped that he could soon put measures in place that would turn things around.

Three weeks after he had phoned Graham Cahill, Gerry was surprised one morning when the man himself walked into the Alexandra Parade office. He had brought Gerry a present all the way from London. It was a surprise for someone. After handing it over he said his goodbyes and headed back down south. By lunchtime that very day Gerry was reading John Johnstone and Alex Burnett's report on their surveillance of Charlie Rice. It was an extensive dossier which gave every little snippet of information on Rice. Gerry was delighted with the standard of their work and, in honesty, had expected nothing less.

Before Gerry could make the next move, Rice beat him to it.

The lad who had been assisting Gerry had told him he was unavailable for the class the following Tuesday night. As a one off, Jim Kennedy had volunteered his services. It was his excuse for a catch up. Gerry didn't know at that time but would later come to the conclusion that the gods had been smiling down on him.

On the following Tuesday Jim Kennedy duly turned up and helped Gerry in instructing the group.

They had a great evening and really enjoyed the session. At the conclusion around 9pm the class all left the building to make their way home. A few minutes later as Gerry and Jim were leaving to get in their cars they were confronted by six rough looking characters, all armed with baseball bats or iron bars. Charlie Rice was sending a message.

Almost by telepathy Gerry and Jim seemed to know what the other man was thinking. Gerry took a step forward only for Jim to move him to one side and step in front. Gerry recalled way back when he and his pal Paul Corrigan had first started training with Jim, his first words.

"The best form of defence is attack."

Jim strode towards the men who had spread out across the car park entrance. He asked,

"Who's the leader?"

Right in front of him stood a gorilla of a man, easily six feet plus who looked to be built from stone. He was carrying a heavy hammer in a menacing fashion. He smirked a reply at Jim.

"I am, old yin."

Without further ado Jim Kennedy took one step back, to give himself room, and delivered a kick straight the big man's chin. He collapsed to the ground like a tree being felled, out cold.

There was a moment's shocked silence and then all hell broke loose. Five minutes later the police arrived in response to a phone call from one of the local residents. By that time Gerry and Jim had made quite a mess of their six opponents, all of whom required hospital treatment. After being taken to Easterhouse Police Office, Gerry and Jim were later allowed to go home after first giving statements. The six men currently at the Royal Infirmary would be charged in relation to the incident.

As the two friends walked towards their cars Jim looked down in the mouth and said,

"Fancy that big guy calling me old yin."

"Well you are grey haired," Gerry laughed.

"Aye, but there's life in the old dog yet," Jim smiled.

The next morning on his daily run Gerry could feel the effects of the previous evening's altercation. His body was sore and he wondered how Jim Kennedy was feeling. Jim may now have grey hair but, judging by the way he had dealt with those thugs, he still had plenty of fight left in him.

After showering and dressing back at the office, Gerry phoned the Gordon Street office. He spoke to Alex Burnett and arranged to pick up him and John Johnstone in the afternoon.

Around 2pm the three men stopped outside an old warehouse in Tollcross, Glasgow. Charlie Rice had been using the place as his office-cum-gymnasium for over a year. Along with his drug dealing empire, it appeared that Charlie had taken an interest in boxing. As Gerry and his associates approached the building the memories came flooding back and reminded Gerry of what he was missing. There were several boxers training as they entered, the smell of the place was just as he'd remembered a mixture of sweat and liniment.

The ground floor was wholly taken over by the boxing gym and ring. Rice had converted the first floor into an office for himself and his associates. As Gerry climbed up the stairs, he saw Rice sat at his desk sipping a glass of champagne. He really did think he was the bee's knees.

Gerry got his dig in first.

"How are your boys feeling today, Charlie?" he asked.

"Fine, Mr Lynch, just fine," Charlie replied.

A few bruised and battered faces standing around told a different story. Gerry noticed the big guy that Jim Kennedy had taken on. He was sipping what looked like a milkshake through a straw. His jaw, obviously broken, was wired shut.

Gerry couldn't resist smiling at him and shouted over,

"The old guy with the grey hair says hello."

He could see that the guy was just about to explode but his injuries prevented him from doing anything.

"Anyway, Charlie," Gerry continued. "I just thought I should pay you a visit and let you know in person, that I intend putting a stop to you grooming weans on the estate to do your dirty work. Next time it will be you getting bruised."

He could see Rice was angry but trying to keep himself in check.

"Obviously you like a fight Mr Lynch, here take these," he said, handing Gerry two tickets. "Two ringside seats for my next promotion in Glasgow. By the way would you care for a glass of champagne?"

Gerry pocketed them without speaking and as he turned to leave said,

"No thanks, Charlie, it's a bit early for me."

Rice picked up a bottle and handed it to Gerry, sarcastically saying,

"Take one for later, Mr Lynch."

Gerry accepted the bottle and then left with Alex and John in tow.

# CHAPTER FORTY- FIVE

**T**wo weeks later, Rice Promotions held a gala boxing evening in a large hotel in Glasgow city centre. Top of the bill was the fighter who Charlie Rice believed was a champion in the making. There was a full card of evenly matched fights and a large crowd had gathered to support the fighters and enjoy themselves.

Ever the showman, Charlie Rice was driven to the event in his Rolls Royce car. He was accompanied by a beautiful young woman who had been hired to be on his arm for the evening. His driver for the night, one of his own men, parked in the underground car park. Charlie and his lady made a grand entrance into the foyer via the lift. The first couple of fights on the lower card had already come and gone. By the time Charlie's future champion had, as expected, won the last contest it was well after midnight. All in all, things had gone well, the evening had been a huge success.

Feeling very pleased with himself, and slightly inebriated, Charlie and his young lady descended back to the underground car park. His driver was there ready to take them home. As the car emerged from the garage and onto the road the whole place lit up. There were marked police cars and unmarked police cars blocking the street with sirens blaring, even the police helicopter hovered above.

"What the hell's going on?" Charlie asked his driver.

"I haven't a clue, boss," he replied.

They were just about to be enlightened by a DCI from the Scottish Crime Squad who opened the back door of Charlie's car. The officer was in possession of a warrant to search the vehicle. Rice thought this was all highly hilarious, that is until the police opened the boot. What they discovered certainly came as a shock to Charlie Rice. Two kilos of cocaine were found, which was bad enough, but also four 9mm semi-automatic pistols, with ammunition.

The car and all the occupants were taken into custody at Stewart Street Police Office. Once there Charlie was given the really bad news. The guns were part of a consignment of army issue weapons which had been stolen from a barracks in 1995 during the troubles in Northern Ireland.

When later interviewed regarding his possession of the guns, Rice obviously denied all knowledge of them. He knew, however, that he had been well and truly stitched up, when the DCI informed him that his fingerprints had been found on all four guns.

The young lady and Rice's driver were released without charge. Charlie Rice knew that his race was run. He was looking at imprisonment for a serious number of years.

News soon got around Easterhouse. The following Tuesday the Chung-Yong Taekwondo Club was standing room only. Eventually all the young lads who had been afraid to attend came back. Even James Gormley came back on his crutches to see what was going on. Once he was fit again, he promised he'd be back training.

Gerry had also made a promise to send Lynne and her family on a holiday to Disney World, once James had fully recovered. He had also helped her to take some steps to make Michelle's quality of life as good as it could possibly be.

Gerry's plan to rid Easterhouse of Charlie Rice had worked to perfection. John Johnstone and Alex Burnett had done a brilliant job watching Rice's every move. Once Gerry had got their findings, he knew all he had to do was somehow get a set of Charlie Rice's fingerprints. Hence the visit to the gymnasium. When Rice handed him the champagne bottle, Gerry had held it by the neck. What Rice didn't notice was he was wearing gloves. Left on the bottle were a perfect set of fingerprints belonging to Charlie Rice.

Where did the 9mm pistols come from?

Bert Williams was a genius when it came to making guns. He had so many parts in his workshop left over from his days under Whitehall. Graham Cahill had simply asked him to construct four pistols and add the serial numbers from identical weapons genuinely stolen in Northern Ireland. It was a simple task to transfer Charlie Rice's fingerprints onto the pistols. Gerry had obtained two kilograms of cocaine from an anonymous source just for show. When the Rolls Royce was left unattended in the car park it was the easiest thing in the world to open the boot and plant the guns and drugs.

All very illegal.

Perhaps it was time Gerry listened to himself and gave up his evil ways.

# CHAPTER FORTY-SIX

Audrey had enjoyed her maternity leave. After she gave birth to daughter Annie she felt her life couldn't possibly get any better. For the next few months she looked after her wee treasure the only way a new mum can. There was no doubt that the Lynch family were very happy. They loved their new home and the family was now complete.

Once her maternity leave was at an end Audrey returned to work and this was when the difficulties began. Brian Wallace had retired and she didn't get on too well with her new detective inspector. They just didn't seem to be the same fit as Brian and Audrey had been. To Audrey, it seemed she was allocated just mundane enquiries to deal with. She wasn't enjoying her work at all. She'd also had an offer to work at the new crime complex at nearby Gartcosh, but turned it down.

Audrey didn't say anything to anyone, not even Gerry. She loved being a police officer but thought that perhaps now having a daughter had changed her prospective. Was it that she just wanted to be a mother?

By this time Gerry, fully fit again, was trying to make up for lost time at QLM and often returned home exhausted. The new parents had put a childcare system into place which they hoped would work. Their idea was that at least one of them would be there at all times to care for Annie.

They wanted to try and raise their own child and not leave it to others. In theory it was a great, but in practice it just created havoc. Work always seemed to get in the way and they began arguing.

Gerry had spoken about hiring a nanny, but they just ended up falling out over the subject.

Annie had started walking just after her first birthday. As she became more proficient she scampered about through a sea of toys scattered all over the house. This usually ended with her landing on her bottom and squealing with delight. Gerry and Audrey struggled to keep up.

One evening when they'd both had particularly stressful days, Gerry and Audrey were sitting quietly enjoying a glass of white wine and watching as wee Annie created her usual havoc. Audrey looked over at Gerry, she had something to say but didn't know if this was the right time.

Suddenly, she thought, 'To hell with it' and it just came out.

"Anyway, I just thought I would let you know that I'm thinking of packing my job in."

Gerry couldn't believe what he was hearing. He looked at his wife as though she were insane. He knew they had been arguing back and forth for weeks now about work and whether to employ a nanny or not, but to leave the force... How could Audrey even consider giving up being a police officer? He had been devastated when he had been required to quit. It was the best job in the world as far as he was concerned.

"What!" Gerry exclaimed. "Are you mad?"

"NO! I'm pregnant again!" she announced.

Instinctively they both looked over to Annie who was trying to struggle back to her feet. She just smiled back at them both. Audrey went and picked up her daughter, holding her close. Gerry stared for a moment at his two girls. At that instant he could swear that he heard his father speaking to him. He knew what he must do. His priorities had changed. Now he had two ladies in his life, it was his responsibility to take care of them.

In the few short years he had been a private investigator he had been shot, assaulted and suffered numerous broken bones. Not that long ago he'd nearly lost Audrey. Lately he had assisted in breaking the law on numerous occasions. Perhaps his wife was right, it was time they both had a change of career. However, first things first, given Audrey's latest revelation.

"In that case," Gerry said, with a huge smile on his face, "I'll make some enquiries first thing in the morning about employing a nanny."

He then shuffled along the settee and took his wife in his arms and kissed her.

"I love you," he whispered.

"I love you too," Audrey replied.

Annie just looked at her parents and laughed.

**THE END**

# About the Author

**G**ordon Waugh was born in Scotland but raised and educated in Yorkshire. Returning to the country of his birth, he served 30 years in the Police before retiring to Spain. He and his wife now live at the foot of the beautiful Campsie Hills. Evil Ways is the second book featuring Gerry Lynch..

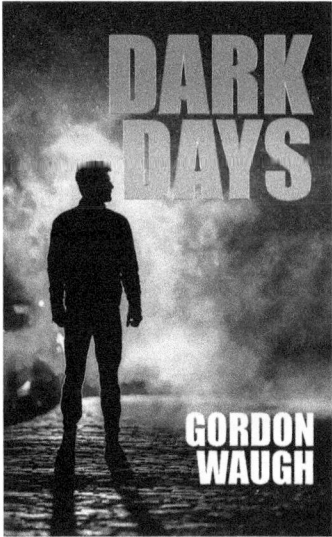

9 781999 322724